LIVES APART

ANNE M. McLOUGHLIN

POOLBEG

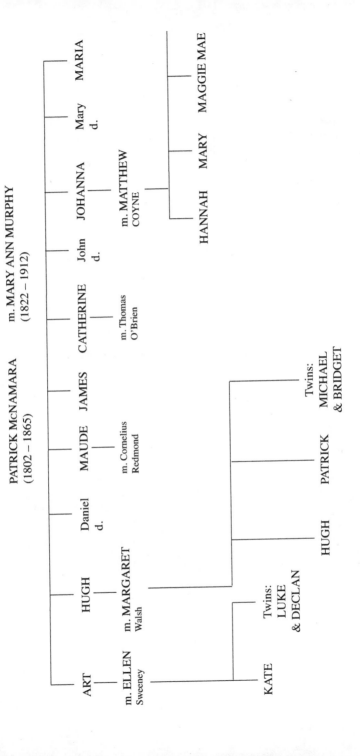

PATRICK McNAMARA
(1802 – 1865)

m. MARY ANN MURPHY
(1822 – 1912)

ART — HUGH — Daniel — MAUDE — JAMES — CATHERINE — John — JOHANNA — Mary — MARIA

m. ELLEN
Sweeney

m. MARGARET
Walsh

Daniel
d.

m. Cornelius
Redmond

m. Thomas
O'Brien

John
d.

m. MATTHEW
COYNE

Mary
d.

KATE — Twins: LUKE & DECLAN

HUGH — PATRICK — Twins: MICHAEL & BRIDGET

HANNAH — MARY — MAGGIE MAE

Published 2020
by Poolbeg Press Ltd.
123 Grange Hill, Baldoyle,
Dublin 13, Ireland
Email: poolbeg@poolbeg.com

A catalogue record for this book is available from the British Library.

ISBN 978178199-400-9

www.poolbeg.com

About the Author

Anne McLoughlin was born in Dublin, Ireland, and now divides her time between there and her home in rural Wexford.

She has written stories for the RTÉ children's programme *Anything Goes*, has published a series of local social history books and written articles for newspapers and magazines.

Highly commended in the Colm Tóibín International Short Story Competition in the Wexford Literary Festival, this gave her the encouragement to begin working on the novels that have been niggling at the back of her brain for years.

Acknowledgements

Many of my ancestors had a great sense of adventure and the courage to follow their dreams in the late 1800's when they faced the possibility that for some of them their journey to America might very likely be one-way. They were the inspiration for this, my first book in the *Lives* trilogy, a family saga that follows the lives of the fictional McNamara family who embark on a similar adventure. While I cannot thank my ancestors for obvious reasons, I would like to thank the descendants of the extended O'Keeffe family in County Clare and in the USA, for their help in filling in the gaps in our mutual family tree and bringing me to the realisation that there is no such thing as an 'ordinary' life.

The 2020 Wexford Literary Festival Committee operated against the odds during a difficult COVID-19 year and continued to run the competitions. Thanks to them for selecting my novel as one of those shortlisted to 'Meet the Publisher' and to Carol Long for setting up the Zoom pitching session when the face-to-face meetings had to be abandoned.

Thanks to:

Patricia O'Reilly, my former tutor in UCD. For anyone who wishes to advance their writing skills her Creative Writing Workshops are just wonderful and great fun. Also to authors Cat Hogan and Derville Murphy for their advice on how to avoid a rookie's mistakes.

Gemma McCrohan, my former colleague, friend and reporter on the *Would You Believe* television series, who read my first draft. She bravely came back to me asking if I wanted her to be honest or kind. I opted for honest and held my breath. Being very familiar with her incisive intellect, I took the chance on being told to keep the day job. "Right," said Gemma. "I suppose you think you've your book written now? Well, you haven't. You write very well. You have great stories. However, you haven't got a book here – you have three! Go back to the drawing board and start again." Thank you, Gemma.

Ann McCabe, a member of my RTÉ Book Club who read an early draft of Johanna's story and gave me great encouragement to keep at it, and advised on some farming traditions and terms. I'm still not sure of the difference between the fork, the pitch-fork and the sprong.

Liam Duffy, French horn player extraordinaire, whose advice ensured I eliminated a few historic errors that had worked their way into my manuscript in relation to the problems that beset orchestral horn players.

Evan Jones for his guidance on crime and punishment in the USA, and the likely consequences of getting involved on the periphery of crime. I alone am responsible and have to take the blame for any historical errors in the book.

Alice Walsh who managed to produce some lovely photographs of a writer who normally hates the usual results.

Conor Kostick of the Irish Writers' Union for his expert advice to an un-agented writer.

Never having worked with a publisher before, it was an absolute pleasure to work with Poolbeg Press. Unfortunately during the process, due to the COVID-19 pandemic, we didn't get to meet in person but I'd particularly like to thank Paula Campbell and my wonderful editor Gaye Shortland for their expertise and encouragement at all stages of the process. Also to David Prendergast for the stylish look of the book and the beautiful cover.

And where would one be without the RTÉ network? The support and encouragement of all my former work colleagues have been second to none – they will never know just how important their friendship is to me – especially the RTÉ Gatherers and Book Club.

Dedication

This book is dedicated to all our ancestors
who bravely emigrated from Ireland to an unknown life
in America in the 1800s.

Prologue

They sat there staring at her. All three faces frozen in silent amazement. The clinking of cups and murmur of voices in the tearoom suddenly audible.

She had never really thought about it before but now, for the first time ever, she saw her daughters as they really were. How had they developed from chirpy, fun-loving children into what she could only admit were three rather lacklustre adults? She wondered if it might have been some mistake she'd made with their upbringing.

The realisation of the effect of her announcement made it difficult to keep a slightly smug feeling under control. A bit ashamed, she could feel it spreading upwards and outwards to the surface. She needed to put a halt to it before it reached her face and oozed out through her pores.

Of course she loved them but had to admit they all needed a good shake-up. She didn't go through all that labour to allow them now to vegetate into narrow lives that believed the world began and ended in Boston, or in New York in Hannah's case. And from what she could see that's the way they were shaping up.

"What?"

She smiled at their perfect unison.

1

"What do you mean '*what*'? You heard what I said."

Maggie's mouth hung open. The lockjaw position was not attractive, Johanna thought, as she waited for them to digest her news.

"To *Ireland*? You're going to Ireland?" Mary's eyebrows rose upwards until they threatened to disappear under her hairline.

"I am. I'm going to Ireland – to County Clare, to be precise." She paused. There was no rush. "Well, I'll base myself in Clare and sure maybe I'll do a bit more travelling around the rest of the country while I'm there."

She waited for a reaction but knew by the vacant stares that she'd lost them at "to Ireland".

"Back to Ireland? At your age?" said Hannah.

Confident now of their full attention, not always the case, it was her turn to look surprised.

"What do you mean 'at my age'? I can hardly do it any younger now, can I?"

"You never mentioned anything like this before." Hannah's eyes were popped. "You never said anything about it when I was home at Christmas!"

"I didn't know then," Johanna replied calmly, ignoring the accusing tone as she pushed aside the thought that her eldest daughter might have the beginnings of a thyroid problem.

"So it's just something you've taken a notion to do?" Hannah's eyes relaxed back into their sockets.

"So you're not really serious about it?" Maggie had recovered enough to join in.

"And why would I not be serious?" Johanna didn't like the suggestion in her tone that they could all relax now and indulge their mother in her never-likely-to-happen fantasy. "Isn't it time I did something exciting with my life?"

"For how long, Mother?" Mary had been watching the exchange and noted the firm set of her mother's elbows on the table.

The others might not be ready for it yet but Johanna could see the recognition dawning on her middle daughter that this might just be something more than a passing notion.

"I don't know. I haven't made up my mind yet." Johanna sat back and beamed at them.

Suddenly she deserved more than half an ear. Not someone to be taken for granted anymore. Not always going to be around to service their needs.

"Maybe I'll stay there. We'll see." She was enjoying this, watching her children glance at each other, suspicion written on each face. She could see what was coming.

"Did you know anything about this?" Hannah's tone was sharp as she looked at Mary. She often missed things. Often got left out. The only one living in another State, they often forgot to tell her bits of news.

"What? No. No, I did not." The accusation in her sister's voice annoyed Mary. "This is the first I've heard of it."

Johanna's chair creaked as she leaned back, savouring the power. She waited until they realised that it was she and she alone who held all the cards.

"But, Mother, you've hardly even had a holiday anywhere. Why would you be taking a big trip like this? You've never left America since you arrived."

"Is that not reason enough?"

"Who are you going with? You can't go alone."

"Why ever not? I left Ireland and made the trip here on my own, didn't I? And I was only seventeen, a lot younger than any of you lot. And did I get lost?" She paused. "How far have any of you ever travelled? Alone?"

She looked from one to the other. No answer to that.

"I thought not."

She waited for it to sink in. For them to take a good look at themselves.

"Do you think I'm not capable?" she went on. "That

I've gone dotty in my old age?"

"It's not that . . . " Maggie was worried that her mother was taking this up all wrong.

"Well, what is it then? I've travelled further than all of you put together, so I'm well able for an adventure. And would you deny me that?"

"Well, no. It's just that it's a bit of a surprise. A bit sudden. That's all we're saying." Mary hoped the casual approach might cool things down.

"Well, that's it then. That's why I called you here so you'd all hear it together." She paused. "And the reason I picked Easter? I thought it would be a good time to tell you when Hannah was here. I didn't want to be accused of telling one or the other of you first." She looked around at each of them. *"I'm taking a trip back to Ireland."* She nodded with each word as slowly she emphasised them. "Yes. And, no, I'm not going alone. Myself and your Uncle Hugh. For the first time in nearly fifty years."

Johanna watched a shadow pass over Hannah's face. Young, single, no ties and it had never occurred to her to embark on such an adventure. The message had hit home there. A moment's pity for her eldest daughter on whom it was just dawning that maybe she was dull. Well, duller than her own mother. Perhaps the news would wake her up, waken them all up, before it was too late. She'd almost delayed too long herself. But then her life had been different. A lot to contend with that they might possibly never understand.

Mary and Maggie, if they were envious, were going to have to live with that. Maybe they should have taken the opportunity when they were free. Now, tied with young children, their chance was a long way off.

"A good way to celebrate the fiftieth anniversary of my coming to America, don't you think?"

4

Johanna stood up. Not waiting for an answer, she took her coat from the back of the chair. Hannah stood to help as she struggled to find the second sleeve.

"Things to do. I'll leave you lot to fix up the bill. I'll be saving my money now. And you can all have a little chat about it when I'm gone." Johanna smiled at them. "I've a hair appointment and then I need to get home and start sorting myself out." She tucked a stray lock of grey hair back into her bun. "I might go for a bob or one of those – what are they? Oh, yes – a shingle cut. Yes, I think that might suit me better."

"Mother. You can't?" Maggie looked startled.

"Why ever not, Maggie? Hannah's bob suits her. Why can't I be up to the minute and me with a nice natural wave in my hair? Anyway, can't delay – Hugh is booking the tickets for next month. I'll let you know the exact date when that's done."

Johanna winked at them and, wiggling her fingers in a playful wave, she turned and left the tearoom.

Chapter 1

Boston, Massachusetts, USA

February 1926

Hugh was sitting in the old squashy armchair by the fire, reading his newspaper.

"How would you like to go home?" he called from the sitting room.

Johanna had invited her brother over for Sunday lunch. It was a regular date. An excuse not to have to invite the grandchildren, much as she loved them. No, Sundays were calmer without them and Hugh was a good excuse as her daughters knew he didn't like the hustle and bustle they brought with them.

Not one to cook himself, he treated her to lunch in a hotel once or twice a month. Just the two of them. A fair payback. She enjoyed that. Not something she could afford too often on her own meagre income.

How would she like to go home? What was he talking about? She had sent him into the connecting sitting room while she washed up the dishes in the kitchen. She wasn't sure she'd heard him correctly, calling in as he had from the other room.

"Sure I am *home! What are you on about?"* Shouting over her shoulder, she put the last plate on the drainer and wondered if her brother had gone daft. Did he think he was

in his own house and it was time for her to leave? You never knew with Hugh. She could hear him mumbling something.

"I'll be in to you in a minute! I can't hear you properly from here!"

She reached for the towel and, drying her hands, went in to where he sat gazing into the fire, the newspaper dangling from his hand.

"What is it you're saying, Hugh? You know I can't hear you from the kitchen."

"How would you like to go home? I mean *home* home." He looked at her. "Ireland."

"What's brought this on?" She was puzzled. "Do you mean for good?"

"No, not for good. No, I was just thinking I need to ease up at work. Well, I wasn't thinking it at all actually – the doctor told me I needed to. That maybe I should take a holiday."

"Well, he's right. But it's not like you to take advice." She looked at him sharply. Her brain suddenly froze. Was he trying to tell her something? Not ready for any bad news, she batted away the worry that was trying to worm its way in. "I've been telling you that for years, but sure what would I know? I can't understand why you're still working so hard anyway, at your age."

"I'm even beginning to ask myself that." He held up the newspaper and turned the page, then folded it in half before laying it on the arm of the chair, as if ready to resume his reading when the conversation was completed.

She hadn't noticed the years creeping up on him. His dapper suits, always dark in colour, lent him a smart well-turned-out air. And although there wasn't a hint of an old-man stoop about him, now that she thought about it the spring had gone from his step. Had she been asked to describe him she'd have said he was a smart-looking gentleman with thinning grey hair. Now, as she looked across at him, she realised that he was completely bald on top. How had she not noticed?

"You can well afford to retire and leave them at it. I'm sure at this stage your sons would like to make their own decisions about the business without you resisting all changes."

"I know, Jo, but it's hard to let go."

"Well, maybe it's time you tried it." She glanced at him. He didn't look in any way anxious. Maybe there was nothing to be concerned about. Maybe he was just getting sense.

"Well, what do you think? How about it?"

She knew by the way he looked her straight in the eye that he was trying to gauge her reaction.

"A trip home? That might be a step in the right direction." Johanna kept the tingle of excitement under control in case she'd misunderstood. He'd hardly taken a holiday since she came to America – well, apart from a few weeks at the beach in the summers when his children were young, but not anything you could call a big trip. He'd only once returned to Ireland on a short business trip and that was years ago after Margaret died. He'd never mentioned the possibility of a return since. The leap now from zero to a major excursion was too big a jump to hope for.

"You're really serious, are you? Talking about Ireland."

"I am. Well, then, if I was to go would you come with me?"

"Sure I couldn't afford it and you know that." He wouldn't be expecting her to pay but she couldn't presume anything.

"Consider it a present, all your birthdays together. I'd never go on my own now, not at my age anyhow." He smiled at her. "I could only go if a youngster like you came to look after me. So how about it, would you come?"

"Would I go? What a question? Hugh, it's what I've wanted all my life. Thanks, Hugh, thank you. I'd love to come." She threw her arms in the air before suddenly pointing at him. *"When?"*

"*Whoa there*, hold your horses. Don't rush me now. We need to plan this." He laughed as he held up his hand.

"Let's not wait too long then." She paused and winked at him. "At your age."

She clapped and, with a little skip, waved the towel in the air and danced off. "They won't believe this. Wait 'til I tell them. I can't wait to see their faces."

He could hear her delight as she waltzed back into the kitchen and smiled to himself.

"Well, that's settled then." Picking up the newspaper with a flourish, he returned to his reading. A companion would make the trip for him, and his sister was the perfect one. His eyes moved backwards and forwards across the first few paragraphs, their contents sailing through his mind without a word settling. If he'd been asked what he'd read he could not have said.

The sound of Johanna humming in the kitchen disturbed him. Not her singing but her obvious pleasure. All those years in between when he'd never concerned himself about her day-to-day life. A pang of guilt stabbed him. How she occupied herself when she wasn't minding his children, her own children or working in his shop, he didn't know. He'd just let her get on with it. All those years. How she'd unquestioningly filled the gap, the huge gaping hole that had threatened to swallow him after Margaret died. His self-centredness appalled him. He'd never given a thought to how it was for her. Really was. And in later years . . . he couldn't even think about that. He'd used money to fix his guilt. All those years, her children's education, the big gestures for birthdays and Christmas and the occasional outing – but never a thought to the in-betweens times. And he knew all about the in-between times. Those were the difficult bits. She'd been there for him but where had he been for her? Too busy to spare the time, too occupied with his own life to get involved. Ensuring she wasn't short of money – that had been his contribution.

Laying the paper down on his knee, he gazed into the orange flames. He'd been blind to it all. A pity he hadn't suggested it years ago, before their mother died. It would have meant so much to her. And to him. Always on the long finger: must do it sometime. But now it had all passed in the blink of an eye.

He heard her steps in the hall and, as his sister's presence filled the doorway, he moved to pick up the newspaper again. He didn't want to read her eyes as she stood there but, more especially, he hoped she couldn't read his mind. Couldn't bear the thought that she might be thinking the same. Why had he waited so long?

"Cup of tea?" She smiled at him.

"That'd be nice, Jo."

He picked at a thread on the well-worn arm of the chair as she went back to the kitchen. A pity he couldn't rewrite history.

11

HUGH

Chapter 2

County Clare, Ireland
1865

The journey was long, too far to carry the coffin the whole way. The dull clomping of the horses' hooves, the only sound, filled the air as they walked the route to the cemetery in silence.

The front mourners, all family, isolated in their thoughts of Patrick, were oblivious to the beauty of the countryside stretching out to their right where the mist, wraith-like, hung over the lake.

Their minds were on the past, every memory unique and precious to its owner. Heads downcast, they saw nothing but the dried clay on which they trod. There was little trace of the gravel laid years before to mark the pathway. It had sunk deep into the earth after half a century of rain and footsteps.

The whispered conversations only started further back along the procession, amongst those friends and neighbours whose sadness sat closer to the surface. As they talked amongst themselves they knew that this day was not just about loss. For the moment, the overwhelming sadness of the event would cloak what lay ahead for the individuals involved. Too early yet to think about the changes it would bring for everyone in the family. The positioning of each, and their futures.

* * *

At eighteen Hugh was already aware how often such shifts in circumstances caused rifts in families. He also knew where he did not want to be, something that might just be a relief to others in the family when he chose his moment to tell them. Art's position would not be contested. Unlike himself, his brother was a natural. Art's future as the farmer in the McNamara family would be secure. The accepted position for the eldest son in such circumstances would cause no ill-feeling. He had seen the red-raw hands of his mother on a winter's morning, carrying in a bucket of milk for the household or taking slops out to the pigs, and the stooped shoulders of his father, a man old before his time.

A future not for him. But maybe today was not the best time to tell them.

Patrick had always been ready to introduce his children to new things. He'd encouraged each of them to try out everything, regardless of the results. His love of music was a gift he tried to pass on to each of them. A few melodies on an instrument, any instrument – the whistle, the concertina or the violin – a few airs that they could bring to any session in any house or to any dance at the crossroads.

Hugh knew his father was proud of him. It was in the little things. Even when it came to music, something that Patrick had failed spectacularly to teach his son as a child, Hugh could remember the wink his father had thrown him after the handful of out-of-tune notes on the fiddle that confirmed it. Not a man to give up easily, he tried him on the spoons but when he watched Hugh, clearly oblivious to the fact that he was out of rhythm with the rest of the group, he had to accept defeat.

"I don't think we'll ever make a musician of you, son."

"Why not, Da?" Hugh looked up at his father, the naive curiosity of a six-year-old radiating from his face.

"Arithmetic. Mathematics. Yes, that's your thing, Hugh, me boy!" Patrick smiled down at him and gave him a pat on the head, flattening the tuft that stood upright. "I think you're going to be the professor in the family. Or maybe the entrepreneur. Yes, an '*on-trop-pron-air*'." Patrick grinned as he put on a grand accent, delighted with his twist on the word.

"What's that, Da?"

"A fella that can't be stopped. The big businessman. I think that'll be you, Hugh. You'll be the one making all the money in this family."

From his early days at school it was evident that figures were Hugh's thing. Always the boy the teacher would call to the top of the class to demonstrate how a sum should be done. The other children didn't seem to resent his being the teacher's favourite. They just grinned on the occasions when a visitor to the school was treated to a performance of Hugh displaying his ability to tot up two columns of figures at the same time. They enjoyed his trick as much as he did showing it off and most of them were glad it wasn't them who'd been called up.

From the time that Art and himself were of any use around the farm, his father allowed them to choose a newborn calf or lamb as their own and take responsibility for rearing it to the point of sale. He always chose a calf. Had a thing about lambs. You could taste the wool when you were eating the meat.

"Now, Hugh, I'm deducting the cost of the feeding from the price you got for the animal." Patrick took the wad of notes from him before they left the fair. "You have to learn the economics of rearing livestock. It doesn't come cheap."

"You're telling me!" Hugh watched, dismayed, as his father peeled off several of the notes from the bundle.

"Here you are. Now don't lose it." Patrick handed him back the remainder. "You can treat yourself to something but don't spend it all in the one go."

"I think I'll get another calf," he paused, a frown forming on his forehead, "or maybe two."

"Good lad. That's the trick. That's the way you build up your herd. That first one was free just to get you started." Patrick smiled, delighted his son had already worked that one out. "But remember I'll be charging you for the feed again and this time it'll be for two animals but that's the way to go, son."

"Ah, Da!" He could see his father was going to be no pushover.

"You get nothing for nothing in this world, Hugh, me boy. You might as well learn that lesson young. It mightn't make sense to you now but it'll stand to you later."

Hugh remembered the enjoyment of those first attempts at buying and selling but, after a few seasons, he was beginning to realise that his interest in figures went way beyond the price of a heifer. Listening to the men gathered outside the church after the Sunday Mass or under the eaves of a thatch in the village, sheltering from the rain, he knew the monotony of such debates would, in time, suffocate him. He didn't know then where or how his life would pan out but he knew it would have to stretch far beyond the boundaries of this parish.

The procession stopped suddenly and Hugh bumped into Maude's back, jolting him into the present. Not sure how he had got behind, he looked and realised she had moved ahead and taken his place behind Art who was linking their mother at the head of the mourners. Stepping onto the grass, he moved up alongside his sister.

The murmuring had ceased. The pathway to the burial

place had narrowed now into a lane not wide enough for the horses to proceed, leaving a fair walk to the cemetery still to be covered. A long way to bear the weight of a coffin on shoulders, but it had to be done.

The sound of men shuffling into place was amplified above the hush of the crowd as they removed the casket. Hugh took his lead from Art and the older neighbours with more experience of the practicalities. They directed him to the front left before taking their places behind, along each side of the coffin. One of the horses whinnied as if giving the signal to sons and neighbours to raise the casket shoulder-high. A final check that everyone had a secure hold and they began the journey, carrying Patrick to his final resting place.

The path seemed unending as the weight dug into his shoulder. They halted twice along the route to rest. One of the older neighbours signalled to a couple of younger men to step forward and change with those who were flagging, but Hugh refused the offer of relief. He would see it to the end. The bruises would heal. He didn't want to miss out on these remaining minutes with his father. The last thing he could do for him.

They slowed as they approached to where his resting place awaited. Hugh stood watching the undertaker make the final preparations as they waited to be called forward to their position. He relished the soreness that spread through his shoulder and down into his chest as if his father was pressing the final goodbye deep into his core.

A few steps forward before the weight was removed and he was able to rub his shoulder. He stood and watched, giving a few rotations of the joint to ease the pain. In the silence he focused on the coffin being lowered into the grave, a moment that would never come again, the last time in his father's presence. Tears stung his eyes but before they had a chance to fall he felt a small hand slip into his. A wave of guilt at his resentment of the intrusion swept through him as he looked down into the little white face of his young sister nuzzling his side. The sight of her, like a little calf, released the tears to roll down his cheeks. Separating his fingers from hers, he cupped Johanna's head and rubbed the brown silky hair with his big-brother hand and took comfort in her closeness.

He had never seen much beyond the sociable gathering at the 'American wakes' in the houses where sons or daughters were preparing to leave for a new life across the Atlantic. Hadn't paid much heed to the mothers' tears nor noticed the fear behind the emigrants' jocularity. Hugh had seen the parties only in relation to their function, enjoyable punctuation marks that provided a bit of fun and entertainment in an otherwise uneventful passing of one season into another.

A feature of life since his childhood when he went to the ones in nearby houses and watched the adults grow wilder as the night progressed, not understanding what it was all about. For a child they were just a break in routine with plenty of sweet treats. For Hugh the seeds were well and truly set at the later ones where a few miles was nothing to travel in order to bid the emigrant farewell. He'd known some who'd taken the long voyage but he'd yet to meet anyone who'd returned to report on it. Not in his short lifetime anyway. This concern was only something that had manifested itself recently in his mind. The realisation of the finality of such a decision. That was something that bothered him. But he had to take the chance or forever remain the hired hand on the farm. It was Art's responsibility now.

JOHANNA

Chapter 3

Knocknageeha, County Clare

1877

"Come on, Jo, no sitting down on the job," Art chivvied his sister now that there were only the two of them left in the field. He could see she was tired but he couldn't afford for her to give up on him now with the weather closing in.

"Can we not leave it now, Art? I'm exhausted." Johanna felt husks of the grain in her hair as she brushed it back from her burnt face. "I'll give you a hand again in the morning."

"We need to get it done now before the rain comes." He knew he was pushing her but, after a week of wet weather behind them and this dry spell providing an opportunity to save the crop, he couldn't afford to risk not finishing it this evening. "Just another dozen or so and we'll have the whole field stooked." He saw her hesitate. "Come on, don't leave me now. I'll sing to you while we're doing it."

"Don't threaten me with that or I'll definitely go." She grinned back at him as she took his extended hand and let him haul her up from where she had plonked down at the base of the sheaves.

"Only for you, Art, only for you." She shook her head at her brother. "But remember you'll owe me for this. I'm good but I'm not cheap."

* * *

She had felt the tiredness flow away in the grimy water and it surprised her. Maybe after tea she would walk out to her favourite place. Pity to waste the renewed energy she could now feel coursing through her.

The bedroom door was open. A rattle of mugs came from the kitchen.

"*Tea's ready!*" her mother called out.

"*Down in a minute!*"

With the dust of the harvest washed off, she stood at the window, drawing the comb through her long wet hair. The threatening black clouds from earlier had passed and the view across the farmland was now golden in the evening sun. A job well done, the stooks of corn cast rows of sloping shadows punctuating the distant field.

She could already hear the shuffle of chair legs in the kitchen below. She took one last look in the mirror. Yes, it was definitely time to change that image. Who wanted to look like that strong, sturdy girl who was staring back at her, the one who could '*do the work of ten farmers*' like they were all so fond of saying. The raw material was there – the features were good but the figure could do with a little trim and maybe she could waft around a bit more instead of using the purposeful stride she knew she had. But that was a job for another day, and with that thought she turned and headed down to join them at the table.

For most of the walk up the slope the steep inland cliff of rock to the left of the pathway was like a wall blocking her view of the landscape on that side. To her right a narrow field of flat grey limestone slabs, like tabletops, led to the edge of the coastline. They ended suddenly at the point where the cliffs dropped sharply to the sea. A limitless view westwards stretched out across the Atlantic Ocean, broken only by the occasional foam-topped wave.

It was a steep climb and, each time she came here, she aimed to get to the top without having to stop halfway to catch her breath. Today, with only a light breeze against her she had made it without resting but her breath felt sore in her chest as she forced herself up the last few yards of the incline. Arriving to the top, she halted just short of the turn where the pathway disappeared behind the rockface from where she knew it began its descent down the far side of the hill.

She bent down to remove a pebble from her shoe. Her ears popped and the blood pounded in her head. Not a good idea to have put such strenuous effort into her walking after a hard day's work. As she stood up, the earth began to sway. She reached out her hand and placed it flat against the rocky cliff. It took a few moments for the giddiness to recede. As her world steadied she flopped down on a large flat slab and leaned back against the smooth rockface, closing her mouth to ease the rawness in her throat. It would be worth it in a minute. It always was.

The stone was still warm from the late-evening sun that had caressed it up to moments ago. From where she sat she could see the far horizon. She'd often wondered about the short stretch of dry-stone walling on the other side of the pathway where it edged the narrow field of limestone slabs. Wondered who had taken the trouble to build it. It didn't appear to have much purpose unless it was just to alert strangers to the turn in the path and not have them walking straight ahead and over the slabs and into the sea. There must have been twenty yards of limestone field so it would be unlikely that someone would do that. Not unless they intended to. It wasn't something she liked to dwell on, although it had happened. She knew that from the whispers picked up in the veiled comments of the older people. No-one really talked about it. At least not openly.

Closing her eyes, she listened. In the quiet she could hear the water lapping and splashing as an occasional large wave broke against the cliffs below. Taking long breaths, she tried to match them with the rhythm of the ocean and, as her breathing grew shallower, the threatened headache from the throbbing subsided.

The sun, which had already been slowly sliding down the sky had almost reached the horizon. She got up from her seat. She'd been caught out before. Not wise to wait until it melted down into the sea and disappeared completely. She'd done that one evening and was caught with having to walk the last half mile home in the pitch black. She ran her hand over the back of her neck. The light perspiration had cooled and she released the locks of hair that had stuck. She looked out at the horizon, feeling the long strands blowing out behind her in the gentle south-westerly breeze. There was still a little time to enjoy the sunset. Crossing the pathway, she stepped over the wall onto the flat slabs. She placed her hands carefully in order to avoid dislodging one of its loose stones as she did so. The gritty surfaces of the limestone dug into her palms as she steadied herself.

Weaving her way, she jumped from slab to slab, across the weatherworn lunar field, thousands of years unchanged. The clouds of sea thrift that had clung to life in the crevices between the slabs were beginning to turn brown now, but there was still a faint echo of pink even this late in the season, a result of the wet summer. She paused to examine the wonder of their survival in this barren landscape.

The squawks of seagulls tore the air. She looked upwards but there was no sign of them overhead. She saw that they were flying in from the sea to land short of where she stood, swooping downwards out of sight to touch down somewhere below the cliff edge. She watched them a while until curiosity drew her across the limestone expanse to

21

investigate their resting place. Nearing the edge, she began picking her steps, testing each slab for movement before putting her full weight on it, going as close to the cliff verge as she dared.

"Come back from that edge!" Her mother's warning voice from her childhood came back to her.

Down below, the waters of the cold, grey Atlantic broke in a white spume against the jagged rocks. An open invitation to anyone standing on the unprotected cliff edge to enter its depths.

The pull of the water below dizzied her. She lay down on her stomach on the slab to break the magnetic draw. Imagine if she fell in! They'd never find her. And if they did they might think she had done away with herself on purpose and she would end up the subject of those whisperings. Maybe even Art would think he'd pushed her too hard. She smiled at the thought. It would take a lot more than that.

Secure now in her prone position she contented herself watching the bird activity on the cliff face below, her head hanging slightly over the edge. She loved that place. The wildness. The isolation of it. Walking out to that spot a couple of evenings a week to watch the setting sun and to wait for her life to begin. The possibilities limitless. Like the ocean itself.

The anticipation of magical shades of the watercolour sky had kept her going as she'd panted her way on the uphill, knowing the orange-and-pink world that beckoned beyond. The vastness, from where she lay now, usually looked as if it was just waiting for her to reach out and fly. That's the way it was most evenings. But not today. Art had been right. The burst of sun had been short-lived. The weather was closing in. The twilight now had grey-and-navy clouds throwing a veil over a vision that may only have been in her dreams.

The drawing of the cloudy curtains brought a slight chill to the air.

Wishing she'd headed out earlier to get the best of the evening she began mooching herself back from the edge, like a child learning to crawl. She smiled to herself, remembering her younger sister Maria's first efforts at movement, the crawling in reverse before she learned there was no future in that.

She waited until she had moved several feet back from the edge before standing up. There was a dampness now in the breeze. She remembered her father's line. Never knew what it meant then. *"You get four seasons in a day here. Sometimes even in an hour."* Definitely rain on the way.

Traversing the slabs, she made her way to the track. She needed to step up the pace if she were to get home before a soaking. Just as well it was all downhill.

Chapter 4

"Will you make me stilts, Hugh?"

Joanna's memory of her brother before he emigrated to seek his fortune was filtered through the eyes of the child who saw him as an all-knowing adult. Never a doubt in his head. He knew exactly who he was and where he was going. And, more important, you knew exactly where you stood with him.

"Not now. I'm busy. But I will after the tea this evening."

She was always sure that he was as good as his word and that evening looked at him expectantly when he stood up from the table and drained his cup.

"Well, what are you waiting for, Jo?" He looked over at her. "We've work to do. Come with me."

She stood still while he measured her with the hazel rods and watched as he cobbled together a rough pair of stilts, putting several of them together and binding them to strengthen each one.

"Now let's try them out." He put them into her hands and held her while she stepped up onto them.

"*Don't let me go!*" Johanna shrieked as the ground below suddenly seemed very far away. "*Take me down! Take me down! I want to get down! You do it first, Hugh! Show me how!*"

"I can't. They won't hold me. They're not strong enough for a big fella like me." Hugh steadied her. "They're only strong enough for little girls."

"Hold me, hold me, I'm going to fall!"

"You're not going to fall." His voice softened. "I won't let you go. When did I ever let you fall? Come on. Try taking a step. The way you're doing it you're sticking it into the ground. Come on – I'll hold on to you. I promise."

Johanna gave a scream as the stilts leaned forward, threatening to topple her onto the gravel below.

"Now you're standing on them. Just lift one. You nearly have it – you're doing fine," he cajoled her. "Now try taking a step. Come on. I'll steady you. Just lift your right foot and bring the stilt with it. You have to lift it at the same time as your foot."

She glanced at him before looking down at her foot. As she lifted it she felt his rough hand wrapped around her own, pulling upwards on the stilt.

"I'm walking, I'm walking!" She started to laugh. "Don't let go, Hugh!"

"I won't. Just concentrate. Now, that's one step. Put your weight onto that foot and we'll try and lift the left one."

"Ma, Da, look at me!" she shouted, taking her eye off the business as she wobbled around the farmyard with Hugh's help.

"Stay quiet now. You need to concentrate. I don't think you're ready for an audience yet. Now, I think that's enough for today. We don't want to push our luck." Hugh lifted her down. "Tomorrow I'll give you another lesson and maybe you'll be able to try it without me holding you."

The stilt lessons, despite her brave progress, almost came to an abrupt end. He'd promised to give her one before she went to school the next day. He had rushed his early-morning chores to accommodate her. She had asked and he had agreed but she forgot. When he arrived into the kitchen to collect her, she was still eating her breakfast. Her heart sank when he stared at her, then put on his cross frown and went back outside. With Hugh you rarely got a second chance. Not a mistake to be made again. With her brother everything was a learning experience. This time the lesson being taught was that there were consequences to your mistakes.

She ran after him. "I'm sorry, Hugh. I forgot." Her face began to crumple.

"Well, maybe after school. If I have time."

She knew he'd make time.

Art was different. Like Hugh he was forever busy with jobs on the farm. But with Art it was always a 'maybe'. But it seldom happened. He meant to help her with her school homework but there was never time. With Hugh it would happen but it was always necessary to make an appointment. You could waste your own time but you weren't going to waste his. That was Hugh's way.

It wasn't just Hugh going away that changed things. Her brother James had followed and then a few of their friends. So gradual at first that it almost passed unnoticed until a hole began to emerge around the farmyard. With each disappearance it got bigger, could be felt like the middle was eroding from life around the place. No longer so many of the young folk calling.

Johanna shook the crumbs from the breadboard onto the slab outside the henhouse and waited as the hens jerked around pecking the scraps. She envied their focus, their ability to live in the moment, looking neither to the past nor to the future. Never looking beyond the next crumb to be pecked.

She watched the bent back of old Francie at the far end

of the yard as he shovelled manure from the cow byre. The slow, methodical jab and the lift and plop of the sequence gave off the same signs of contentment. Not something she could settle for.

The sound of Art's twins, Declan and Luke, drifted in from the front where she knew they were playing under the trees and she could hear her mother chatting to Art's wife Ellen, and the high voices of her sister Maria and Art's young daughter Katie. It wasn't that she was alone but she missed the youthful vibrancy and banter of the young men who were no longer around. Nothing left but the high voices of the youngsters, the chatter of the women and the slowness of old Francie. He had always worked on the farm but had been drafted in more frequently in recent times to help Art. A lot of the work was beyond him now but he was doing his best to make up for some of the loss of the young labourers. Not that he could fill that gaping hole in the middle. No, she was left alone to do that but no matter how much she loved life there she couldn't do it. Didn't want to even attempt to. Not on her own.

Unaware of her presence, Francie stopped. He drew a sleeve across his brow and leaned on the handle of the fork, looking at his morning's work, the mound of manure piled beside the outside wall of the byre. There it would stay for months weathering and rotting down in time for spreading on the fields.

"You look ready for a cup of tea, Francie?"

He looked over his shoulder, eyebrow raised in surprise.

"Ah, Jo, I didn't see you there." His brown weathered face crinkled. "I could certainly do with it." He lifted the fork, jabbed it into the manure and followed her into the kitchen.

Francie was a man of few words and they had the tea together with no more than a couple of pleasantries exchanged. She knew that's the way he liked it.

"Must be lonely around here for you now, Jo."

His comment came as a surprise. Not something she'd have expected him to have noticed. Nobody else had. Recently she'd come to wonder if she was invisible.

"It is, Francie. I really miss them all."

"Sure, I miss them myself. Miss the bit of banter." He lapsed into silence.

At least someone understood. It wasn't a subject that was easy to introduce into conversation with her mother. Mary Ann had her own problems with most of her sons so far away, Maude in Wexford and Catherine living-in, training in the Big House, and even though it was only a few miles away she only got home once a month.

"Ah sure, Mary Ann, you still have Johanna at home. There's nothing like a daughter around the place."

It was these comments from neighbours that worried Johanna. Everyone taking her life for granted. It set her thinking after Francie left the kitchen. The isolation facing her was alarming. It had all happened in such a gradual way as to go almost unnoticed, until she realised she had no-one to go dancing with anymore. Only the old men and women were left in the neighbouring farms. Very few of her school friends had stayed around. Most had gone to the cities – a few to Dublin and others had gone to Galway and Limerick and Cork. It wasn't enough to see them when they came back for the week or fortnight holidays. There was a lot of in-between time. The spark had gone out of the place and not a lot she could do to replace it.

She hadn't always felt like this – like she was waiting for her life to start. She hadn't given it much thought before, just assuming that everything would happen in its own good time. If she were honest it wasn't that she hadn't given it much thought – she had never given it any thought until the friends and neighbours had started to dribble away. Not just the ones who had gone to the cities but the others who'd emigrated to England and America. Only the odd one at first then it seemed to have become contagious, until now she seemed to be the only one who hadn't caught the bug. For the first time ever Johanna looked at herself in detail, picking apart what was left of her life now that the links were disappearing. Not a lot remained.

It wasn't that she missed anyone in particular other than her brothers and sisters. It was more the cumulative effect that increased the emptiness. It had happened little by little until it became something she couldn't put words on until now, when it seemed to have grown into something she could no longer ignore. This big nothingness that she was left behind with.

She'd only been five when Hugh went and now, at seventeen, what had she done since the rest of them had all disappeared as well? Not a thing, other than grow up. Not idle. Not unhappy. Just nothing of any significance. Not one marker to say she had ever passed this way. Apart from Art, her brothers had never known the adult Johanna. James rarely made contact except at Christmas. Kept details of his life to himself. Always changing his address so it was hard to stay in touch.

Hugh was a different story. The twelve years since he left Ireland had moved fast for him. Marrying Margaret, a girl he met on the voyage, they already had two children. He'd saved enough money from working several jobs, every penny a prisoner with him until he arrived at his goal and was able to open his own grocery shop. He was now planning his second one. Their father had been right. Hugh was the businessman of the family.

If Johanna disappeared now they would never have known her as anything, not as a person, nothing other than a blip of a child in their lives. Not a lot to be said about her.

Maybe 'a nice little girl' – that was it at best.

Her achievements didn't stand up well when compared to those who'd gone away. Gone to lives that held the excitement of the unknown unlike her own predictable future. Dull years of sameness stretching out ahead. Nothing would change if she didn't make it happen. Her life might never start, never jolt itself out of the repetitive pattern of each day, month, season, unless she did something. No-one else was going to do it for her. She couldn't give in to the guilt that niggled about leaving Art and her mother another hand down on the farm. They had managed when Hugh and James had left. They would somehow manage to replace her. She would have to push that to one side if it wasn't to paralyse her. The necessity to make a life. She'd never given it consideration before, just assumed it would happen, like the sun rising and the night falling. No effort needed. No decisions to be made. It would all just miraculously unfold. But the problem was – it wouldn't. That was the truth of it. It had taken a long time for that to dawn on her. She needed a plan, some sort of a programme for the future. What was she waiting for? For a sign to come from somewhere? Well, she might just be left waiting.

The clouds had taken on a soft cream as the afternoon melted into evening. She remembered an old farmer telling her how the light of the sun followed you across the country, sinking later here on the west coast of Ireland than on the eastern side. It was while she was thinking this that it happened. All of a sudden when she was least expecting it. For once she wasn't even thinking about the future. No warning that this particular evening was going to be any different from a hundred others. Nothing to indicate that this was the day the sign would come when the possibilities for her life ahead were to be revealed to her. Had she been asked to describe it she would have said it was like a biblical revelation.

With the evenings drawing in now, soon she wouldn't be able to come out for a walk after the supper. She stood to take one last westerly look out over the sea. A sudden burst of bright evening sunlight, like white lightning breaking through the clouds, startled her. She watched the flare ignite a million candles to twinkle on the surface of the ocean. A scene of amazing clarity – a manifestation at the edge of dark. She could see it for what it was. How she hadn't recognised it before puzzled her. The sparkling lights of America calling her. That's what the draw to this place had been about. A message that had waited, postponed itself until she was ready. Until she was ripe for it. *America*. Her big brothers. And the start of her life.

Chapter 5

Boston

1877

Looking at the choppy grey expanse between her and the familiar land that was slowly disappearing into the distance, she wondered if this had really been such a great idea. As she heard others around her on the deck arguing if it was Cork or Kerry they were looking back at, she wondered if she might catch a last glimpse of Clare before Ireland disappeared from view.

The contradictions and confusion that had been hopping around her head when the time came to leave rattled her. Balancing the thought of no future at home with the unknown adventures that awaited did little to relieve the wrench in her gut as she said goodbye and queued to board the vessel for the start of her journey to America. Never did an afternoon in the Lake Field, paddling about in the little old rowing boat between the rushes seem more attractive. And back home for the tea at five o'clock.

Leaning on the rail, she watched until the land was absorbed into the mist. She stayed on deck, keeping a long low cloud that hung on the horizon in her sight, unwilling to let it go until reality could no longer be ignored. There was no turning back now.

Away from the comfort of the familiar, the concentration

required for figuring out how things worked on the voyage helped settle her. Finding her way around the ship, which way to turn as she exited the cabin, which corridors led where, which stairs led to the various decks, how the mealtimes worked, each small detail a new experience.

It was surprisingly easy to get to know people. Lots of them, like herself, were first-timers and once that link was established it was a relief when she discovered they all shared much the same anxieties. The voyage provided an opportunity to make a few possible contacts but many conversations ended in disappointment with the discovery that only a few were destined for Boston. And they weren't always the people she felt comfortable with. Not the ones she'd have chosen as travelling companions anyway. Many were stopping in New York and others continuing on to Philadelphia or Chicago to join relatives. It would have been nice to have someone to share the next leg of the journey with, but the way things were shaping up she would just have to rely on her own abilities. She spoke the language. That was what she kept telling herself every time the panic began to rise.

"Haven't you a tongue in your head?" Her mother's voice, a reminder for keeping the anxiety under control.

She'd been dreading breaking the news to them but after a couple of false starts she got her mother alone one evening.

"Ma, I've something to tell you." She hoped the anxiety she was feeling didn't show on her face.

"This sounds ominous." Mary Ann glanced up from her knitting.

She could see from her mother's expression what she might be expecting.

"It's not what you think." Not sure if this was going to make it easier she blurted it out. "I'm thinking of going to America." There it was, said.

She watched as her mother processed this. Maybe she shouldn't have said she was only *'thinking'* about it.

Mary Ann took a deep breath and put her knitting aside. "Well, Johanna, you're going to be missed here. You know that. Art will miss you and so will I."

She hoped her mother wasn't going to put objections in her way. This was hard enough.

"How am I going to tell Art?"

"Leave that to me – I'll break it to him gently," her mother reassured her. "You have to do what you want to do with your life, child. You have only one and you have to do what's best for you."

It hadn't been as difficult as she'd imagined, although she knew her mother's heart was broken. Another of her children leaving. She doubted if she herself would be so brave or selfless under the same circumstances.

As her voyage neared its end an impatience to get moving nagged. Her eagerness for life to begin conflicted with the picture she'd had of her arrival on the new continent.

"I can see myself standing on the platform, a forlorn figure all alone with my battered old suitcase and nobody to meet me." There, she'd said it. Revealed the image that had loomed so large in her head, the one that she'd tormented herself with for days.

"Of course he'll be there to meet you." The woman smiled. "Doesn't he know you're coming? Are you meeting him in New York or Boston?"

"Boston. He's too busy to travel down."

"Well, you needn't worry. They're always delighted to have a relative from Ireland visit."

"Well, I'm not exactly here on a visit. I'm here for good."

"All the better. Some of them, especially the men, would never admit it but they do get very lonesome for home. They love someone coming over. Anyone at all will do." The woman caught a loose strand of hair that had blown free in the breeze and tucked it behind her ear. "So what are you worrying about? You're his sister, he'll be thrilled."

"I wouldn't be so sure." Johanna looked doubtful. "He hasn't seen me since I was a child. I daresay he won't even know me."

"Well, isn't he in for a nice surprise then? A lovely young lady." The woman stood back and looked at Johanna. "Believe me, I know. I've been that person on the quayside, wouldn't have missed a relative arriving. Sure I'd have been building up to it for months and would be waiting there for hours before the ship was due."

"So this isn't your first time coming over then." It wasn't a question. It made sense now. The unselfconscious way she carried herself. They'd only ever exchanged greetings as they passed each other. Tall and erect, a middle-aged woman doing her morning walks around the deck and always alone.

"No – I've been living in America for years now but this was my first visit home to Ireland." She looked at Johanna. "I can pick out the ones leaving for the first time. There are quite a few on the ship and they all look like you. Worried and unsure. But you needn't be. It'll all work out. I've never regretted it for a minute. It's a good life over here. Well, it can be if you're prepared to work hard."

Johanna leaned back against the rail. She wished she'd met the woman earlier. Not wasted all that time worrying unnecessarily.

As the woman had said, Hugh was there waiting for her when she alighted from the train. She scanned the crowd, wondering if she would recognise him in the throng on the platform. The last picture she had of him was the day he left Ireland. Hanging onto her mother's hand, she'd watched her big handsome brother in his best suit – his only suit – and his thick wavy brown hair blowing in the wind as he said his goodbyes. She remembered her mother's eyes, her wonder at their redness, herself oblivious to the possibility that she might never see her brother again. The space between the child and adult, a distance too wide to span, right there on the quayside in Ireland. It was like it had all happened yesterday. And now she was here. Family. But a stranger meeting a stranger.

As the crowd thinned she spotted him, or spotted someone she thought might be him. The Boston businessman in his dark topcoat and felt hat walking towards her was not what she'd been expecting. Only the smile that brought one corner of his mouth slightly higher than the other was familiar. It was obvious that time had not stood still for him. Shaking her hand he placed the other arm around her shoulder in a half hug before reaching for her case. Their hands became entangled as he took it, surprising her with the softness of his. A momentary flash of his big rough paws, ingrained with farmyard dirt, as he played card tricks with her. That brother no more. Long gone.

"Welcome to the United States of America, Johanna." He studied her face. "A bit of a change, eh?"

"It surely is." Not sure if he was referring to himself, her or from where she'd come. Embarrassed by the way he boomed it out, she glanced around. No-one had noticed. Everyone else was engrossed in their own bustle of greetings.

"How did you recognise me?"

"The freckles. You never lost them, Jo." He smiled at her. "And you're the very spit of our mother. Tell me, how are they all at home?"

"Good. Nothing's changed much there. The farm is still how you left it."

36

"Well, Art was never a man for change." He laughed. "And how was the journey? Not too rough, I hope?"

Before she had a chance to reply he'd headed off with her case, weaving his way through the crowd. She picked up her cloth bag, and with her eyes clinging to the felt hat ahead she tried to keep up without bumping into those gathered in untidy groups on the platform. Everything was happening fast. She would have liked to stop and watch the activity for a minute but Hugh seemed in a hurry.

She didn't notice the brown bag that lay on the ground. As she tripped a hand reached out and caught her before she hit the ground. By the time she'd got over her fright and turned to mumble her thanks, the owner of the hand had disappeared into the crowd. A ripple of irritation that Hugh hadn't waited ran through her when she realised she had lost sight of him. Her head swivelled in panic. No sign of the hat.

"Go to the nearest door and wait." She could hear her mother's words on the rare occasion when they visited Ennis. "If you get lost wait at the door and I'll come looking for you. Don't go out onto the road. You needn't worry, I won't leave the shop without you."

She must have said it to Hugh too when he was small. A few deep breaths. Surely he'd remember their mother's warning.

She made her way to the first exit. Standing there, she managed to quell the rising anxiety by thinking about the impression she gave with her tumble. No need to add terror to it. Anything to calm herself. She wondered if she looked the same as when he'd first left, only bigger? The notion that she'd not thrown off her childish appearance did nothing to increase her confidence as she glanced about her. How long could it take for him to miss her?

She saw the raised hand beckoning a moment before

she recognised the hat. She waved back, smiling. At least one thing hadn't changed. Even if his smooth exterior belied it, he still remembered that Mother knew best. Not something she would point out. Not yet anyway. She needed to get to know him better. She kept her eyes trained on him this time, relying on his guidance as they worked their way through the throng.

His sophistication made her proud to be associated with this man of the world, but at the same time it worried her. Maybe this was all a mistake. From the little conversation they'd had so far she thought she'd caught a slight American twang, a sharpness at odds with the soft Clare lilt. But maybe she'd imagined it. She hoped she had. Too many thoughts whirling around her head. She was tired now and the changes seemed all too sudden and too many for her. And she was only here an hour.

With the innocence of youth that expected everything to simply fall into place, she hadn't given any thought to the practicalities beyond her arrival and staying with Hugh. That coming to America was only the first step was something that had completely eluded her. At home things just happened, or didn't, and you just went along with it. She had expected that her future here would come naturally. Just like a flower opening in expectation of bees and insects visiting, she hadn't seen the need for plans. Up until now.

Looking out the window of the carriage, the sophistication of the city frightened her. It suddenly dawned on her what a sheltered life she'd been living. Galway had been the only city she'd visited. She'd never even got to Dublin. Maybe she should have stretched herself a bit more before starting out on this adventure. She couldn't see herself ever fitting in here. Everyone walking along seemed to know what they were about, the certainty of their destination decipherable on their faces. The ones with the newspapers under their arms striding with a purpose. The languid couple ambling along admiring the trees. The woman stopping on the pathway, her arm linked through her man's, laughing up at him as he smiled at her. They all fitted. She couldn't imagine the day would ever come when she would fit as comfortably.

The freedom of the unknown, which had added to the excitement before she left home, now suddenly seemed frightening. Too many choices, too many possibilities. Here nobody had expectations of her. There was nothing to hold her back. But now, to someone with no strategy, no destination in mind, that limitless freedom was overwhelming.

Chapter 6

They had travelled in silence except when Hugh pointed out a landmark. She didn't know if it was deliberate, to give her a chance to absorb her first impressions, but she was glad he didn't addle her with talk.

"We're almost there. We're coming up to the Boston Common now." He glanced at her. "If ever you get lost that's the place to head for."

Had he read her mind? Or maybe the worry was written all over her face. Although the streets were wide, the rows of buildings gave a feeling of travelling along reddish-brown-brick corridors. The Common was a relief. An oasis of grass and trees. At last something that she could relate to.

"Everything you'll need to know for the moment radiates from here and the house isn't far away so you'll be within walking distance. You'd only need to ask someone to point you in the right direction."

By the time they had rounded the next couple of corners she had already lost her bearings until suddenly Hugh indicated a black iron gate.

"There she is. Waiting for us." The brightness in his voice told Johanna more about his life than any words might have. Not that he had yet offered any insights.

Margaret stood leaning against the frame of the open door. She looked relaxed, basking in the sun that lit up the front of the house, as if she'd been waiting there a while. Johanna looked out at the tall, elegant woman with dark upswept curls waving at them. It took a few seconds to recover. She didn't know what she had expected but it certainly hadn't been someone so beautiful. Hoping her mouth hadn't been hanging open, she smiled and waved before standing up. She reached across for her luggage, fussing with it before lifting it up, hoping Hugh would get out first and lead the way.

"It's OK. I'll look after that. Go on up and meet her."

She wished he'd come with her. Introduce them. Stepping down from the carriage she looked back at him but he was paying the driver.

Nearing the gate, it struck her that she would be the first family member to meet his wife. Her lack of forward planning suddenly seemed like a huge oversight. Would this be a woman to whom she could give a gift of the fruit cake that had travelled across the Atlantic Ocean in her bag? What if Margaret didn't like her? Then she wouldn't be able to stay here for any length of time.

"Johanna, you're very welcome." Margaret came down the steps and met her halfway up the garden path, enveloping her in a warm hug.

Over Margaret's shoulder Johanna noticed the two fair-haired children, dressed in matching knee breeches and white shirts, half hidden in the shadow of the hall.

"The children have me pestered asking when you were coming, although you wouldn't think it the way they've gone all shy now." Margaret turned and beckoned to them. "Come down here, boys. Come on and meet your aunt."

They stepped out onto the sunlit step and the older boy began descending.

"Wait, Hughie – take Patrick's hand!"

The younger one tottered on the top step, uncertain of his footing. Margaret ran back up the steps and took his other hand. Johanna, forgotten for a moment, watched as the three looked downwards, negotiating each step.

"That's it, big step. Good boy."

As they reached the bottom, the younger boy disappeared into the folds of his mother's skirt, the only visible evidence a chubby suntanned fist grasping a clump of the material.

Margaret reached behind and drew him forward. A thumb stuck in his mouth, he looked up at Johanna from under long brown eyelashes, at odds with his blond hair.

"Now, boys, say hello to your Aunt Johanna – she will be staying with us for a while."

The formality startled her. The niece and nephews at home just called her Jo. She didn't feel old enough to be 'Aunt'.

The older boy, who looked about six, held out his hand. The care with which he watched his positioning of it suggested an earlier rehearsal. Johanna smiled at him, reached out and gave it a warm shake.

"Pleased to meet you, Aunt Johanna." The child squinted up at her, shading his eyes from the sunlight with his free hand.

"And I'm very pleased to meet you too."

The child smiled at her.

"Don't just stand there, come on in." Margaret lifted the toddler and, turning, carried him up the steps as the older boy led Johanna up.

Johanna glanced behind to see her brother leaning on the gate, beaming. He'd been watching the reactions of the two women meeting and in an instant Johanna knew that it was her reaction to his beautiful wife that most interested him.

"And what's your name?" she asked the little boy.

"I'm Hugh. Like my dad. They call me Junior sometimes. But it's usually just Hughie." He paused before continuing. "You can call me Hughie."

As they walked along the hall, two big blue eyes studied her from over Margaret's shoulder.

"And what's *your* name?" Johanna smiled at him.

"His name's Patrick," Hughie jumped in. "He's three but he's shy. I'm six and three-quarters."

"Big boys!" Johanna glanced from one child to the other and saw Hughie eyeing her cloth bag.

"Can I carry your bag?"

"It might be a bit heavy?" Johanna handed it to him. "Here, try it."

"That's not heavy."

He struggled, holding it to one side with his two arms, bumping it against his legs with every step. Her mother's fruit cake might be in crumbs by the time they reached the kitchen.

"And Patrick, he's Paddy," Hughie said. "But we're not allowed to call him that." He giggled.

"Hello, Patrick." She reached up and stroked the chubby hand resting on his mother's shoulder. "And, hello, Hughie Junior." She smiled down at him. "I'm Johanna and you are allowed to call me Jo."

"I think I prefer Auntie Jo."

Usually observant but with so much to take in on arrival, Johanna hadn't immediately noticed that Margaret was pregnant. It wasn't until breakfast the next morning that she had an opportunity to mention it.

"When is the baby due, Margaret?" The completeness of the family unit worried her – they mightn't want her around for long.

"Nearly another two months to go. It can't come soon

enough. *They*. It's twins." Margaret was stirring the porridge at the stove. "Have you thought about work, Johanna?"

"Well, not really, but I've heard there are plenty of jobs." A butterfly tickled the inside of her stomach. She felt rushed and had no idea where to start.

"What sort of work do you have in mind?"

"Anything really. I'm not qualified for anything in particular." She wished she'd thought this out better, prepared herself in some way. "I suppose I'm capable enough at most things . . . I learn fast . . . " Her voice trailed away as her abilities at home on the farm suddenly seemed out of place here.

"Would you be interested in working as a children's nanny?"

"But wouldn't I need experience?"

"Well, you could always get it." Margaret paused. "I've an idea I want to put to you, Johanna, but say if you don't like it."

Once Margaret had set eyes on Johanna, she knew. Hugh seemed happy enough when she put it to him. Over the years an awareness had crept into the relationship, an understanding that he was happy with any decisions she made in relation to the home, content to leave most of those arrangements to her. If she needed something she asked and he never queried the necessity, just went along with it, trusting her judgement.

"How would you feel about helping here with the children? I need someone and I'd prefer it were family." She glanced at Johanna as she ladled out the porridge. "It wouldn't have to be permanent. Just while you're finding your feet." She paused. "It would be a paid job, of course."

"But I couldn't take money if I'm staying here," said Johanna, taken aback.

"Of course you could. You see, the way it is, Johanna, if

you don't take the job we'll have to get someone else and they'll have to live in. And we'd have to pay them anyway. It would suit much better if it were you. I'd feel more comfortable having someone in the family that I know I can trust ..." she looked across at the boys before winking at Johanna, "with my precious darlings. And it will give you the experience you'll need for the future."

"Well, if you're sure?"

"Sure I'm sure." She could feel Johanna watching her face for any sign of doubt as she sat down. "Now, let's eat up the porridge before it gets cold."

If she could have glimpsed the thoughts in Johanna's head she'd have seen her doubts melting away. A job. Being part of a family. She'd have felt the relief in the safety of it all – that what was on offer was exactly what Johanna needed for the moment. Freedom could wait until she found her feet.

Chapter 7

Taking the children out each afternoon while Margaret went to bed for a rest was one of her duties. Observing lots of other girls her age doing the same thing, it hadn't taken Johanna long to realise that up-and-coming business people all had a live-in servant or 'domestic'. And she had no doubt but that her brother was on his way up in the world.

She soon learned that Margaret had come from a different world. A large house that had been passed down through the generations, outside Galway city, where her father was a doctor. She and her siblings, growing up, had even had a governess but unfortunately her father had a taste for the drink and the horses and managed to run them into debt, almost losing their home in the process. Her eldest brother managed to save them from ruin by turning the house into an hotel for the upper classes but at that early stage it hadn't been enough to support them all.

"Was that what made you come to America, Margaret?" Johanna was surprised that it had been necessity rather than a search for adventure that had motivated her sister-in-law.

"Partly. I helped out but once he got the business up and running I could see myself stuck there if I hung around long enough and it wasn't a life that appealed to me." Margaret shook her head. "Besides that, my father was still a bit of a problem and I wasn't prepared to watch him do the same thing again."

"And did he?"

"Didn't get the chance, I'm glad to say. He died shortly after I arrived here. Oh, that sounds awful. I didn't mean it like that." She sounded sad. "Ah, he wasn't all bad. Just foolish. I *was* very fond of him."

"And were you glad you came?" Johanna needed reassurance.

"Well, if I hadn't come I'd never have met your lovely brother. So, yes, very glad."

It was almost always the Common Johanna took the children to but, afraid they might get bored with the same route for their afternoon stroll, she varied it a little. She soon realised, however, that the children didn't seem to care where they went, just as long as they were moving. Patrick was happy to suck his thumb and watch everything that passed. The thumb was released every now and then from its watery home to point to the 'birdie' or the 'dick'.

"Dick! Dick!" Patrick's arm shot out the first day, pointing to the ground.

"What's 'dick', lovie?" She looked around for a clue. "I don't know what it is you want."

Hughie had run ahead so Johanna continued pushing the pram, moving slowly forward along the pathway, hoping what 'dick' was would become evident.

"*Dick! Want dick!*" The level of urgency rose with each shout, threatening to develop into a wail, and the child squirmed around in his restraints, pointing backwards. "*Want dick!*"

Hughie ran back towards them across the grass, taking a leap forward after every short run.

"Did you see that, Auntie Jo?" His breath came out in gasps. "I did big long jumps."

"You're a great athlete altogether."

"*Dick! Dick! My dick!*" The shout went up again as she began to move forward.

"Do you know what he means, Hughie?"

Hughie ran behind them towards a large tree and, picking up a twiggy branch that had blown down onto the grass, handed it to his brother.

"This is what he wants. Here's your stick, Patrick."

"My dick!" Patrick grasped it in his pudgy hand and waved it about, looking up at Johanna, a big smile lighting his face.

"So that's what you wanted." Johanna leaned forward with a teasing grin. "Silly Jo didn't know what it was. But I'll know next time. Isn't it well I had your big brother here to teach me?"

"It is!" said Hughie.

"I think we'll have a little sit-down for a few minutes. What do you think?"

"Alright," said Hughie.

Johanna wedged the pram into position near a bench so that Patrick, happy with his stick, had a good view of the passing walkers, something to keep him entertained.

Hughie sat on the bench beside her and looked around.

Hugh Junior had the type of enquiring mind that produced an endless stream of questions. Mostly about Ireland which, surprisingly, he seemed to have a good grasp of geographically. It was the minutiae that fascinated him and provided her the opportunity to sound more interesting than she'd ever have given herself credit for.

"Why is everything so green in Ireland?" he asked now. "Dad says it rains a lot. But it rains here too."

"Yes, but I'd say you haven't seen anything like as

much rain as we get in Ireland and you're living in a city."
She hadn't really given it much thought before. "We live in
the countryside where there's nothing but field after field.
There wouldn't be a shop – or stores nearby, or streets like
you have here, so there's lots and lots of green."

"What? You don't have stores? Where do you buy things?"

"Well, we do have stores, but not near where we live.
Only in the towns and villages. We'd have to travel a long
way if we wanted to buy something. Where we live is
mostly countryside . . . fields and hedges and trees. That's
why it's so green."

"Where do you get your food?"

"We grow most of it and we have animals for milk and
meat and eggs. We go into the town once or twice a month
and buy what we don't have on the farm."

"Dad said there was a potato famine and lots of people
died." He looked up at her. "What's a famine, Jo?"

From his expression she couldn't be sure that he wasn't
testing her.

"*Emm* . . . how would I put it? A shortage of food, yes,
that's it, Hughie. There was a shortage of potatoes because
they all rotted in the ground."

"Yes, that's what Dad told me." He nodded knowingly.
"But why were the people hungry if there's lots of land?
Couldn't they grow other stuff? They didn't have to grow
just potatoes."

"You're right, Hughie, they didn't, but that's what they
were used to sowing and potatoes were a good healthy food
and could feed a family well for a whole year. Some of the
people did plant other vegetables though, like carrots and
cabbages."

"Dad says *millions* of them died?"

"Well, let's just stick with one million, Hughie, but
many of them had to leave Ireland and come here." She

smiled down, seeing there was no stopping him. The questions came fast once he was on a roll.

"Why didn't they kill the animals and eat them?"

"Well, some people didn't have animals. Others had hens and maybe a cow but if they killed them for meat they wouldn't have any eggs or milk. And some would have to sell their animals to get money to pay the rent on their cottages."

She'd hoped he wasn't going to hone in on the death aspect of it, glad now of the mobility of his mind which allowed him to hop from one thing to another.

"How could they afford to come to America if they didn't have enough to eat?"

"Some of them might have had some money but others would have had to borrow it from other members of their families who were better off, and promise to pay it back when they got a job in America."

"Were you hungry?"

"No. The famine happened before I was born." Johanna smiled at the concerned face looking up at her. "Your dad was born towards the end of it but we were lucky we had other crops and vegetables and we had animals." If this child with his enquiring mind was going to be satisfied she'd have to start engaging her brain more.

"I'm hungry."

"Well, then, maybe it's time we should be heading for home," she said with a grin, "before we all die of starvation."

The heavy rain had stopped mid-afternoon, leaving the streets washed, and by six o'clock a late sun had evaporated the wetness, leaving the pavements fresh in time for the opening of Hugh's new store. Johanna had worried most of the day about her new outfit and shoes. They wouldn't stand up to much hardship if she had to slosh through the torrents.

It wasn't planned that she would attend, but in the

days leading up to the big night it became obvious that Margaret would not be well enough.

"Take Johanna instead, Hugh. I really don't feel up to it and I don't think I'm going to make a miraculous recovery in time." Margaret sipped her tea. "And there'll be a lot of standing around."

"Ah, I don't know. If you can't come I might just go alone." He made no attempt to hide his reluctance. "Jo wouldn't be used to that sort of thing."

"Well, she'll never get used to it if you take that attitude. We all had to start somewhere." Margaret's determined look left him in no doubt. "You weren't always as sophisticated as you are now. It was me that knocked you into shape, remember? Anyway, she'll love it and even if she doesn't she'll learn something new."

"I'm not sure." He tried again. "She won't have anything suitable –"

"To wear? Don't you worry about that. That's my territory." His wife's firm tone confirmed he was not going to win. "She'll be like a princess by the time I've finished with her."

"OK, OK. I'll leave it to you to make sure of that." He accepted his defeat with a smile.

She waited until she was alone with Johanna to break the news, closing all opportunities for her husband to attach himself to his sister's reluctance and avail of the chance to leave her at home.

"You're going to have to go, Johanna. Even if I'm feeling better Saturday I couldn't stand around." Margaret paused and looking across recognised the need to quash the hesitancy she could see taking hold. "It'll be a whole new experience. You'll enjoy it. Anyway, someone has to go to support Hugh and you're the only other family he has here in Boston."

"I've nothing to wear." It was out before she realised. Hoping it didn't sound as if she was asking for anything after all they had done for her. "Well, nothing that might be fancy enough."

"That's easily fixed. The least of our problems. Hugh says you're to buy a frock for the occasion – he'll pay for it. You'll have to do him proud."

"You'll have to come with me to pick it." The very thought of entering one of the smart fashion stores alone as a buying customer terrified her, but one look at Margaret's tired pale face told her that she might have to.

"We'll see. I'll do out a little map for you anyway, how to get to the store, and I'll arrange an appointment with Miss Myers. She manages the women's fashion department." Margaret saw the unsure look on Johanna's face. "Don't worry, she knows me well. I'll ask her to look after you personally and put all purchases on my account. You'll be fine. She has a great eye for what looks good. Be guided by her. You can rely on her to find something to suit you."

"*Mmm.*" Johanna looked doubtful. "She'll have her work cut out with me."

When it came to business and social events, Hugh didn't know the meaning of the word 'doubt'. This was so obvious an attribute in his line of business that Johanna often wondered if they were really part of the same family. Hugh just stated what he wanted to happen and expected others to get on with it. Including herself. Just plough on ahead.

"*No point in looking back. There's no future in that.*" His motto. She'd heard it from him a couple of times when she'd brought up the subject of home. He might be her brother but he wasn't one to entertain a discussion on homesickness, no matter how lonely she was feeling.

He seemed to have forgotten what it was like to be faced with doing something for the first time. For him insecurity was fairly much unknown territory. What was obvious to him was still a mystery to her.

"How will I get there?" The question sounded stupid, even to herself, when he asked her to pick up a jacket from the tailor's.

"Work it out, work it out, woman. You'll never survive here if you go on like that."

She preferred Margaret's gentler way of teaching the ways of the world, guiding with simple tips almost without appearing to. Step by step. One thing at a time.

"Ask the man in uniform at the door to direct you to the frock department. That's what he's there for. Once you get there just ask for Miss Myers."

"But what if she's busy?"

"Say you'll wait. Tell them you have an appointment with her. She's expecting you. Introduce yourself to her. Then just draw a breath and stop talking and worrying. Simple as that." Margaret smiled at her. "Miss Myers will take it from there. Nothing to it now, is there?"

"It just seems so much easier at home. We're less sophisticated there." Johanna made a face. "Am I really that much of a hick?"

They both laughed.

Chapter 8

The evening had turned chilly. Johanna, pulling the wrap around her shoulders, sat back in the chair and read over the letter, hoping she hadn't left out any important news.

Dear Mama,

I hope you are all well, as I am. Sorry the last letter was so short but I just wanted to let you know that I arrived safely. At that stage I didn't have much to write about because I'd only arrived and I hadn't seen anything. It was even an adventure to find where I could buy a stamp and post the letter. How simple am I?

It took me a while to recover from the voyage but I am beginning to settle well here, thanks to Hugh's wife Margaret. It is a pity that you cannot meet her because I know that you would like her very much. Apart from being beautiful, she is very warm and friendly and that has made such a difference to me because I was so nervous when I first arrived. Sometimes in the evenings she plays the piano and we all sit around listening. You'll be relieved to know that I don't offer to sing even though she has tried to persuade me to join in the lovely Moore's melodies that she sings so well. I've told her that I'm a crow as my sisters so often assured me, but she doesn't believe me and I've no intention of opening my mouth to prove it. Her singing reminds me so much of when Maude used to entertain us at home on Sunday nights before she got married. I've been meaning to write to her but I promise I will do so soon.

Hugh is well and very occupied with his business but he sends his love and says he is sorry he doesn't get to write very often. He seems to be very well thought of over here.

The children, Hugh Junior and Patrick are both lovely. In the beginning young Hughie was very polite and formal but now that I've got to know them better I can see that they are full of mischief. Hughie is a very bright little boy, always asking questions. I think Hugh likes to teach him about the world because he knows quite a lot and the little imp is always testing me. They are always nicely dressed in what seems to me to be very refined clothes. No rough coarse materials that would scratch the skin off you like we'd be used to. They are real little Americans not like our Irish ruffians at home. We have some good times together. I really enjoy looking after them and I take them to Boston Common most days. It's a lovely big park with lots of trees and a lake nearby.

Life here is very different. I haven't seen very much of the city yet but I hope to do so soon. So far what I notice are the crowds in the street and the stylish women. You would never see the likes at home. You know, the way our women dress in navy or grey or black if they were going anywhere special, whereas here they look much more bright and cheerful. People don't say hello to you in the street like at home, unless they know you and that takes a bit of getting used to. I suppose it's because there are so many that you'd have the head nodded off you if you were to greet everyone.

*There are lots of shops (they call them stores here).
Some of them look so fancy that you'd be afraid to go into
them in case they'd ask you what you were doing.*

*I nearly forgot to tell you, in the house with the turn
of a tap you have running water. No more going to the
well with a bucket for me.*

*Tell all the others that I miss them and the neighbours
too. I will write soon again when I have some news. I am
going to the opening of Hugh's new store on Saturday. I
am feeling very nervous about it and I wish Margaret was
coming but she isn't feeling very well. Nothing serious
but I will tell you all about it in my next letter and about
my visit to one of those glamorous stores I mentioned.
Margaret sent me on my own to get an outfit for the
occasion – it's gorgeous but that was some experience I
can tell you.*

*It was lovely to see James again. He came over on a
visit from Philadelphia and stayed a couple of days. I gave
out to him for not writing home so I think you might have
a letter soon from your son, at least I hope so. He told me
he learned a lot from Hugh, got a very good training here
in the shop but I think he got itchy feet and wanted to
strike out on his own. He is now managing a store where
they sell all sorts of hardware. I think that interests him
more than groceries. James was always good at making
and fixing things so I can see how he would be more
suited to that sort of establishment. I thought he looked a
bit tired and pale but he said that he was just working
very hard and needs a bit of a holiday. He seems happy
though so there is no need for you to worry.*

With all my love
Your fond daughter
Johanna

"Am I alright?"

Margaret watched from the bed as Johanna did a final check in the cheval mirror. She relaxed back onto the lace-covered pillows, exhausted after completing the finishing touches to Johanna's upswept hairstyle.

"I don't look like me." Johanna twisted her head from side to side, admiring the elegance.

"Will you stop checking the mirror! It is you. You should wear your hair up more often. You've a great thick head of hair. You look just beautiful."

"I think that's stretching the truth a bit."

Margaret laughed. She was glad Johanna had taken Miss Myers' advice and bought the blue dress. It brought out the colour of her eyes.

"When you arrive at the opening just walk in with Hugh, as if you are meant to be there. Don't creep in like you've been caught in your apron. You look great. Hold your head high."

Johanna wasn't sure if she could pull this off. She tried walking up and down the bedroom.

"Slower. You're not rushing out to do the milking."

Johanna laughed as she turned to try again.

"Head up. Don't let it poke forward – you don't want it to arrive first."

"Oh, I wish you were coming. You could remind me of these things."

"Well, you're not on your own. Hugh will be there. This is your first social occasion here. Enjoy it."

"Well, I'm not sure I can go that far. If I survive it I'll be doing well."

"We'll settle for that then. Now off you go. I need a rest after all that." Margaret laughed. "By God, you're hard work!"

Chapter 9

The smell of polish and paint wafted through the door as they entered. A few staff members stood behind the counters, watching as an officious woman buzzed from counter to counter doing her final brisk checks. Every now and then she lifted an item and wiped the counter with a duster or realigned a display before standing back and checking that everything was perfect.

"Good evening, Mr. McNamara." She slipped the duster into a drawer behind the counter as she greeted him.

"Evening, Miss Doyle." Hugh looked around him slowly, taking in every detail. "Great job. The place looks very well, very well indeed."

"Thank you, Mr. McNamara." She glanced around in an effort to include the other workers.

"I know now why I appointed you supervisor." He smiled at her. "You've excelled yourself."

"I'm glad you're happy with it. I have to say the staff have all worked very hard to achieve it."

"That's what I like to hear. It shows, it shows." He smiled. "Thank you all. It is much appreciated. And keep up the good work – this is an important night for all of us."

Within minutes the new store was buzzing with the

chatter of people well-known to one another. Johanna followed Hugh around for the first ten minutes as he spoke to men in suits and members of staff in shop uniforms. He introduced her as his sister initially. It was only when he stopped introducing her as they moved around the various groups that she realised she had hardly uttered a word to anyone. She just nodded and smiled and with a mumbled "How do you do?" shook hands if they seemed so inclined.

She was annoyed that she hadn't given it enough thought beforehand. If she'd done so instead of fussing about being shy, she might have had the wit to equip herself with a few lines to prolong a conversation. Instead she found herself totally lost when the introductions ceased. The length of the handshakes took on a strange importance. She began to notice the differences. Some brief and business-like before they turned their eyes and attention back to her brother. Others uncomfortably long. These lengthy ones left her not quite knowing when she might extricate her hand without appearing rude. But once released, without the support of the formality, she was on her own again with little chance of breaking into a conversation.

"Why don't you take yourself off to have a look around the store, Johanna?"

His suggestion came as a relief, even though she knew he'd said it because he'd had enough of her and her inhibitions. Before she managed a response she found herself staring at his retreating back as he moved off to join a couple of important-looking men at the far side of the room. She watched the chat fade as the group turned towards him on his approach. It was at that moment she realised the power of her brother's success.

A stony-faced businessman stood alone, scanning the crowd for a familiar contact. His head swung upwards, the opposite of a nod, but with the same meaning, his face breaking into a smile. There was no reason why he would have singled her out but, as he weaved through the crowd, for a moment she thought he was heading to her. It was as he drew closer, excusing himself as he passed her, that she realised his smile had been for an acquaintance who stood behind her. She had recognised his relief at finding a kindred spirit and wished that she too could find someone to talk to.

"Look like you are meant to be there." Margaret's words came back to her as the heads of the crowd began to swim before her. She would have to shift herself, move, mingle, anything to quash the anxiety. Plastering a half smile on her face she forced herself to make eye-contact with one or two of the staff as she moved through the crowd. Courage deserted her as they all seemed to have someone to chat with. Hoping to look like she had a destination in mind she headed for what looked like an interesting shelf display of teas, coffees and confectionery. She breathed in the aromas of the spices as she walked along the counter, the exotic nature of the display a million miles from Ennis in County Clare.

She slowed her step. There was no need to rush. She needed to pace herself if she was going to be here for the next hour or two. The details on the containers provided a prop, picking them up and reading them gave her an opportunity to feign an interest while she nursed her inadequacy.

After a few laps of the shelves she glanced around to see if anyone had noticed. A few members of staff were the only ones to cast a look in her direction. She hoped they hadn't counted her rounds.

She felt like hugging the one young shop assistant who actually stopped to talk to her and ask how she was enjoying her stay in Boston. Unfortunately Miss Doyle then signalled for the girl's attention, interrupting their brief conversation, and she was again on her own.

"Look like you are meant to be there." She tried Margaret's

words again, this time to drown the thought that maybe they were thinking that she was about to pilfer something. It wasn't working. She'd have to try another tactic. Maybe try to imagine she owned the place.

She smiled at anyone who looked in her direction, strained muscles pushing up her cheeks. She held it one second, two seconds. Down. Slowly. Did it look as artificial as it felt? Trying to make the smile reach her eyes she hoped her desperation wasn't radiating out her eyeballs. When would this be over? Why had she agreed to come?

A young man in a brown shop-coat strolled in her direction. She watched the trace of a smile widening into something just less than a grin. As he drew closer she glanced over her shoulder to see at whom it might be directed. A group of suited businessmen were gathered in an uninviting huddle behind her. Guessing it was not them, she turned her head to find him stopped in front of her.

"No. It's you I've come over to talk to." He laughed into her face. "You look a bit lost. I doubt that I'd be very welcome in that group behind you?"

"*Mmm*. I suppose they are a bit off-putting, aren't they?" Her voice came out hoarse, the result of her lengthy silence. To cover her embarrassment she gave a little cough and hoped it would clear her throat.

"What do you think of the new store? It's much bigger than the other one, isn't it?"

"It is indeed." She ran her eyes over the full expanse while she recovered. "Much bigger and better."

Silence fell between them as he leaned back against the counter.

"You're from Ireland?" As soon as she'd stated the obvious she felt foolish.

"How did you guess? And there was I thinking I'd picked up the American accent like a native."

61

"Well, the red hair is a bit of a clue as well. Sounds like Galway. Am I right?"

"You're fairly sharp." He grinned at her. A curl bounced down onto his forehead as he cocked his head to one side, reminding her of a young lad in her class at school whose tousled mop had been allowed to grow longer than normal to hide sticking-out ears.

"I'm from Clare."

"I know." He raised his eyebrows, looking straight at her.

"You're fairly sharp yourself."

Aware he was studying her, she moved sideways out of his eyeline and leaned back beside him. She could feel the curved edge of the counter digging into her back but the relief of having someone to talk to overshadowed her discomfort. She settled herself against it, careful to avoid disturbing any of the produce on display behind her. A moment of doubt entered her head, a fear that he might have misread her move and think she didn't want to continue chatting. She turned her head as if glancing around the room, hoping to catch a glimpse of his expression. He looked totally relaxed.

She searched all corners of her mind for a topic, one that wouldn't seem forced. There was nothing there. Her brain was blank. With no conversation to introduce, a panic rose up slowly through her. It seeped up towards her head. She wasn't sure where it might go when it reached her crown – but she needn't have worried – her companion interrupted her thoughts.

"You're Mr. McNamara's sister, aren't you?"

Relief flooded her. She turned her head to face him, grateful for his intervention.

"That's right. His wife couldn't come to the opening so I came instead."

"I'm Matthew Coyne. I'll be moving over here to the

62

new store." He looked at her. "I don't suppose you'll be working here too?"

"No. I'm looking after his children for the moment anyway."

She noticed the shadow of what seemed like disappointment cross his face. Totally unexpected, it caused a thrill to run through her.

"Sure that was probably a stupid question anyway." He blushed. "I don't expect the sister of the boss would be working as a shopgirl anyway."

"Well – I don't know – more likely he wouldn't employ me because I've no experience of shopwork." A sudden rustle in the crowd interrupted her. "Oh, I think he's going to make a speech."

Johanna watched Hugh go behind the counter and climb up on the wooden steps reserved for reaching the high shelves. He glanced over towards where she stood.

"Looks like it." Matthew nodded and turned. Picking up the little brass bell from the counter he gave it a shake. It rang in the silence that enveloped the gathering as Hugh, bringing his fist to his mouth, gave a little cough before announcing the welcome.

Watching her brother address the crowd from his podium she felt proud. This important businessman in his expensive suit was her brother. Thinking over Matthew's comment she hoped she wasn't going to turn into a snob, travelling on the coat-tails of Hugh's success.

Chapter 10

Margaret lay in the bed, day after day, her pallid face blending with the creamy whiteness of the lace-edged pillows. The birth of the twins, a boy and a girl, had left her drained.

"I don't know what's wrong with me, Jo. It's not like when Hughie and Patrick were born." Her voice was feeble. "I was exhausted then but this time is different. I just can't put my finger on it."

"Well, there's no point in looking at me for an answer, Margaret. Sure what would I know about childbirth?" She tried to make light of the situation but could see that her sister-in-law was beyond making a joke. "What did the doctor say?"

"He says it's my heart. He warned me about it after Patrick was born. There's always been a problem – it's a family thing but carrying twins has made it worse. It's made it a bit weaker."

"And is there nothing can be done for it?"

"Not a thing. It's something I've got to live with and not exert myself too much."

At a loss to know how to jolly her along, Johanna moved the lace-trimmed basket over to the side of the bed.

"Maybe if you have a cuddle with the little ones you'll feel better." Johanna passed Baby Michael to her, afraid to allow her hold both at the same time in case she dropped one in her frail state. "Maybe you'd try giving him a little feed."

She hovered around, tidying the dressing table and rearranging the vase of flowers, removing a few heads that were beginning to drop their petals. She watched from the corner of her eye and could see Margaret wince as the baby latched on to her breast. She'd give it a few minutes and see how it went.

"Maybe it's Baby Bridget's turn now to have a little cuddle with her mother and a drop of milk."

She took the bundle and settled Michael back in the basket, then passed the baby girl over to her mother, thinking that Margaret, lying back propped against the pillows, looked like a woman whose life had been sucked out of her.

"Maybe we'll talk to the doctor again about the wet nurse. What do you think, Margaret?" She said it gently, knowing how reluctant her sister-in-law had been when it had first been suggested.

"Maybe we should." The slow nod confirmed her defeat.

Hugh was busy. His time, taken up with the new grocery store, resulted in him leaving the practicalities of running the house to a terrified Johanna.

The managing of the home wasn't a difficulty. The worst that happened was the odd day she didn't get around to cooking the dinner on time and they had to go hungry until she got on top of things. Her brother never complained.

"Don't worry, Jo, it's not a hotel. We won't starve if we have to wait a bit," he reassured her. "Here, boys, pass me one of those apples and sit down at the table and I'll show you something."

He took a knife from the drawer and cut the apple in half.

"Now what have I got?"

"You've got pieces of apple?" Hughie offered.

"Yes, I've got two pieces of apple. This is *half* of the apple. And this is the other *half*. Now, Hugh, let Patrick tell me what have I in this hand?"

"Half apple. Can I have half apple?" Patrick smiled up at his father.

"You can indeed, Patrick. That's very good. Here's your half apple." He handed it to his son. "Now, Hughie, if I cut your half in two what do I have?"

"You have two pieces. Can I have the two?" Hugh smiled.

"You can, but wait." He cut the piece in half. "See, I've cut it into *quarters*. Here you go. Two quarters make a half." He glanced at Hughie who had his hand out, not sure if his son quite understood, but not wanting to labour the point when they were hungry. "Now, you can eat that while we're waiting for Johanna to finish making the dinner."

"And what about you and me, Hugh?" Johanna looked over her shoulder and laughed. Her brother was never one to miss an opportunity to teach his sons mathematics. "Or would eighths be too complicated yet for your little geniuses?"

She sometimes worried about the upset for the children, with their mother in bed all the time now. But the boys could be managed easily enough, and Hughie seemed to understand the shift in the atmosphere. Understand might be too strong a word to put on it but he appeared to sense that all was not well and that they should behave.

She had overheard him cajole his little brother as she came down the stairs after seeing to Margaret.

"We have to be good, Patrick. Stop shouting. The babies are asleep and Jo will be annoyed if we wake them."

"Why?" Patrick whispered.

She knew he was starting out on what would most likely be a list of questions but at least the volume was reduced.

"Because if you wake them they'll be shouting too."

She couldn't have put it better herself.

"Why?"

"Because . . ." A pause followed. "Oh, I don't know – because they're always shouting. Come on, we'll play with the toys. Which one do you want?"

Good man, Hughie.

No, the boys weren't the problem. What petrified her was finding herself fully accountable for the survival of the two completely dependent little bundles as their mother lay flat and disinterested upstairs, too weak to concern herself as to what was going on. That was a different matter altogether. No granny or neighbours to run to if anything went wrong. Johanna had never envisaged this situation, had never thought how the responsibility for such things might be left to her.

The most experience she had of small babies was of Art's children before she left home. She'd often minded them for short periods. At home – with Granny next door in case of emergencies – of which there had never been any. Not when she was in charge anyway. It was only now with no rescuers nearby that the possibility of a disaster occurring emerged as a huge concern in the absence of familiar props around her. This unexpected situation had her feeling more of a stranger than when she had first arrived in Boston. Then she had only herself to look after. If she'd failed, no-one else would have suffered.

In the evenings Hugh spent most of his time after work sitting beside Margaret's bed coaxing her to sample the little dainties he brought home from the grocery store. He often succeeded where Johanna had failed. She sometimes wondered if Margaret was just humouring him, but it didn't matter once she ate something. She hung onto that thought for the small comfort it gave her. A sense that somehow Margaret felt comfortable enough with her not to have to pretend.

Today she was making soup – recently the only thing with which she could tempt Margaret's taste buds. The only food that she seemed able to swallow.

Johanna gave a final stir to the soup and removed the saucepan from the heat. Taking the potato masher she plunged it into the saucepan. As she did, the liquid splashed the front of her apron, a few spatters scalding the back of her hand. She dropped the masher into the pot but managed to retrieve it before it sank beneath the surface. Wiping the handle on the tea towel she raised herself on her toes in order to pack enough power to mash the vegetables to a pulp. The potatoes yielded under the pressure. Today they were nice and soft as she pressed slowly, watching as they emerged upwards through the holes in the masher. A rare moment of satisfaction amidst the pressure.

Johanna laid down the tray on the sideboard on the landing and knocked gently on the bedroom door. There was no sound from within.

"Are you awake, Margaret?" With a half whisper she put her head around the door. The knock had been unnecessary. The door was already open but she didn't want to give Margaret a fright in case she hadn't heard the footsteps on the stairs.

"I've brought you something nice."

The feeble response was barely audible. Johanna saw the effort it took for Margaret to lift her head to look towards the door. She watched as it just fell back onto the pillow, the effort too much to sustain.

"Here, let me help you sit up before I bring in the tray."

In a few strides she was across the room and, placing her arm under Margaret's back, she raised her up into a sitting position before straightening the pillows behind her and slipping in an extra one. She always worried that the fragile bones beneath the nightdress might snap as she carried out the manoeuvre.

She patted the pillow in place. "Now, how's that? More comfortable?"

"Grand. That's fine now thanks, Johanna." Margaret looked at her, eyelids heavy in a slow blink. "More comfortable."

"Hold on there while I get the soup." The trace of the smile that crossed Margaret's face cheered her. "Well, sure you'll hardly be going anywhere, I suppose." Johanna grinned at her.

Returning with the tray she sat on the side of the bed and took up the bowl and spoon.

"Would you like to try it yourself or will I give you a hand?"

"I'm very tired. Maybe you'd . . ."

Johanna gave a stir to the skin that had already begun to form on the surface. Taking up a spoonful she scraped the underside of the spoon against the edge of the bowl to remove the drips before leaning in and feeding it to her sister-in-law. Margaret closed her eyes and rolled the soup around her tongue before swallowing it.

"Oh, that's lovely. Very tasty." She opened her eyes and looked towards Johanna, ready for more. "Lovely and smooth. You make the best soup, Johanna."

"My mother's recipe. You can't beat it." She knew how Margaret liked it since she became ill. Well pulped, no lumps and cooled down.

Today had been a good day. A little improvement. She'd be able to tell Hugh when he arrived home. Always his first question. The second only came because the boys would run in to meet him as they heard him in the kitchen talking to Johanna.

"How were my little men? Were they good today?"

He never asked about the babies. It was almost as if the twins didn't exist.

Chapter 11

Apart from the occasional slight improvement, each day was much the same. Margaret neither improved nor deteriorated – too ill to enjoy her babies despite Johanna's best efforts.

"Isn't it lovely to have a little girl after all the boys?" Johanna smiled down at the baby fingers stretching out against the pearly pink cheek. "Would you look at her, isn't she gorgeous? I think she's going to be like you, Margaret."

There was no response from the bed.

"Aren't you gorgeous, just like your mama?" she cooed before glancing up. "Would you like to hold her for a minute?"

Before her sister-in-law had a chance to protest she placed the baby in her arms and put a pillow under her elbow to support the weight.

"They've just had a feed and the wet nurse has gone home for the moment. She'll be back later for the night feed."

"Isn't it a bother for her, all this coming and going?"

"Don't you worry about that. She's glad of the work and she only lives a few minutes' walk away so it suits her."

Margaret watched the eyelids flutter and half open as her daughter dreamed in her arms. Johanna hesitated, pleased to see a smile on Margaret's face. She waited a few moments before going over to the cradle to get Baby Michael. A small success. A little bit of progress to tell Hugh about when he came home.

The doctor called twice a week and reassured them that her recovery would be a slow process and they would just have to be patient and not expect miracles overnight.

Hugh had woken early. The pearly grey of the overcast sky was visible through a chink in the curtains. It was only in recent days that Margaret requested that they be left open a little at night – said she liked to be able to see the stars and the moon when she had difficulty sleeping and to watch the morning drift in.

Reluctant to disturb her, he propped himself on his elbow and watched her beautiful sleeping face. For a couple of minutes he resisted the urge but, as the time to get up approached, the temptation became too much and he reached out to stroke her cheek. The marble cold of her skin shocked him and he stared, the stillness of her body raising his suspicion. Placing a hand on her chest, the warmth of his palm felt like it would burn its way into the coldness of her body.

"Margaret, Margaret, wake up!" He shook her shoulders, half afraid to use too much force in case she was in a deep sleep and he would hurt her. "Wake up, love, wake up!"

He shook her harder, panic rising as he failed to rouse her.

"Johanna, Johanna, come here! Come quick!"

From her bed, Johanna could hear the shout coming down the corridor. It was the tone that sent a chill down her spine. Without waiting to put her slippers on, she ran across the landing barefoot in her nightgown.

"She can't be . . . I think . . . Johanna . . . quick . . ."

Hugh was kneeling on the bed, leaning over Margaret,

his face wide with terror. He looked up at Joanna, willing her to tell him that he was mistaken, that what he knew to be true was not the case.

Her heart pounding, Johanna took Margaret's white wrist and felt for a pulse.

"Margaret, Margaret, wake up . . . wake up, Margaret . . . we're here . . ." She ran to the dressing table and grabbed the hand mirror. Moving to the bedside she held it to Margaret's face and waited. "She's not breathing."

"I think she is. Try it again, do it again, Jo."

She knew, but more to satisfy him than with any expectation she replaced the mirror again in front of Margaret's face as Hugh held her to him. She took a deep breath to still the thumping of her own heart and put down the mirror. She took Margaret's wrist again but there was nothing.

"Hugh, Hugh, she's gone." She said it as gently as she could.

"*She's not, she can't be.*" His stricken face looking up at his sister radiated a childish hope that broke her heart.

Aware that the bewilderment in her voice may have made the words come out as a question rather than a statement, she knew she would have to say it again.

"She's gone, Hugh, I'm sorry, there's nothing we can do. She's gone." It felt cruel to say it so firmly, but she had to leave him in no doubt. It was clear he didn't want to believe her.

The sound of a door opening down the corridor broke the moment. They looked at each other, startled.

"Don't let them in. Don't let the boys in, Jo."

"I'll see to them." She ran the sleeve of her nightgown across her eyes, just in case, even though they felt dry with shock. She gave Hugh's shoulder a squeeze before going out to intercept the boys, careful to close the bedroom door firmly behind her.

* * *

Johanna changed the twins and put them back into their cradles while the boys sat at the table eating their breakfast. The wet nurse was late this morning. Of all days.

"Why was Dada shouting?" Hughie had already asked the question. "Why was he calling you? What did he want?"

Her lips parted to answer but she hesitated, unsure how to reply.

"Your mama isn't well . . ." A partial truth to buy time.

His question required no further elaboration as Patrick, at that moment, knocked over his glass of milk. She could have kissed him. The child's enquiry might have opened up the conversation but she wasn't equipped to provide answers. Not yet anyway. She couldn't deal with what had happened herself.

"I want to go in and say goodbye to Mama before I go to school." Hughie slid off his chair, wiping his milky moustache.

"Hold on a minute, pet. You can't disturb her. Anyway I think we'll give school a miss today."

"Why? I'm not sick?"

"I know, lovey, but . . ." She hesitated, fearing the terror would show on her face. She wondered if the break in routine at the breakfast table might have given the children a clue that something was amiss. She could only stall them for so long.

"Come here and I'll give that face a wipe – you're all breakfasty." Maybe it hadn't been a good idea to allow her brother to stay upstairs. She wished he'd come down now. The doctor would need to be called and the news would have to be broken to the boys and she didn't know how to do it. Didn't want to have to do it. They were *his* children. He should take responsibility for the task. It shouldn't come from her.

"I think your father has something to tell you, Hughie. He's still upstairs. He'll be down in a few minutes, but you can go out to the garden for a little while and play while I find him. Take Patrick with you, he's finished his breakfast too."

She lifted him from his chair and giving his hands a quick wipe ushered the two boys out the back door.

She stood at the bottom of the stairs and looked up at the dismal grey of the landing. The space so filled with a silence that to call his name seemed like a desecration. She put her foot on the first step but found herself unable to take the second. Closing her eyes she willed herself to continue. There was no choice. The children wouldn't stay outside for too long and she couldn't move forward with anything until they had been told.

Chapter 12

The bedroom door was closed. Her hand in the air was ready, but unable to knock. Dreading encroaching on his grief, the door a barrier against the awfulness that lay behind it, but she had to do it. There was no response to her gentle tap. She waited. Maybe he hadn't heard.

"*Hugh?*" She listened. Could hear a slight rustle from the other side of the door. She tried again, wincing as the sound which seemed to amplify with each knock.

"*Hugh?*" She turned the handle slowly as she called him and gently pushed open the door.

He lay on his side on the eiderdown beside Margaret, holding her cold hand, not looking up at Johanna.

"Sorry, Hugh. Sorry to disturb you but we have to do something about the children. Young Hughie wants to come up."

"He can't." Hugh sat upright, shock written on his face.

"I know, but he won't understand that. I've sent them out to the garden to play for the moment, but you're going to have to tell them sooner or later."

He looked at her, his eyes pleading.

"No, Hugh, I can't. Please don't ask me." It came out as a sob. She watched as he dropped his head onto his hand.

"Come on, Hugh. It's better to tell them now. I can't keep them out there for much longer."

He didn't move. She waited.

"I'll come with you," she said.

She heard the sigh as he shifted and sat on the edge of the bed looking down at his feet, his two hands propping himself up.

"Come on," she said. "We'll do it together."

Without giving her an answer he stood up slowly, turning to look back at his wife.

"Can I leave it to you, Jo? You take them up."

"No. You have to come with us."

"I can't believe it. I still can't believe it." More to himself than to her, the tone of resignation was echoed in his face with all hope of life gone.

He was still hunkered down in front of the two boys. Big globs of tears had begun to roll down young Hughie's flushed cheeks, while Patrick, thumb in his mouth, glanced at his big brother, unsure what to do, not quite understanding what he had been told.

"I can't do it, Jo."

"Hugh, you have to. You can't expect me to do this on my own. You're their father. It's you they need, not me." Johanna gripped his arm and pulled him upright. "Come on."

Nudging him in front, she took the boys by the hand and led them through the hall. Hugh stood aside as they reached the bottom of the stairs. She raised her eyebrows at him but went up in front with the children, checking over her shoulder that her brother was following. She stood back to let him open the door of the bedroom, feeling the boys pulling in behind her skirt. She prised loose their grip on her hands and bending down she put an arm around each.

"You needn't worry, your mama just looks like she's sleeping. You can say goodbye. I'll come with you."

They allowed her to lead them in. Hugh was standing by the bed, looking down at his wife. He brushed a lock of hair from her forehead and glanced at the boys, his face white with worry.

Johanna looked at him and saw he was waiting for her to do something.

"I'll help you up onto the bed so you can say goodbye." She took Hughie's hand and guided him up. "Kneel down, Hughie, yes, that's right, beside her."

"Will I wake her up?" The child looked up at his father.

She could hear a strangled sob emit from Hugh's throat, unable to answer his son.

"Lovey, you won't waken her. That's the sad thing. Your mama won't waken up again. She's gone to Heaven."

She lifted Patrick up onto the bed, catching him as he stumbled against his brother.

"Move, Hughie. Want to see Mama." Steadying himself, Patrick gripped his brother's back.

"You can give her a kiss, Hughie. If you want." She put a restraining hand on Patrick.

"Hold on there, pet, until Hughie says goodbye. And then he'll move over and let you get in closer."

Hughie kissed his mother on the cheek.

"She's very cold," he said. "Put another blanket on her, Dada, she's very cold. I don't want her to be cold."

Hugh, rooted to the spot, looked at his son, powerless to respond.

"Don't worry," Jo said. "Your dada will put one over her after we go downstairs."

As Hughie climbed down onto the floor again he looked up at her.

"I want her here. I don't want her in Heaven." His tear-streaked face reflected all their wishes.

"I know you don't." She whispered the words down to him. "We all want her here. But she's gone, love."

The cry of a twin alerted her to life downstairs. The normality of it came as a guilty relief. She wanted to run away. It wasn't her responsibility to deal with any of this. She had no experience of this type of situation.

"*All you can do is your best. There's no right way of doing things.*" Her father's words rang in her head. Although she hadn't been much older than Hughie, she still remembered them. Always his answer when they tried to avoid a challenge. "*The lessons you'll remember most are those where you learn from your mistakes.*"

What could she do? Turn her back on the little anxious faces or muddle along doing what she could, however inadequate that might be. There was no-one else, unless Hugh had a plan, but his crushed shoulders told her otherwise.

The increasing volume of the mewling baby from downstairs took on an urgency as she lifted Patrick down from the bed. The two children stood looking at their father. Oblivious now to their presence, Hugh sat on the side of the bed stroking his wife's cheek. They looked up at Johanna with eyes that expected her to take charge.

"Let's go down and see what the twins want, will we?"

In the hours and days that followed, Hugh wandered around the house. A ghost with no purpose, a man incapable of functioning. She could hardly recognise him. Such a transformation from the way he had been – in charge of everything.

Johanna had no idea now where to start. Margaret would have known.

"Do whatever you think, Johanna."

The only answer she could force out of him. No clue

what to think or do, she wished he'd revert back to his previous role as decisionmaker.

Organising a funeral was something she had no experience of. At home it all just happened, centuries of old traditions seemed to automatically fall into place. The priest, the undertaker, the gravediggers, the sandwich-makers, all known to everyone. Like a well-oiled machine, neighbours moved into their roles. A seamless operation where everyone seemed to know their place, their duties, what was needed, and in what order.

With her brother's failure to function she didn't know where to begin. The doctor confirmed heart failure and provided the necessary documentation. Nothing any of them could have done. He advised on practicalities which Johanna put on a list. She left it on the kitchen table in the hope that Hugh would make a start but it sat there untouched throughout the day. He passed in and out through the room in a trance-like state. It was as if he didn't see the piece of white paper with the black writing. Or had any interest in what it might say.

Johanna checked regularly for evidence of his usual method of crossing off jobs completed, only to find the list unchanged. She picked it up, read through it to see if she could do anything but all needed a decision before they could be put into action. Afraid to draw his attention in case it upset him, she adopted a different strategy. Task by task she asked him for a decision on what was most urgent and immediate.

"What time do you want the Mass?"

"I don't care."

That clearly didn't work.

"Nine o'clock or eleven? Which would be best?" She looked across the room to where he sat in his armchair gazing out the window, face blank.

"Whatever you think."

"Right. Eleven o'clock it will be then. Give people time to get ready. I'll confirm that with the priest."

The new approach proved more satisfactory in that it allowed her to move things forward in between comforting the children as best she could.

The boys asked questions of their father but like herself they couldn't reach him. They began coming to her instead and seemed satisfied with the simple explanations she offered. At least they appeared to accept them. For the moment anyway.

With the babies it was as if they had nothing to do with Hugh. They might as well not have existed. Their needs were left to her, to rely on her own devices. No time to think about it, just plough on and hope for the best. If she were to look further ahead than the next feed she was afraid she would be paralysed with fear.

To bring a semblance of normality to the house during the time of the wake she organised food at regular mealtimes. The children ate but not Hugh. She made him sit at the table with them and put a plate in front of him but all he did was pick at it in silence. Sometimes she doubted herself. Why was she persisting in behaving as though things were normal when nothing was? Nothing would ever be normal again. Not for the children. Nor Hugh. But she didn't know what else to do.

Carrying out what needed to be done was the easy part. She could function with the chores, but in the dead of night the panic set in. This wasn't at all what she'd planned. Her picture had been one where Margaret had recovered, however slowly, and resumed her place as head of the domestic side of things, gradually taking over again. Now left with the total care of the babies and two little boys constantly asking questions and wanting her attention, she felt herself drowning under it all.

* * *

Returning from the cemetery in the carriage, she leaned her head against the seatback and watched the horses' breath vaporise into the frosty air. The wet nurse had agreed to stay in the house to mind the babies while the funeral took place. Johanna hoped she would stay on for the rest of the day – a welcome break from a responsibility that threatened to crush her.

Hugh was lost in his own thoughts. The boys were quiet and she was too tired to wonder what bewildering ideas they had in their little heads. Hugh had wanted them to be left at home but Johanna insisted it was better that they attend the funeral. Taking advantage of her brother's apathy, what would have been a battle in normal times was easily won. It might be the last memory they had of their mother. Possibly the one thing that would trigger other memories of her in years to come.

The clip-clopping of the horses was soothing and she felt herself drift into a slumber as her head drooped.

Chapter 13

Too cold a day for strolling she moved briskly along the pathway, free of the encumbrance of the children for an hour. Hugh had agreed to keep an eye on them while she ran a few errands.

Johanna had noticed him from a distance, seated on the wooden bench. He had no hat and his wispy hair was too thin to provide any heat for his head. The old man, his coat collar turned up against the wind, raised his head and looked up as she drew near. She had seen how each time someone passed a glimmer of hope softened the wrinkles in his face. Hope of what she had no idea and she suspected that neither had he. It was the lonesomeness in the half smile that got her as if he wanted someone to see him – needed someone to acknowledge his existence on that park bench. Far too cold a day to sit, she could imagine the cold seeping through the wool of his threadbare coat.

She might not have paid him much attention except that he reminded her of old Donie the Singerman, who used to sit on the wall outside the village church at home. Always hopeful for someone to chat to whenever he visited for a few days. Most likely did the same in all the villages and towns on his traversing around the countryside throughout the year. To places where the people were familiar with him and his ways. For him each area around the west of Ireland had a particular season. The summer months Donie kept to the coastal areas in the hope of making some money by entertaining the holidaymakers along the sea front with his ballads. As autumn drew near he moved inland to avail of the harvesting season. He'd make a show of helping out with a bit of labouring to ensure a place to rest for the night. He was of little use with the physical work but the farmers, used to his harmless ways, always allowed him to sleep in an old barn or outhouse. Saving the crops meant long days, often extending into late evening, but they looked forward to the supper and an hour or so with Donie singing for his as they parked their weariness by the fireside in the kitchen.

The first day he'd arrive in the village on his annual round he'd be a bit shy sitting on the wall, as if he thought no-one would remember him from last year.

"Have you e'er an auld ballad for us, Donie?"

It wasn't much but all it needed was one passer-by to shout out to him and he knew he wasn't forgotten. He was welcome in the village again. That first acknowledgement was all it took to have him belonging, to have him back, part of them again.

You could pick out the Irish anywhere, even out of their element. No mistaking them. And this man seated on the bench in Boston Common was definitely out of his. The ruddy, wind-pinched complexion of his Celtic face with its sandy-haired eyebrows and stubble confirmed his origins. Not the most attractive-looking race. Only now in the mix of cultures could she see it. The Irish standing out for all the wrong reasons. She hoped her Irishness wasn't so obvious.

"It's a chilly enough afternoon, isn't it?" Johanna nodded at him, her breath visible as it hung on the cold air.

"It is, girleen, it is." He blew on his bare hands and rubbed them together.

His pale blue eyes watered. She could see the abandonment in them fading as he looked up at her.

"It surely is."

The way he added it after a slight pause as if to prolong the conversation caught her heart. She wasn't sure why the gratitude in his smile bothered her. It had stirred an uncomfortable awareness that the value of her greeting meant so much to him, a guilt at knowing she had almost passed him by. Her acknowledgement of him had been received with an appreciation over and above its worth.

It was only after she'd moved on, feeling a slight remorse that she hadn't made more effort to prolong the conversation, that she began to think about the number of immigrants in the streets. She'd noticed them before but more as a novelty. She'd never really thought how it must be for them. Only ever thought about herself and her own efforts to fit in. But she had the back-up of family.

Without realising it she had slowed down and the cold was beginning to penetrate. Something about the man on the park bench had caused a shift. The confidence she'd managed to build up since she'd come to Boston, most of it unconsciously, was now unseated, replaced by an unease that had surreptitiously crept in. She looked back at him and saw that he'd resumed his previous posture, looking up at the passers-by. She considered going back, but that might have him realising how pitiful he appeared and she didn't want that. If she saw him again she'd stop.

He was old. As if he should be at an age when he'd arrived somewhere. Not sitting on a park bench looking lost and rudderless, left to drift along on a sea of loneliness. It worried her how he might have ended up there. How easily it could happen. She needed a signpost, someone to point her in the right direction. That was something he might never have had.

It wasn't just the Irish that she noticed. There were the brown and black-complexioned, some with lost vacant expressions on their faces as they walked along. They weren't all like that but she began watching for those who were. What lay behind the haunted looks of those who hadn't integrated, who didn't belong here and maybe never would? It left her wondering if they might be reflecting on memories of warmer climes and loved ones left behind? She hoped she didn't have the same sad expression on her face. She'd have to watch that. *"Look like you are meant to be here."* Margaret's words came back to her.

Dear Mama,

You have no idea how much I miss Margaret. And if I miss her this much I cannot imagine how it must be for Hugh. He doesn't talk about her, he has just gone into himself. I'm very worried but I don't know what to say or do to help him. He doesn't seem to notice the children so they are depending on me and I'm afraid I am not up to the job of replacing their lovely mother.

The twins are so tiny and they need so much of my time that I'm afraid I may be neglecting the little fellows, but there is so much to do. Some days I can't get the babies to stop crying and I put them into the pram and take them out for a walk to try and get them to sleep and it sometimes works. Oh, Mama, I wish you were here. You would know what to do. Please write to me soon with some advice because Hugh is no help and who could blame him? He is devastated over the loss of his beautiful wife.

I have no other news for the moment. I haven't time to do anything else.

Your loving daughter
Johanna
P.S. Please give my love to everyone.

Something changed in the days that followed.

She hadn't heard from home. It was too soon. Maybe it was the letter, putting her fears on paper that helped. The muddle of recent times seemed to disperse. The lonely space that she occupied seemed to have melted away. What had been one big problem now divided up into individual ones. There were questions and recognising that was a start. Now perhaps she could begin to look for answers. Tackle one thing at a time.

Her brother was the first challenge. Like a wandering soul in a desert, there was no point in looking to him for a lead. Not at the moment anyway. She was going to have to make the decisions, like she did at the time of the funeral. No more waiting. One of them would have to start functioning and it clearly wasn't going to be Hugh.

She listened to the tinkle of the spoon on the cup as she stirred her tea and gazed out the window. The grey outside was beginning to lift, allowing a weak beam of light filter through. Laying the spoon on the saucer, she decided on her first action. She would tell him what was to happen and unless he had a better idea she'd put it into action. He mightn't like her taking over but if he didn't he had an option. Go along with her or suggest a better plan. His choice. As simple as that.

That moment of revelation was like seeing around a blind corner. She leaned back on the chair, her arms resting on the table and breathed deeply. She was pleased with herself as she felt the weight lift. Her mind idled and in that space she could see now where she was. The before and the after. She had grown up. It had taken something as awful as this to discover that at last she was now a fully developed adult, no longer just the younger sister that he was helping out. She'd crossed the dividing line. It was all behind her. That dependent girl no longer existed.

Chapter 14

The house had become a big empty shell. As soon as they entered and closed the door behind them it seemed like they had stepped into this great desolate hole. Johanna wondered if they all felt as she did. Wanting to turn and run out again. But where to? It was like the whole centre had gone out of their world. Sometimes she considered that it might be easier not to go out at all so they wouldn't have to face the emptiness on their return. But that was no answer either.

"It looks very dark, Johanna? Why are there no lamps lit?"

It was young Hughie who put his finger on it as they headed for home after their walk one evening. They had stayed out later than usual. Dusk had begun to fall and the greyness of the street was punctuated by glimmers of yellow-white light filtering out from most of the windows. Except theirs. That was one of the contributory factors.

"Up you go, boys." She closed the gate behind her.

"Don't want to go in. No like dark. " Patrick stopped at the bottom of the steps, refusing to budge.

"Well, you wait there a moment. I'll soon fix that." She looked down at him. "Hold Hughie's hand and I'll go in and light a lamp."

She watched Patrick's face threaten to crumple.

"Look, go up a few steps and hold onto the railing with your other hand and wait." She bent down to him. "You'll be fine. It will only take me a minute and I'll come out and get you."

She was glad they hadn't figured out the real reason for the gloominess, that it wasn't just the warmth of light that was missing. For the moment, it was the best she could do to put a temporary fix on that for them. It wouldn't be so easy to replace the bigger things.

Disguise it she could, but it was impossible to escape the deadness that permeated the place. Something that at first had filled the entire house, as the weeks went on began to dissolve and lately it seemed to just attach itself to specific areas within each room. Like a still, cold air trapped in spots. Frozen. Around the chair in front of the drawing-room window where Margaret liked to do her embroidery. The sofa where she'd sat. The chill remained in those spaces even when the fire was lit.

Hugh and Johanna were sitting in the drawing room in the evening as they usually did. With nothing to say to each other. It was always worse when the children were in bed. Leaning forward she placed a log on the fire and watched the flickering as it caught alight. She rubbed her hand on her skirt before picking up her crochet. She held up the lace, checking her handiwork. Margaret had shown her the basics and she'd picked up the knack quickly. Always had a flair for handicrafts. Only a few more rounds to go and the runner would be completed. It had been intended as a present for Margaret for her dressing table. She'd had to force herself to get interested enough to work on it again once she realised there was nothing to be gained by dwelling on what might have been.

The crackle of the fire was the only sound. Not a word

exchanged between them. She wove the crochet hook in and out, the repetitive action leaving plenty of space for thoughts to wander through her mind. Thoughts that rarely strayed far from recent events.

"Any news today in the shop?" She made conversation, knowing it was just to relieve the sound of the stillness. Had to keep trying and suffer the discomfort of his lack of response and learn to ignore the feeling that she was intruding on something.

"No."

Even as she asked she could have anticipated his answer. The most gentle of sentences sometimes seemed loud, like they might shatter the fragile silence. As if she had shouted, making her wish she hadn't opened her mouth. Knowing Hugh was unwilling to make the effort, she suspected her attempts irritated him. But most times she knew he was just unable to.

Sitting together at the fire, each alone with their thoughts, sometimes she would forget. There were interludes when the yawning gap would fill as her mind moved to other places, other things that needed doing. These short spells allowed unconnected thoughts to drift in to fill the hole.

"Do you remember the day I got stuck in the gate, when I was small, and you had to . . ."

It had happened a couple of times. A half-uttered sentence. Stopping, realising the awkwardness of trying to share her thought, her memory of his prising apart the iron bars to release her little head. One glance in his direction as he sat across from her staring into the dying flames of the fire was enough. A reminder that he hadn't arrived at a place where there were any such breaches in his wall of grief.

For weeks she watched as he went about his daily business white-faced. Never a mention of Margaret's name as if to do so would render him incapable of proceeding. The brittle shell that surrounded him left her afraid to mention his wife's name. That was something that would have to change, but maybe not just yet. In the meantime, while there was little she could do for Hugh, she would concentrate on the children, continuing as she was going, already cuddling them more than ever, as much for her own comfort as theirs.

"Just one more story, Johanna. Tell us one more about Mama before we go to sleep."

Hughie was old enough to understand the stories she told them. She tried to keep the language simple enough for Patrick although she wasn't sure if he followed them or not, but he seemed to be happy enough to listen and the hum of her voice sufficed to soothe the twins. She sang Margaret's songs, the boys not seemingly bothered about her lack of talent, and she filled the kitchen with her baking smells, something she was good at. Each night she placed their mother's shawl or nightgown in their beds. She didn't tell Hugh about this cocoon she was creating in case he thought it strange. She just wanted them to have the scent of their mother so they would feel her still with them and prolong their memories. That was the best she could do.

Hughie was six, not much older than she had been when her father died. How little she remembered of him. *Da*. A hazy memory of a full house, hushed voices and lots of ham and wheaten bread and sweet cake on the table for visitors and suddenly he was no more. The feel of his hand as he ruffled her hair. The way he would throw her up in the air and pretend he wasn't going to catch her. Her own shrieks of laughter at the pretend game. But no face. She couldn't remember his face. Sometimes the smell of his pipe came to her, but only for a second, fading as he had over the years.

Not sure now if it was her imagination straining to cling on to memories or if she really remembered them. No longer able to differentiate between what she'd heard and what she'd experienced, she was determined to reduce the possibilities of this happening to Margaret's children.

She sat by the window. The brightness in the sky with the lengthening evenings allowed sufficient light to work by without lighting the lamp. She dropped a stitch and as she adjusted herself in the seat the ball of crochet cotton fell to the floor, pulling with it the loose thread, unravelling the last shell of the pattern she had created.

Leaning forward she retrieved the ball. She caught the lost stitch on the hook before resting the work on her knee. Maybe Hugh would remember more about their father, before he vanished completely from her memory. She glanced across to where he sat at the fire. His relaxed face behind the newspaper caused her to hesitate. It was the first time she'd seen the absence of the misery that had been etched on his face recently. Maybe she should leave well enough alone. Endure the silence she'd got used to with the passing days. That was why, as she settled back to her crochet, she was unprepared when it happened.

"Well, what will they think of next? There's a lad here shooting pictures of a horse and trying to make motion pictures of them!"

Johanna glanced up surprised.

"Did you read that, Margaret?"

Johanna stared over at him. He was still looking at the newspaper, oblivious to the words that had come out of his mouth. Frozen in the chair, her mind rigid, it was only her lack of a response that made him look up in the direction of the window, to where he expected his wife to be sitting, sewing in the fading light.

Something told her that to utter a word would be the wrong thing to do. Best to act as though she hadn't heard him. It was clear he had totally forgotten her. In silence she resumed her crochet, knowing he didn't even see her, the pain evident on the face that stayed turned towards the window, his gaze off somewhere she had no knowledge of.

Johanna was torn. The incident bothered her. The daily domestic routine had to continue but as the weeks and months passed she became more aware that something was happening. So subtle was it that without realising, in her attempts at filling the gap from as many angles as possible, she had been closing a trap on herself. No loud slam, just a gradual silent sealing of her fate.

The selfishness of the thoughts that came into her head disturbed her. Not something she could discuss with anyone. Her own fault for having made herself indispensable. Not something she could admit to, but a halt had been put on her life now, to any changes she might have planned for the future. Not that she had many plans. Yet. But this stop to her life, a life that was only just starting, panicked her. And somehow it didn't seem fair.

Chapter 15

The evenings had got cooler and she could hear the sound of the leaves as they rustled in the light breeze while she leaned against the doorframe. The dark outline of the trees silhouetted in the moonlight reminded her of home. The way herself and her mother would open the back door when they were finished clearing up the kitchen after feeding the harvesters who had spent a long day in the fields. They would make a pot of tea for themselves and sit outside on the granite bench and enjoy it in the silence of the twilight.

Was her mother looking up at the same moon now? Wanting to believe it, she pushed aside the thought that her mother was probably fast asleep in bed.

Hugh was out at a business function.

"Don't wait up for me. I might be late."

She was glad he was occupied with his businesses but the balance seemed wrong somehow. She didn't say anything for fear he would take it the wrong way. That something interested him or at least was starting to interest him again was a positive thing. It was just going to take time. She just hoped not too much.

Before all this happened it had been on her mind,

wondering when she was going to get a life of her own. Forever the sensible one, the reliable one, she had got tired of that image before she left home. She was well aware of how she came across. Too old for her years. A new country had given her the chance of a new start. A whole new Jo. She had toyed with the idea but it seemed silly now to think she could have shaken off her 'practical' cloak. At home she'd envied some of her friends their butterfly ways. Had studied them in the hope of finding an escape, some way of introducing small changes that would go unnoticed until she had shed her dependable skin.

"How do you get away with it?" She'd asked the question one sunny Saturday afternoon when she called to her friend's house.

"Get away with what?"

"Whitewashing the barn. I see your sister is slaving away at it? I'm usually that person."

"Oh, that!" Her friend laughed. "The last time I did it they complained that I did a bad job, missed out bits."

"So that's the technique then." Johanna wondered how she hadn't worked out this before now.

"Yes, it is. You need to listen and learn. Your problem is that you always do things well. When you're asked to do a job never let it be perfect. Leave it just short enough that you'll not be asked again. They'll go to the reliable one next time. Like you." Her friend laughed. "Unless they're absolutely desperate they'll avoid me. Works most times."

Even at school, she was the one the teacher always called on for help.

Johanna had given her friend's method a try when asked to help tidy the classroom or dust the desks but it always went against the grain. To leave things half done, even with jobs that weren't important like cleaning windows or polishing the furniture, it just felt wrong. Added to which, at home there was no-one else to do the jobs. Maria was too young, Art and her mother too busy and the rest of them all away.

"That's my problem. I feel guilty if I don't do my best. Like why bother doing it at all if you're not going to do it right?"

"Well, that's the first hurdle. You'll just have to get over that," her friend advised. "I did."

"Yeah, but you're not like me. You obviously had no difficulty with that." She grinned at her.

"What? Are you saying I'm lazy?" Her friend's eyebrows shot up. "Try harder, Jo. It becomes easy with practice. Believe me. I'm living proof of it."

"But why am I always the 'if you need something done properly ask Jo' one?"

"It's meant as a compliment."

"But I don't want compliments like that. I often feel like telling them 'No, go and ask someone else to do it for you'."

"Well, instead of feeling it, why don't you practise getting good at my method?"

"*Mmm.* I have and it doesn't work. It really annoys me that I'm never the one they'd expect to do something wild?"

"What sort of wild do you have in mind?"

"I've no idea. Just some sort of recklessness." Johanna shrugged. "Just something, anything. God, I must be dull if I can't even think of anything wild to do – but I'm tired of always being made to feel I'm indispensable. I'd much rather be a butterfly like you." She directed a playful punch at her friend.

A navy cloud drifted across the moon. Johanna heaved herself away from the doorframe and went inside, closing the door quietly.

To change that impression. That was why she'd come to America – well, one of the lesser reasons anyway.

The overwhelming cultural differences that presented themselves since her arrival had highlighted her inadequacies. The effort required to learn and fit into her new life overshadowed her plan for an image change and circumstances had pushed it to the back of her mind. She doubted that her competence was evident here – her farming skills, however useful at home, had possibly contributed to her general lack of polish.

What she had failed to notice during the growing familiarity with her new life, hidden under all these layers, was a slow building of her confidence. Only now, in the light of the tragedy that had thrown their lives into disarray, did she remember. Now was not the time for the introduction of a change of personality. That would have to be postponed. At least until Hugh had taken back control of his family. How long that would be she had no idea, but with each passing day she found herself back in the same old reliable role.

She ran her finger over the surface of the table and felt a sticky blob of jam left after the children's supper. She turned and, taking the damp dish cloth from the drainer, scrubbed at the jammy stain before running the cloth over the entire table in case there were any more invisible remains of the day.

She sat down again and watched the last of the clouds pass across the yellow-white orb which, as they cleared, left a slant of moonlight across the table.

She traced the crack in the table. With her nail she scraped out the pastry remnants that had gathered.

She was annoyed with herself for her pettiness, for even thinking it, but why was it up to her again? The one to make the compromise.

A sigh escaped. It looked likely that she would never really be able to make it happen. She seemed destined for what would appear to be her true fate. Sensibleness. No amount of wanting would ever make her the 'exciting' one?

Ashamed at her self-centredness, she knew now was not the time to be wanting to fulfil ambitions. She stood up from the table and, going to the sink, emptied the cold dregs of tea and rinsed the cup. Patience was what she needed. Her personal changes could wait. More important matters had to take priority now.

It was almost eleven o'clock. Hugh was still not home. She would leave him a note.

Hope you had a good evening. Can you leave a dollar for the morning – Hughie needs it for schoolbooks.

Money was not a problem. There was always cash left for housekeeping in a brown earthenware jar in the kitchen. She could have used this but she needed an opportunity, an excuse to involve him in the children's activities and this was one. Afraid if he was shielded from the daily events now, the gap would become too wide to be filled in the future. It was proving more difficult with the twins. He still acted as if they didn't exist. She pulled the note towards her and added an extra bit of news.

The twins were babbling today and I think I heard Michael say his first word. You'll be pleased to know it sounded like Dada.

A bit of a white lie but Johanna didn't care if her efforts to force him to participate in their lives were transparent. She too missed Margaret but the void left was too big for her alone to fill. Whether her brother liked it or not, he was going to have to resume his role as a parent again.

Chapter 16

Even without the red hair Johanna would have recognised the twinkle in the blue eyes. It was all she could see of the face above the top of the cardboard box.

"The boss asked me to deliver these."

Matthew had called to the house with a box of groceries from the store.

"Oh, thanks." She went to take the box from him.

"Mind, it's heavy. I'll take it in for you." He dodged her extended arms, forcing her to move aside to make room as he stepped into the hallway. "Says I'm to deliver them twice a week and I'm to check with you what's needed."

"Well, come along into the kitchen 'til I see what's in this."

Peering over the top of the box, he followed her.

"Tell me if there's a step. I wouldn't want to measure my length."

"No steps, just straight ahead."

"You don't remember me, do you?"

A thrill ran through her that he would harbour such a doubt. Savouring the thought, she hesitated, toying with the idea of taking the advantage. A glance back over her shoulder, the box lowered enough now for her to see the sight of his disappointed look struck a chord, reflecting something she was well acquainted with. That feeling of being eminently unmemorable forced her to let go of the temptation to torment him.

"Oh, I do." She grinned. "Of course I remember you."

The box landed on the kitchen table with a soft plonk.

"It's Matthew, isn't it? How could I ever forget you?" she teased.

"Only too easily." He began opening the flaps on the top of the box.

"How are you getting on in the new shop?"

"Oh, it's going fine. Everything fresh and exciting. Lots of new faces." He glanced across at her and smiled. "Customers, I mean."

"Of course." Johanna watched as he shuffled, not sure whether to stay or go, the self-confidence he'd displayed at the opening of the new shop deserting him in this unfamiliar territory. Her territory.

"I suppose I'd better be off then."

"Are you not going to stay while I check what you've brought?" She began to take the items from the box. "Would you like a cup of tea while you're waiting, before you do your next delivery?"

"I'd love it but maybe I'd better get back or the boss will be asking why it's taking me so long. Maybe next time?"

"Maybe. I can give the list of requirements to 'the boss' anyway for the next delivery." She smiled. "Thanks for bringing these."

She followed him to the door and watched as he mounted his delivery tricycle. She glanced at the McNamara name on the side of the box that sat on the front to hold the groceries. She'd seen it before and it happened each time, the swell of pride at the sight of it. Her family name, known in their local townland and village in Clare, but here advertised on the streets of Boston. They, or at least Hugh had made a mark.

"Bye, now." His foot on the pedal, Matthew settled himself and began cycling off down the street.

She saw him release the handlebar, confidence restored, and without looking back at her wave his right hand in the air, like he knew she was still standing in the doorway. Embarrassed, she stepped back into the hall and closing the door behind her leaned against it and laughed.

Johanna found herself mouthing it as soon as his key sounded in the front-door lock.

"How were the children today?"

The same question each evening. Her brother going through the motions.

"Did they behave?"

The unvarying pattern when he returned home from work.

Nothing more than that. She supposed she had to be satisfied. At least it was a start. Hugh's question, she knew, was intended as blanket coverage. A ruse to hide the fact that he rarely looked into the cradle.

"As good as you'd expect." Johanna continued buttering the bread as her brother looked out the window to where the boys were playing in the garden. Without looking up, she sensed him starting to move off. Time to introduce another of her new tactics. Allowing him three steps towards the door before straightening up from her task, she turned towards him. Aware it might seem like she was wielding a mallet but she didn't care. The time had come to employ the more direct method.

She'd given him the chance but he'd failed the test. He hadn't availed of the few seconds' pause to exhibit an interest in the babies in the corner of the kitchen, the only leeway she was allowing him. No more would he be permitted the pretence of the twins being included in the general enquiry. She'd tolerated that for too long and it hadn't worked. Time now to close off his hiding place once and for all. And hers.

"The twins had their first taste of real food today." Johanna looked him full in the face. No room for escape, no opportunity for him to disappear into the parlour and hide behind his newspaper.

"Did they now?"

"Yeah, they did. Potato. Little Bridget was inclined to spit it out but Michael loved it." Her steady gaze held him on the end of her leash, demanding a reaction, unwilling to release him until she got more.

"*Hmm*, must be the Irishman in him." He shuffled uncomfortably into a half turn. "What are you going to do with the knife? Stab me?"

As he raised his brows she could see a hint of amusement in his eyes. She looked at the butter knife, unaware it was raised in front of her, pointing directly at him. She replaced it on the edge of the butter dish.

"She'll get used to it, I'm sure. But *he* liked it?" he said.

His half smile revealed a confidence in having got control but she didn't care. It had worked. The diversion had allowed him to ask the question more comfortably.

"A spud mashed up with a bit of butter. Who wouldn't like that?" She walked over and tickled each twin under the chin. "You'll like it next time, won't you, Bridget?"

She swung her head around in time to catch a faint softness melt her brother's face. A small improvement. Enough for now. She knew enough to know he wasn't someone to succumb to pressure. Another attempt and he might buck on her if she didn't release him.

"Go on into the parlour. I'll give you a shout when the tea is ready."

Putting the kettle to boil she smiled, pleased with herself.

A small change from the normal rigid body stance, not allowing himself to react or maybe not able. In those instances she had seen a fleeting shadow of pain undo the glazed hardness of his face. A momentary flicker, before he moved away, quickly, as if afraid to stay looking in case he might not blame them. And at that time he needed someone to blame. No, looking at him now, slow but sure was the way to go. Too soon to expect that he might reach down to them. Progress. Slow but it was working.

There had always been an aloofness about her brother. She remembered it from her childhood. Even then he was businesslike. She had loved his company but you knew instinctively not to mess with him. Not at all like Art. You could trick around with him and he would tease back, fooling about with you until work called. Open displays of affection were definitely not Hugh's thing, so to expect that to change now would be a step too far. This wasn't the time to be trying to figure out why Hugh was so different. With all that had happened it was clear she would have to accept his lack of engagement or at least some level of it. She'd have to settle for his taking an active interest in the boys' schooling although it bothered her that they must miss their mother's hugs. An occasional show of tenderness from their father would go a long way towards easing that loss.

Chapter 17

"What date is it, boys?" Hugh called from the hallway.

"The first of the month?" Hughie sang out and looked at his brother, who knew the routine but had no idea what it all meant – their faces shining as they waited for their father to come into the kitchen.

"And how do you know it's the first of the month?"

"Because you've brought us a present like you always do on the first of the month."

"Not quite the answer I'd like, but I suppose I'll have to settle for it, for the moment." He grinned across at Johanna. "What are you teaching them at all?"

Hugh planted his leather case on the table as the boys scrambled onto the chairs.

"And what month is it?" he teased them, hand poised on the lock, unwilling to open it until the correct answer was given. The twitch at the corner of his mouth, a hint of a smile as he pretended to walk off with the case, his eye catching Johanna's as she mouthed the correct answer to the boys.

"November." Hughie grinned.

"'vember." Patrick took his lead from his brother.

The new books had been carefully selected. That they

weren't just picked off the shelf carelessly was evident. All had been chosen with each of the boys' level of ability in mind. The ritual of the books for each of them was, she guessed, as close to a show of affection as he could manage. Something to build on.

Hugh helped them enjoy the books and set new words for Hughie to learn each week. He concentrated on the pictures with Patrick, helping him increase his vocabulary. He encouraged Johanna to supervise their learning in the afternoons. It became a pattern where he checked on their progress, setting tests at the end of the week and rewarding their efforts with a chocolate treat which he brought home from the store.

The total care of the babies though still remained with Johanna.

"And how are the twins? No problems, I hope?" He had started to make a point of asking about their welfare and progress, but they were still 'the twins'. Time now to ratchet things up.

"Here. Hold Bridget while I change Michael."

"I was just … " Hugh pulled back, opening his arms in a way that indicated he wasn't going to take the baby.

Ignoring him, Johanna plonked his daughter firmly against his shoulder, ensuring he had a good hold of her before moving away. The suddenness of her action successfully quenched any protest. He mightn't be quite ready for this but she was.

"Here, sit down." She pulled out a chair. "It's more comfortable to hold her sitting down. Just mind you don't bump her head on the edge of the table. She's more agile than you might expect."

After lunch on Saturday she put the twins down for a nap. Taking out her best frock, she held it up against herself.

Checking in the mirror, she toyed with the idea of changing into it. Why not look her best?

She laid it on the bed and, removing the hairpins, released her hair, admiring the way it cascaded over her shoulders. Picking up the brush she cocked her head to one side and began working it through the length of the tresses, wincing as it caught a knot. Untangling it, she gave a few more strokes until the brush began to glide smoothly. She admired herself, pleased with the silkiness under her hand.

It took only a few seconds for the doubt to enter her mind. What if Hugh came home unexpectedly? Hand with the brush held aloft in the air, she wondered what he'd think if he saw her looking like she was going somewhere special?

"Johanna, stop it." Before the misgivings could implant themselves she waved the brush at her reflection. "Remember, Johanna, you're an adult now. It's none of his business."

Replacing the brush on the dressing table, she picked up the frock once again and holding it up to her gave a twirl in front of the mirror.

"You do look good, Johanna. Well, maybe you aren't going somewhere special but you are meeting someone special so why shouldn't you smarten yourself up and let Hugh go and hump off with himself?"

"Thank you, Matthew." She moved to take the box from him at the door.

"I'll carry them in for you."

As she had hoped he waited for her to step aside before entering the hallway.

"Is that cup of tea still on offer?"

"I thought the boss would be after you?" Johanna followed him down the hall. His back view pleased her with the sunlight filtering through the window at the end of the corridor, glinting on his red-gold curls.

"This is my last call. I've all my deliveries done so I can fit it in. That's if you're offering of course. And, by the way, my friends call me Mattie."

Chapter 18

Sunday was his day off. His and Mattie's. She didn't have one. At least not formally. But she'd decided it was time to establish something.

"Hugh, I need to go out tomorrow afternoon for a few hours. Will you be here to keep an eye on the children?" She'd needed to make it clear she wouldn't be taking them with her.

"I suppose I could." He'd glanced up from the newspaper, a look of surprise on his face. "Going anywhere interesting?"

"Just meeting a friend." Too soon to mention who the friend was. Establish a pattern first and see how it goes. "We're not sure yet where we're going."

That had been a few weeks ago and despite her regular outings she still hadn't had the courage to introduce Mattie's name into the conversation.

Unplanned as it was, leaving most of the parenting to his sister as Hugh did yielded a positive. For Johanna. It took a while before it dawned on her but when it did it was something of a revelation. A talent she'd been unaware of – the discovery of something she was particularly good at. Mothering. It both pleased her and worried her. Why could it not have been a different flair she had? No, she didn't really mean that. It had been lucky for the children under the circumstances. But just her luck that it couldn't have been something that would not hold such a tie, now that her life seemed to be taking off. She was afraid to ponder too much on it but the possibility that she might be moving on was exciting.

"You need to involve yourself more. Do things with them. Without me always having to be here." She had to set the wheels in motion, just in case it happened.

From the look on his face she realised that her brother had no idea. Something that had occupied her thoughts for months hadn't even entered his mind.

"I'm doing the best I can."

"I know you are but you're going to have to try harder. Spend more time alone with them. Take them places." She stood at the sink, drying the dishes, trying to make it sound casual. "It doesn't have to be anywhere fancy, just do nice things with them like taking them for a walk. Look at the swans in the park or whatever. It doesn't matter what, the children just like to be out and about. They'll find things to amuse themselves with."

"Do you think I have the time? I'm running a business." His voice rose. "Don't you do all that with them?"

"I do but that has to change." Had he not noticed the difference in her? Or had he deliberately ignored what was happening under his nose? Seeing he was making no effort to hide his annoyance, she changed tone. A softer tactic might yield better results. "You're very good at teaching them about the world but it's important that they build up memories of things they did with you so when they get older they won't feel they've lost out . . . well, because of the situation." She waited but the set of his jaw told her this wasn't working. Not something he was prepared to take on board.

"It's selfish just to think of yourself in all this, Hugh." She winced at her own words.

"What do *you* know?" he exploded. "You've never been through anything like this. I've lost my wife. You've no idea what that's like. You've never lost anyone." His face was suddenly red with rage as his hands flailed the air. "You're just a child, never even loved anyone."

His words stung. A moment of realisation that in his eyes she was still nothing other than the small clinging child waving him off to America. At that second she realised he had completely misunderstood. He thought she was referring to the children. Had no idea that it was her own life she was talking about.

She held back, watching the heat evaporating through his pores. His lack of awareness of her situation shocked her. She should have told him about Mattie. This was her own fault. Not a subject she could dare mention to him now. Definitely not the right time. She had upset him enough. Better for the moment to leave things be. He wasn't ready for more yet.

"That's unfair. You know that's unfair, Hugh." She allowed a silence before continuing in a quiet voice. "I may be a lot younger than you but I do know what love is. I'm not making little of your loss. But, Hugh, the children have suffered a loss too and they're not old enough to understand it. You have to consider them in all of this."

"I know, I know. I can't understand it myself. I can't even begin to consider how it must be affecting them." He pulled out the chair and sat down heavily. "And I'm sorry. You didn't deserve that. It was unfair of me." He paused. "I know it's an awful thing to have to admit – pure selfishness. But that's how it is. I can't think outside the pain." Placing his elbows on the table, he propped his head on his splayed-out fingers, running them back and forth through his thinning hair as if to massage away the agony.

"We can talk about it again, Hugh, but you're going to have to try. They've lost their mother. They can't lose their father too. And I'm no substitute no matter how hard I try. I love them dearly but I'm only filling in."

"Sorry, sorry, Johanna. You're right. I don't know what I'd have done without you. You didn't deserve that – any of it." He put down his hands and looked at her. "What you said, well, it's not nice to hear it but you're right. I know you're right."

"I know it's hard, Hugh." She put her hand on his shoulder. "Don't think for a minute that I don't understand. I do."

"It's just that I don't know what to do. I don't know where to start."

"Look, how about this Saturday we all go for a picnic, around the lake? If the weather is good."

"I need to go in to work on Saturday."

"That's where you're wrong, Hugh." She shook his shoulder gently. "Don't forget you're the boss. You don't have to go to work. Put someone else in charge for the day. Do something with your children. It would be a start."

"I don't know."

"Well, I do, but it's up to you. What do you want them to remember of their childhood when they get older? That life stopped when they lost their mother?"

He closed his eyes as if to block out the image.

She released his shoulder and moved to the sink. "The longer you leave it the harder it'll be." It was cruel but she ploughed on. "The gulf will be so wide you won't be able to span it."

She stood leaning her back against the drainer and watched him as he bent forward staring down at the table. A beaten man. He didn't look up but she knew he'd accepted what she'd said. Enough for now, she turned back to the sink and picked up the tea towel. She left the silence hang as she

111

began drying the dishes, the clinking of plates the only sound in the room.

It was a couple of minutes before the chair legs scraped the floor. She placed the last of the crockery on the dresser before turning around towards him.

"Right. I'll say nothing to the children other than we'll be going somewhere at the weekend. A surprise. Just in case it's raining." She injected a lightness into her voice, hoping it didn't sound false. "And if it is we'll just go somewhere else with them. I'll leave it to you to sort out your business. But Saturday is for the children. Alright?"

"Alright." It came out almost as a whisper.

The boys sat in the middle of the floor, playing with their toys. They'd been to the park earlier where Hughie practised walking on the stilts he'd got for his birthday. Johanna had diverted the threatening tears after a fall and kissed the grazed knee.

"Do you know your papa made me a pair of those when I was a little girl? They weren't fancy ones like yours – they were made from the branches of a tree."

"And were you able to walk on them?"

"Well, I had to practise hard but I wasn't very good at it and then they broke."

"And did he make you another pair?"

"No, sure he was gone to America by that time."

He took them from her when they reached the hall door.

"I want to walk along the hall in them."

"That's not a good idea, Hughie. You can stand them up in the hall, with the walking canes."

"No, I want to walk on them in the house."

"They're not for playing indoors," she said firmly as they entered. "We'll go to the Common again tomorrow if it's fine and you can try them out again." She knew by the look on his face that he wasn't satisfied.

"Come on now, who wants a drink of milk and a surprise?" She headed for the kitchen before he had a chance to protest.

"*Me, me, me! Milky!*" Patrick clapped his hands and ran after her.

Hughie followed reluctantly, then heard his father's key in the door and ran back to meet him.

"Papa, I walked on the stilts today and I was able to do five steps before I fell down!" The words came out in a rush.

"That's good. You're getting the hang of it then." Hugh hung his hat on the stand.

"I only fell a few times. Look, my knee. Auntie Jo washed it."

He ushered his son back into the drawing room.

Johanna could see by his face he wasn't in good form. The mess spread out when he came in from work wasn't going to ease his irritation.

"Come on, lads, tidy up those toys into the box. We can't have your father falling over a stray ball and breaking his neck now, can we?" Johanna had a way of halting the criticism before it passed her brother's lips.

"Not unless Papa promises to buy me a cap gun." Hughie directed a bull-faced challenge to his father.

"You've already got enough toys to play with. You've just had your birthday present." The warning in his flat voice was lost on his son.

"Well, I don't –"

"Enough. No blackmail in this house." Hugh almost barked it.

She knew the signs. Her brother was in no mood to be defied.

"What's blackmail?" said Hughie.

"Forget about blackmail. I can tell you something,

Hughie, you'll not always have what you want. There's no contentment to be found in that." A hard look settled on her brother's face.

She knew that look, needed to intervene to stop the whine that threatened to enter the child's voice.

"Come on now, Hughie, help your brother. It's a two-man job. That's it, Patrick, everything into the box. Good boy."

Johanna saw the hurt look that crossed the child's face and the puzzlement at his father's words. Hugh had seen it too. She hoped it would make him regret the harshness of his parenting. It was not the first time.

It was something that bothered him in the dark evenings when he sat alone and Johanna and the children had gone to bed. He'd sit there pondering the advisability of making the future too easy for them. Life was hard and, while he didn't want to labour that fact, it was important his children didn't grow up soft, unable to cope with adversity. The line between tipping the scales on the heavy side with chores and responsibilities and allowing the boys to turn into useless articles was difficult to find. He tried to aim for fair – not sure if he always achieved it.

It was hard to remember they were just children when delegating tasks, to remember not to expect perfection. He remembered his own father, always happy to settle for results that were suited to the ages of his children. He needed to accept that but his patience wasn't the best. Not since Margaret . . . it was good that Johanna was there to balance it out.

He hoped his children knew he loved them. He'd always known his own father did but Da had been made of softer stuff. Maybe he needed to practise some of that. It was important that they knew how indispensable they were to him, even when he was tough, but the look on young Hughie's face earlier made him doubt it.

Chapter 19

The lifting of the burden from her shoulders had a gradual effect on them all, a change that started with that first forced picnic. The adjustment was so delicate that at first it was hardly noticeable. It made no real sense anyway because she still had responsibility for her little charges for most of the week but that simple move lightened up the weekends and made it easier to introduce other changes.

"You take the boys to Mass with you tomorrow, Hugh, and I'll take the twins to the park." She hadn't told him that Mattie's presence on their walks on a Sunday morning had turned into a regular pattern.

"Mattie helped us to feed the ducks in the park."

She had watched her brother's raised eyebrow when Hughie or Patrick happened to mention him.

"Did he now?"

It had happened a few times with variations. Now might be a good time to move things on a bit.

"Would you mind if Mattie came to lunch next Sunday?" She threw it out in the direction of the newspaper.

"I don't think that would be a good idea."

She detected a flicker of annoyance in his voice.

"Why ever not?"

"I don't believe in mixing business with pleasure. I see enough of him at work."

A few throwaway comments over the weeks had alerted her but Hugh's tone now confirmed that he might not be particularly impressed with Mattie.

"It's not a good idea for me to mix like that with the staff."

Her irritation rose but showing it might just cause a row. No, best to stay calm if she was to be successful in achieving her aim.

"Well, you won't mind me taking the afternoon off then to go out with him?" She'd started so she'd finish, hoping the sarcasm in her head wasn't reflected in her tone. "We'll have lunch out and you can look after the children." Leave him in no doubt that he was being left to his own devices in the kitchen. See how he liked that.

"No, that's fine. You need more time to yourself."

His easy agreement took her by surprise. Immediately regretting her bad thoughts, she glanced across to see if he had noticed the stubborn set of her face but he appeared buried in the news. Just as well.

"*Mind you don't cut yourself.*" Her mother's reprimand echoed in her head.

"*What?*" Polishing the sideboard with a soft cloth at the time, Johanna had stopped in puzzlement at the remark.

"*With the sharp edge on that tongue of yours. You'll need to watch that.*"

She heard the rustle as he put the paper on his knee.

"Look, Johanna, you've been more than good to us, to the children."

The look on his face was not what she was expecting as it mirrored back her own feelings of guilt. Her mother had been right. The sharp tone. Maybe not the right time for it but it seemed to have worked.

"I'm glad I've been able to help. And you know I love being with them."

"I know. We couldn't have survived without you." He glanced at the children playing with their toys on the floor. "It's just Matthew, he's a nice lad. Nothing wrong with him, but he's not a great worker. A bit lazy . . . well, maybe lazy is too strong a word . . . maybe too easygoing for his own good. Not much ambition in him."

Johanna let it go. Life wasn't all about work. Maybe in Hugh's book it was but now was not the time to point that out to him, not the time for that battle.

Mattie was happy to play with the twins any time he called with the groceries. He'd whistle a tune from behind the baby carriage, watching for their reaction as they looked around to see where the sound was coming from. He made funny faces at them and seemed to get as much fun from these games as the babies did. She watched him fill the hole that her brother was unable to. A hole that still her brother wasn't fully aware of despite her pointing it out to him in all sorts of ways.

Johanna never suggested entertaining Mattie in the house again. She met him outside twice a week. In the evenings they went for walks or an occasional visit to the theatre and on a Sunday they met for afternoon tea, leaving Hugh to interact in whatever way he could manage with the children.

Hugh watched his sister blossom. A reminder of a life he'd had, emotions that he might never experience again, a happiness he could never imagine himself feeling again. Watching her glow did little to ease his emptiness. On the contrary it served only to highlight his own loneliness. The reason for it was obvious and while he was glad for her he couldn't eradicate completely the twinges of envy that niggled.

What he could see with Mattie and his sister worried him. It was something that would change all their lives, not just hers, if it continued to progress. It was unreasonable to allow the fear of her leaving put an obstacle in her way. Trying to dislike Mattie wasn't going to change that. There was nothing disagreeable about him. Quite the contrary – he was a decent lad. And the lightness of her as she went about the household chores told him all he needed to know. He couldn't take that from her. He'd been thinking about his plan to let Mattie go after his last warning at work. If he were honest maybe it was fear that had influenced him and caused too harsh a judgement on Mattie's performance.

The Sunday she brought Mattie into the house he knew. He was in the drawing room reading his book, a big historical tome. Out of the corner of his eye he saw the nudge she gave Mattie as she propelled him through the open door.

"I'm just going to say goodbye to the children before we head off, Hugh."

"Don't be too long." Mattie threw a pleading look over his shoulder and caught her smile at his half-whispered warning before she closed the door.

It wasn't just the suit that told Hugh that the day he'd been dreading had arrived. It was the way Mattie was running his finger inside the collar of his shirt as if it was in danger of choking him.

"Sit down, Matthew. Sit down 'til she's ready." Hugh put his bookmark in place and, closing the book, laid it on the circular side table beside his armchair. He had a certain sympathy for the lad. This wasn't going to be easy. Not for either of them.

"Well?" Johanna stood in the doorway, coat on. "Are we ready?"

Mattie was propped on the edge of his seat. The shy grin on his face when he turned told her the job was done and everything was alright.

"I hope you'll both be very happy." Hugh stood up from his armchair and took a step towards her. Extending his hand, he took hers in a firm handshake. The tightness of his voice might have sounded insincere, delivered as it was without a smile, but the slight redness of his eyelids told her what this was costing him.

"Don't say anything to the boys until I get back, sure you won't? I don't want them to be worrying that I'll disappear suddenly because I won't."

"No, we'll tell them together."

"You know, I'm happy to continue minding them for the moment, if that's what you want."

"Don't you know it's what I want? I'd like that – of course I would. And so would the children." Hugh gave a slight smile. "How could you doubt it?"

Mattie glanced at Johanna, unsure if the conversation was finished. Hugh turned and picked up his newspaper from where it lay on the arm of the armchair. With his back to them he brandished it in the air, waving it at them before turning to settle back into the soft cushion.

"Go on, off you go, the pair of you! Sure maybe we'd have a toast to celebrate when you get back later . . . if you're not too late."

"Why don't you invite Matthew over for the dinner on Sunday?"

Spoken to her back as she washed up the breakfast dishes as if there had never been a problem. That was as much as Hugh ever said about him. But it was enough for Johanna. After that Mattie was included every Sunday.

"Mind your eye." Mattie would never let a nose-poking job go unremarked when he saw a small finger excavating.

His joking amused the boys while having the desired effect. More fun than their father's stern insistence on good manners.

Mattie had arrived now at a stage where, while he may not have been totally comfortable with Hugh, he was somewhat at ease with him. It had taken a while to achieve but he recognised the boundary, a polite relaxation while never crossing into casualness with him in the way he did with the children. A stranger observing might never have been aware he was an employee. It was just something in the way Hugh's conversation with him was kept to the necessities that, while courteous, made it unequal. So subtle a distinction that neither may have been aware but it told Johanna how marrying Mattie would place them on a different level. Up to now she had been the boss's sister. Now she would be Mattie's wife. An almost imperceptible difference but one that would demote her to a lower position nonetheless. A lower rank. Of inferior status to her own brother.

ART

Chapter 20

Knocknageeha, County Clare, Ireland
1887

The journey in the pony and trap had been silent, the travellers buried deep in their own thoughts. Art was conscious that the only words he had uttered during the entire drive had been those of encouragement to the animal.

The last few minutes in the house had been awkward. Luke had been hanging around the house all morning, afraid to go off to play in the fields in case he missed his chance to say goodbye to his sister.

"Will you go and see if you can find Declan?" Art saw the reluctance on his son's face.

"Don't go away, Katie, before I come back. Sure you won't? Promise me."

"Of course I won't, you noodle." Kate gave him a hug. "Go on. Off with you."

"Are you sure you have everything?" Ellen checked with her daughter as Art helped them into the trap.

"Yes, I have all I need." Kate knew her mother was against her decision but it was what she had to do.

"You are sure this is what you want, Kate?" Art asked. "There's still time to change your mind. Your mother and I won't be disappointed."

The set look on Kate's face confirmed what he already knew.

"How many times do I have to say it?" She picked up the tartan rug from the bench seat and placed it over her mother's lap, unfolding it to cover her own knees.

"Where is that Declan?" An impatience crept into Art's voice. "Wouldn't you think he'd make it his business to be here to say goodbye?"

Luke rounded the corner of the house alone, his face anxious in case they had departed.

"Well, where's your brother?" Art said as Luke approached the trap. "I'll never understand that boy. He knew Kate was leaving after breakfast."

"I can't find him. He's not anywhere around." Luke shook his head, disbelief on his face that Declan could do such a thing. To go missing when he might never see his sister again. "He must be gone off somewhere."

"Did you give a good shout over the fields?"

"Yes, I did."

"Well, we can't wait any longer or we'll be late." Art climbed up into the trap with a grunt. As he picked up the reins he spotted Kate's lonely case standing on the ground. "Here, pass the case up."

Luke lifted it, surprised by the lightness.

"You're not taking a lot with you, Katie," he said. "Is that all?"

She smiled down at him. "The Lord will provide."

"Bye, Katie." Luke put his two hands to his mouth before opening them as if releasing a dove and blew a kiss up at his sister. He felt water pooling somewhere beneath his eyeballs, causing his eyes to float.

"Say goodbye to Declan for me, won't you?" she called over to him as he backed away towards the house.

"Here you are." Art handed back the small case to Kate, his eyes downcast.

"Father, I'm certain. It's the right thing for me." She

spoke softly, knowing he couldn't bear to meet her eye.

The last words spoken. Nothing more to be said. The departure could be delayed no longer. Giving one final look over his shoulder to see if Declan had appeared he gave the reins a shake.

Kate looked around at the passing landscape, taking in as many precious signs of nature as she could memorise, conscious that this might be the last sighting she would have of these familiar fields.

Ellen saw nothing except a yawning emptiness. The mother and daughter relationship, maturing over the last few years, was about to be severed as cleanly as if an axe were to fall, its keen blade separating the two halves forever. The anticipation of the adult companionship of her daughter cut short – only now did she realise how much she'd been looking forward to it. All the hope of the future and her only daughter was choosing to leave her in this way. The emptiness of it was overshadowed by the annoyance at not being able to do anything about it.

The pony's trot, music to Kate's ears and a rhythmic comfort to her father, was not so for Ellen. Building up to a thundering in her head it made her want to shout at the pony to stop his clattering. Knowing it would be of no help, she settled back against the seat to nurse her misplaced anger and to wallow in her selfishness in wishing things were otherwise. If another neighbour mentioned how great it was to have a nun in the family she couldn't be sure she'd be responsible for her actions.

The clouded grey sky of earlier was beginning to break up as the edges lightened to a white fluff. She held her face up to catch the ray of weak sunlight struggling to get through and concentrated on her breathing. No one had interfered with her choice in life. She would just have to settle her mind and try to accept her daughter's decision.

The clip-clopping of the hooves receded until it became a lulling which hovered over the trap. It floated in the air until their thoughts merged in a silence, all linked by a moist sadness. One that accompanied them on their journey knowing it was to be the end of the familiar life together, a life that they would all miss, a loss that would leave a permanent hole in the family. Her resignation allowed for these last minutes, if not exactly happy, to be spent together in a not unpleasant manner.

Giving one's innocent daughter away at the top of a church aisle was something of a loss, but one with an expectancy of joys to come. Art didn't want to think about giving her away to the Church itself. A bereavement of sorts. For him anyway.

He turned his thoughts to Declan. An anger rose up in him. For once could his son not do as he should? Was there no emotion in him at all? Wouldn't you want to say goodbye to your only sister, especially when you didn't know when or if you would ever see her again?

"Are you mad or something?"

Ellen and Luke had spoken together, almost shouting across the table in shock.

Art just looked at his daughter. If he was aware of the horror on his face he was too shocked to bother hiding it.

"*What?* You're going to be a nun?" Luke looked at his sister in disbelief.

"It's what I want." Kate's answer was barely audible. It was worse than she'd anticipated.

The way parents boasted about having a nun or priest in the family was all that she had been familiar with. She wondered now if they had all had the same shocked reaction when their daughters announced their intentions or if it was just her family.

124

"Will you have to wear all those black things and get your hair chopped off?" Luke was the first to recover, his curiosity getting the better of him.

"Not immediately."

"You need to really think about this, Kate," Art said.

His softened tone told her that he felt sorry for her. She looked across at her father, avoiding her mother, not wanting to see the anger in her eyes, the resentment at her decision. She was comforted that he at least understood her disappointment, realising that she thought they'd have been pleased.

"Whatever put this into your head?" Her mother's face was screwed up with annoyance. "Or whoever?" She looked ready to take on the culprit.

"No-one did. I decided myself." Kate raised herself from the slump she had slipped into and faced her. "I've been thinking about it for a long time and I've spoken to one of the nuns. Several times."

"And you said nothing?"

"I needed to be sure first."

"It's a very big step, love," Art said. "Think it over and we'll talk about it again." He stood up from the table. "I need to go out and get the cattle in."

It was only much later that Art remembered Declan's reaction. Or lack of one. He had just shrugged at the table that day when she broke the news. Never said a word. Nothing at all. He'd continued chewing his meat and gazing out the window as if she'd said she was going out to feed the hens.

Declan was always a peculiar child. So different from Luke. Hard to believe they were brothers, much less twins. Would rarely look you in the eye during normal conversation. Only in situations where he thought he was on top would he allow such eye contact. Ask him to do something and he'd

125

behave as though you hadn't spoken. His hearing had been checked and no problem showed up. Playing peaceably with other children seemed an alien concept to him. A football game was never that when Declan appeared. Teamwork didn't come into it. The ball would immediately be kicked out of play to where none of the others could get it. A sandcastle was something to be jumped on after the others had spent time building it. Art had tried to teach him that there were consequences to such actions. Pointed out that one of the consequences was that he would never make any friends.

"What do I care?" Tossed off with a shrug.

The worrying part was that Art could see that he genuinely didn't care.

His classmates simply didn't like him or his behaviour. It was like he spooked them. A sense that there was something they should be a little afraid of even though he hadn't actually done anything. At times he was defiant. But unlike most other children he took his confrontation to the extreme. Couldn't, or wouldn't share a plaything. Would hold on as if his life depended on it.

The incident with the garden fork was the one that worried Art most. He had instilled in the boys the message that forks were not for playing with. That the tines were lethal. The only time they were allowed to use one was under supervision if they were helping to turn the hay or shift the manure. No messing about with it in your hand.

"Let go of it! We're not allowed!"

Art could hear the shouting of his sons before he rounded the end of the cowhouse.

"And who's going to stop me? Now you let go or I'll make you." There was no mistaking the sneer in Declan's voice.

The metal prongs of the fork were inches from Luke's stomach as the two boys tussled beside the dung-heap.

Declan had a firm grip on the wooden handle. Using his advantage, he pushed his brother backwards towards the stained whitewashed wall of the barn.

"*Stop!*" Art ran forward, horrified as Declan, at his shout, released the handle.

The unexpected freedom, combined with Luke's pull, bull's-eyed the prongs into his belly as he fell backwards against the barn wall, knocking the wind out of him.

He slumped to the ground.

In three strides Art was beside Luke and as he bent over him he heard it.

"*Huh!*" The dismissive tone of Declan. "*That'll teach you!*"

Fury rose up in him. He straightened just in time to see a smirk on his son's face as their eyes met.

"Go and get your mother."

Declan stood there.

"*I said go and get her. Quickly.*" There was no mistaking the urgency in Art's voice. He watched the insolence on his son's face fade just as he turned and ran towards the house. After the first few urgent steps, as if he knew his father was watching, he slowed his run to an exaggerated slow pace.

"*Quickly, I said. Damn it, boy! Run!*" Art shouted as Declan disappeared from view around the corner of the barn.

He gently removed the fork from Luke's hands. Relieved that it came away easily, he lifted up his son's jumper to check if the prongs had penetrated.

"I wasn't . . . play . . . fork . . ." The words came out in the breathy whisper of one whose lungs had emptied.

"Don't talk, son. Save your breath. You're not in trouble." Art patted his shoulder. "I saw what happened."

Four dirty brown marks dotted his stomach. No blood. That was good. Less chance of infection but he'd be well bruised later.

"I think you're alright. It didn't go into you. You'll live this time." Art smiled down at his son. "You were lucky."

What bothered Art more than the incident itself was Declan's lack of concern.

"Do you realise it could have been a whole lot worse?"

"Well, it wasn't." Declan stood up from the table and made to move off.

"Where do you think you're going? Get back here." His son's attitude, as if nothing had happened, as if that was the end of it, infuriated Art. "It was no thanks to you that it wasn't."

"Luke should have let go. It was his own fault."

"You shouldn't have had the fork in the first place." Art glared across at him. "Are you even sorry?"

Declan's shrug fired him to continue.

"You do realise you could have killed him if the prongs had gone into him?" Art's eyes were wide in amazement at the lack of any remorse. "I know you didn't do it on purpose, but don't you even care?"

He stared at his son in the hope of finding even the slightest sign of empathy. He searched, but in Declan's demeanour he could find not a trace.

"Can I go now?"

Art looked away in disgust as his son walked to the door.

"Ellen, there's something wrong with that boy." He shook his head. "There has to be. I'll never understand him."

Chapter 21

1865

From the day of his birth Art's future had been mapped out for him. He was the sort of easy-going lad who just accepted this inevitability without it ever entering his consciousness that other options might exist. He went with the flow, putting one foot in front of the other and plodded through life, day by day, season by season – not someone given to analysis, he wasn't even conscious how much he loved the feel of their changes on his skin and in his nostrils. He was simply content that this was the way of things. The freezing breath on the winter air as welcome as the sweet smell of summer clover.

As the eldest son it was assumed that Art would step into his father's shoes and run the farm when the time came. Neither he nor anyone else questioned it. It was something that would happen in the distant future, a place far away on the horizon, when their parents' strength waned. A common enough presumption in most of the farming homesteads around, but not one that Art had given much thought to until shortly after his twentieth birthday when his father suddenly dropped dead. No warning. Nothing. Just slumped forward in the middle of the dinnertime conversation. Leaving like that, without so much as a signal that something was wrong.

The shock of Patrick's death reverberated through the tightknit community. It was the way neighbours immediately came together, taking over the household and farm chores and helped keep the lives of the McNamara family running fairly smoothly in the days that followed, that carried them through the tragic time. It wasn't until the comfort of their support had dispersed that the truth of the situation became evident. A houseful of children left behind to be looked after by Mary Ann with no option but to entrust the running of the farm to Art who was not yet ready for the responsibility. Something both she and he were well aware of.

"You're the man of the house now, Art. You'll need to look after your mother and the young childer."

If another old fellow said it to him he'd swing for him. The numbers of them who mouthed the platitude on their way into the wake was mounting and each time delivered as if it were an original thought. He began to lay bets in his head as to whether the next one would say it or not.

He splashed a drop of milk into his mug and wandered outside to have his tea in peace. He needed to clear his head, couldn't take any more of the blather. The pink and orange streaks left by the setting sun threw a soft light over the fields, silhouetting the hedgerow trees on the horizon. He could make out the shapes of the animals in the distance, some moving about still munching the grass as if nothing had happened. As he leaned on the fence he heard a sound behind him and hoped it wasn't someone come to join him. He needed a few minutes alone.

"So this is where you've got to."

He was relieved it was his mother. He wasn't in form for making small-talk.

"They're very good, but I'm worn out from all the chat." She leaned on the fence a few feet away from her son and lapsed into a silence that only the distant mooing of a cow filled.

130

"If I hear once again what a lovely corpse your father makes I swear I'll scream."

Art glanced at her. She was shaking her head but he could see that she managed to crack a smile.

"It's the 'man-of-the-house' one that gets me." He grinned at her.

"Don't worry too much about that one." His mother gave him a nudge. "I'm still the boss."

"And sure don't we all know it, Mother?"

The annoyance at the mindlessness of the auld lads' comments served a purpose, taking his mind off his grief and the enormity of what lay ahead. Batting the remarks away was, he supposed, one way of not letting it in. But they were right and there was no getting away from it now. He was the man of the house whether he liked it or not.

He took the last swig of his tea and spilled the dregs onto the grass.

"Come on, Ma, we'd better go back in and face them." He put an arm around her shoulders. "Sort the rota for who's going to sit up with the 'lovely corpse' for the night. Sure, I suppose if we didn't laugh we'd cry."

He lay there on his back, on top of the eiderdown, hands clasped behind his head. He had just handed over his place in the wake room to Hugh and headed to the bedroom for a couple of hours' rest. He didn't bother to take off his clothes – it was hardly worthwhile – he'd have to get up to see to the cattle in a while. No point in going into a deep sleep so he'd left the curtains open, preferring to watch the slow lightening of the universe as dawn broke. He breathed deeply and with each inhalation the earthy smell of the forest floor, as strong as if he were standing there collecting the kindling for the fire, hit his brain. He couldn't be sure if it was coming in through the open window or was a scent of long ago.

* * *

Kicking through the russet leaves, his mother didn't mind that it took twice as long to complete the task. Happy to wait while he pulled his wooden cart behind him, there was never an urgency to interrupt his enjoyment. He could still hear the snap of the dry wood ringing through the woods as she put her boot on one of the bigger branches, breaking it to fit into his little cart.

From the time he took his first toddling steps he remembered the tricks they'd used for him to develop his farming skills – as effortlessly as if they had been games. He was quick to learn when his mother demonstrated how to handle the hens firmly and quietly and not to drop the eggs into the basket but to lay them down gently. He had watched with fascination the thick yellow liquid of the broken yolk seep into the tea-towel and congeal the first time he tried.

"See, that's why we need to be careful or else we'll have none for the tea."

She'd only had to show him once how to avoid a jellylike mess and he had the knack.

"Let's see how many eggs we can collect today." Mary Ann always gave him his own basket, lined with a tea-towel and when he wasn't looking she would slip a few of the ones she'd collected into it.

"I've got four. How many have you, Art?"

"One, two, three, four, five, six, seven, eight! *I won!*" He smiled up at her.

"Good lad. The hens must like you."

The innocent scenes played through his head. A balminess in them perhaps because they involved just himself and his mother. Maybe they could do this together too.

He pulled the eiderdown and blankets from under him

132

and slipped between the cold sheets, snuggling into the warm downy softness of the pillow where his head had just lain. He turned on his side, pulling the blankets up over his shoulders and tucking his arms under their warmth. As he closed his eyes he wondered if she too lay in the next room, unable to sleep. Was she also thinking back and wondering now if he was up to the job?

The days coming up to the funeral time had been busy. Not much time for thinking. It was in the exhausted quiet of the night with sleep eluding him that the notion crept in, the fact that he had never made choices about his life, had never even thought about it until now. Too busy growing up and allowing things to just happen to have given consideration to the fact that he might have had options.

They came to him often as he worked alone and sometimes at the stage between wakefulness and sleep. Memories of times spent with his father cleaning out the byre, a job he'd done so many times with him.

"Don't worry, Da, you've trained me well." He'd heard the put-downs of other fathers and realised how lucky he'd been with his.

"Don't worry about it. You can't expect not to make mistakes. It's all about learning from them."

His first day ploughing. His father dismissed Art's disappointment at the wavy furrow that snaked out from the plough.

"Mistakes are how you progress. The man who's perfect has nowhere to go. Now turn that horse and let's try the next one and take your time, son. It'll come."

The memory of that day returned. The pride of having moved on from the babyish chores with his mother.

"Time to do man's work now, Art." He could still feel his father tousling his hair. "Come with me and you'll see what job I have for you."

133

"Where are we going, Da?"

"We're going down the fields." He looked down at his son's face smiling up at him. "To build a wall, lad."

"Don't let him lift anything too heavy now, Pat." Mary Ann looked worried.

"You needn't concern yourself, missus." He looked over at his wife, giving her a wink. "He'll be well able for the job I have for him."

Down in the field the rocks looked very heavy. As heavy as the disappointment that quenched his enthusiasm. He wouldn't be able to carry them. Not ready for this work yet.

"Now, young man. We're going to build a bit of a wall. You and me." His father took him by the hand and sat him down on a large flat rock. "And piers too. To hold the new gate."

He sat beside Art and took out his pipe.

"Where's the new gate, Da?"

"It's not made yet, Art. No point in making the gate until you've something to hang it on."

Art watched his father go through the pipe-lighting ritual, recognising the slow drawing-out of the process. He lasted a minute before the torment of it became too much.

"Can we start now, Da?"

"In a minute, Art. In a minute." His father tapped the pipe against the rock, emptying out the last remnants of ash before refilling it. "But the first thing you need to learn before any job is to have patience. You can't just rush into it. You need to think how you're going to approach it first."

"But don't we just lift the rocks and put them on top of one another?"

"Well, we could, but the wall might fall down if we did."

He remembered the way Da had looked down at him, as if waiting for him to digest the idea.

"You have to have a plan. A strategy. You see, son, you have to select the correct stones, not just any old stone will

134

do. They need to wedge into one another. Good and firm."

Art surveyed the field of pale-grey stones. Large flat ones lay as if they had been planted in the earth. Some the size of footballs lay loose, scattered like they had been left there mid-game, while others were piled in mounds. Patrick had stayed silent long enough to give him time to take in their project, the interruption coming just in time to stop him being overwhelmed by the size of the task.

"Take a look over that wall behind us, son." Patrick checked his pipe. It had gone out. He pressed on the tobacco to ensure it wasn't smouldering before replacing it in his pocket. "That field used to be just like this one and now look at it. A right feed of green grass for the cattle. And hardly a rock in it."

Art picked his way through the rocks and stones and standing on his tiptoes checked over the wall.

"Was it really like this one, Da?"

"Indeed it was. And I bet you've looked at that field hundreds of times and never thought that it was once just a field of rocks." Patrick paused. "So you see it's not something we'll clear in a day. Sure that one behind would have taken weeks to do. It was my grandfather who cleared that one. Now what we need to do is to break it down into small jobs." He looked over at the boy still standing looking over the wall. "So what do you think the first job is that we have to do?"

"I don't know, Da." Art's concentration was on a loose stone on the top of the wall. He leaned gently on it and rocked it. "I thought you'd just decide to build a wall and then get on with putting it up. I didn't know you had to think about it first." He was beginning to lose interest.

"Well, you do, son. Otherwise all your hard work might be wasted if you do it wrong." Patrick looked at Art's puzzled face. "Now, where do we need the wall? You have to think what it is you want the wall to do. Is it just to

135

divide up a field where you're going to plant the spuds or is it to keep the cattle or sheep from escaping? How big do you want the field? Where should the entrance be? Things like that are important to decide on before you begin." He stood up. "Enough talking. I think we're ready to get going. It may be all in the planning but now it's time for action."

"What can I do, Da?" The slump in Art's shoulders lifted.

"Well, son, what I need you to do first is to go around the field and collect all the smaller stones. The ones that are no bigger than two goose eggs together." He held up his hands and looked at Art through the perfect oval made with his forefingers and thumbs. "You can put them in a pile there." He pointed. "We need to collect different shapes and sizes into separate piles first. Put the flatter ones over there." He indicated where with a nod of the head.

It was a memory he went back to over and over. It helped him sleep sometimes even before he allowed himself reach the pleasure of that last day when they both stood together and admired their handiwork.

"Now, son, stand back there and look at what you've achieved. Not only have we the wall built but the field is cleared of rocks, ready for the planting of the spuds." Patrick's contented voice was in the room. "Two jobs for the price of one."

The sense of accomplishment that made the heat and drudgery of the job worthwhile. A lesson for life.

Sleep drifted over him but in a reluctance to let his father go he tried to catch other memories as they threatened to slip away. Removing the dead trees from around the farm and splitting them into fire-logs with an axe, that was the day he knew without doubt that he wanted to be a farmer. The master's teaching and building of his confidence had been so painless as to be almost invisible. No job on the land at which he, Art, wasn't an expert. As sleep carried him off he felt the hand slide from his grasp and was content to let it go.

Chapter 22

1866

"No, Art. I've no intention of moving into your mother's house." Ellen was emphatic. "I told you that from the time you proposed so don't act all surprised now."

In a move against tradition Ellen had her own ideas about their accommodation. Ideas she'd been nudging him about for a while.

"Come on, she's very easy to get on with." He slipped his arm around her shoulders and smiled down at her. "I thought you liked her."

"I do. Very much. And that's the way I want it to continue." Her face was set in a way he knew there was no budging. "I've nothing against Mary Ann. She's a lovely woman, but I know how those sorts of arrangements can turn sour. And it doesn't take long. Sure I've seen it at home."

"It'll be different with us," he pleaded. "We can make it work."

"No, Art, that's what they all say. We won't even be trying to make it work because it's not going to happen. Get that into your head. I have another plan."

"A plan? What sort of a plan?" He stood back, holding her at arm's length. "This is new. Am I going to like it?"

"You will." She smiled back at him with the confidence

of a woman who knows she has won. "Trust me, you will. Eventually."

"*Mmm.* I hope so."

"We can do something for ourselves with those outhouses at the back. They're not being used for anything."

"They are so. There's the wood pile and –"

"Not anything important. Nothing that can't be rearranged. No, we can do something with those."

"I love the 'we'."

"I'm not looking for anything fancy – just give me my own hall door. That's all I'm asking."

"It's a plan alright." He rubbed his chin while Ellen hesitated, waiting for him to digest it. "But my mother will think it strange. Us living in an outhouse when there's a perfectly comfortable farmhouse available to us."

"Leave her to me. I'll persuade her it'll be to her benefit. And I'm sure it'll suit her."

"And how do you plan on doing that? She's sharp, my mother. She'll see through it."

"Well, it's not as if she's going to be lonely. Sure hasn't she enough of her own children still living at home?" Ellen grinned at him. "Don't worry, by the time you're finished with the outhouse it will be a home, and by the time I'm finished with her she'll be happy with us in separate accommodation. I'll leave her in no doubt that I mightn't be the easiest to get on with."

"Now you tell me!" Art laughed.

And so Art renovated the outhouses and they married. A year later their daughter Katie was born.

Chapter 23

1873

Solid and dependable were qualities that anyone who knew him, if asked, would attribute to Art. Unfortunately, hand in hand with these particular qualities came a stubbornness. Once Art made up his mind about something there was no changing it. And so it was with the dog.

Ellen hated the way the dog skulked. He followed her around the yard, never with her, always trailing behind with a way of crouching low that she didn't trust.

"You must have done something to him one time."

"So it's my fault, is it? Nothing to do with the sneaky old way of him?"

Art always defended the dog even when Ellen had hard evidence to the contrary.

"He wouldn't let your mother in the gate this morning."

"He doesn't like her – she's always shouting at him."

"Oh, blame her, that's right! She's going to be the one to bite someone, I suppose? I'm sure he gives her good reason to shout. I've been telling you since he did it the first time when it was Johanna he took a dislike to and that was over a year ago and your sister had done nothing to him."

The strange thing about the dog was that whenever Art was present he behaved perfectly, even when someone came to the door. When he wasn't around, the dog wouldn't let anyone on the premises, running at them, teeth bared, leaving them in no doubt but that they were about to be torn limb from limb.

"Well, it's only natural. He's guarding the place and protecting you all when he knows the master's not here."

"We don't need protecting, thanks. Not from the fellow coming for eggs anyway. The dog snapped at him and sure he knows that young lad. Doesn't he come here every few days to collect them?"

"Ah, he must have given him the boot or something?"

"He didn't. I saw what happened."

"You're imagining it. He wouldn't hurt a fly, sure you wouldn't?" Art rubbed the dog's head resting on his knee.

"Well, he did. And he drew blood. Only I was there he'd have eaten the young fellow. There's a wicked nature in him – you need to get rid of him. I don't like him around the children."

"Ah, what are you talking about! He loves them. He's going nowhere. He's my pal, aren't you? My old friend."

"I'm telling you he'll attack again one day and it might be more serious next time. Are you going to wait for that to happen?"

Ellen had been in control of the dog up until now but lately she noticed a change that she didn't like. Whenever someone called in she'd call the dog off, but recently he'd begun to ignore her. And while it worried her, it annoyed her more that it didn't seem to bother Art, even when she admitted to being afraid of the dog.

It was night-time when he arrived back to the house. He stopped to admire the luminous light shining in the yard. The full moon bleached the colour from everything, transforming the scene into a shimmering silver picture.

He could make out the shape of the dog asleep in the middle of the yard. He went over to rouse him and shift him to the shed to lock up for the night. A spade lay on the cobbles a few yards away as if someone had thrown it there in mid-task. The metal of the spade was wet and the moon was reflected on its shiny dark surface.

"Get up out of that! C'mon, get up and off to your bed!"

As he nudged the dog with his boot, he noticed the same wet substance on the stones beneath the animal's head. He reached down to give him a shake and in that same instance, feeling something sticky on his fur, he realised that his dog was dead. Battered to death.

His roars brought his mother from the farmhouse across the yard.

"What's after happening? Who did this to my dog?"

"You can forget about the bloody dog! It's your daughter that's the problem." Mary Ann's voice shook with fury. "You wouldn't listen, would you? We all warned you often enough."

Although the livid red scar down the right side of Kate's face had faded to a silvery mark, it was something Art could never get away from. It accused him across the kitchen table every day. On Sundays he always got into the pew last so that he would sit on her left but at home he couldn't change his usual place at the dinner table without it being obvious. It wasn't the ugliness of the mutilated skin he wanted to avoid, it was the guilt.

He once saw Luke gently run his finger down the length of it.

"Is it sore, Katie?"

"No, it doesn't hurt. I don't even remember it's there unless I look in the mirror."

He wanted to do it himself, to stroke it gently until it

went away, but he could never bring himself to touch it. Didn't want to remind her.

She was an easy child to hug, not something he'd ever thought about, just something they'd always done. The natural feel when their left cheeks met.

"You're all scratchy, Daddy." Kate would complain. "You need to shave."

It was the way they had always done it. Left cheeks. And for this he was now grateful. He couldn't bear to think of the scratchiness of his beard against her delicate scar. Grateful it was something that didn't have to change to accommodate her disfigurement. And his shame.

Easier to appreciate why Ellen couldn't forgive him so easily for what she saw as ruining their beautiful daughter's life. No difficulty comprehending this because he never forgave himself.

After the initial shock wore off Ellen never mentioned it. But he could see the way she looked at Kate when she thought the child wasn't watching. Could see the pain on her face. It was enough for him to know that it was best not to talk about blame. He was on his own there.

Chapter 24

1887

At the convent they said their last goodbyes, Ellen inconsolable at the thought of the future. Had it been a teaching or nursing order it wouldn't have been so bad, but the enclosed convent life behind the metal grille was not what she'd had in mind for her only daughter. Being barred from contact with the outside world was, for Ellen, like an end to life itself. She had made that plain.

Art stood in red-eyed silence. Locked in the past, he could see it all. The day it happened. Kate's lovely face taken from her. This time her life taken from them. She never appeared to hold him responsible. Had simply grown up appearing to accept her disfigurement but he'd always wanted to ask her how she really felt. Wanted to ask if it had anything to do with her decision. The question he couldn't ask. Would have to live forever not knowing the answer. A question that would always be in his mind.

HUGH

Chapter 25

Boston

1882

If Hugh missed Ireland it was a sentiment that was never allowed to gain a firm foothold. Not that it was batted away in any conscious sense. If it ever existed, with a future full of promise, there was no time for a young man in a hurry, like Hugh, to ponder on it. His ambition and sense of adventure sustained him, carrying him over any momentary pangs. If ever there had been a time when the excitement had begun to wane, the soaring of his heart on meeting Margaret put paid to that and made for a seamless crossover into the next phase.

The desolation at her loss didn't diminish easily nor fast. The edge wore off but his heart remained punctured in a way he knew would never completely heal. It was through these holes that the occasional yearnings for home now slipped through. Longings he couldn't afford to wallow in for fear they would paralyse him. Building his business empire was the only way he knew to ensure he could keep going. The sense of satisfaction at seeing it grow fulfilled the busy daytime part of his life, but the hollowness within him that came to the fore as he made his way home in the evenings was something else. That was more difficult – and hadn't eased. Something he was sorry he hadn't talked more about at the time. Hadn't been able to but he should have tried. It

144

was too late. No-one would want to know now. And pathetic, that was the last thing he wanted to come across as. The lonesomeness had turned into something he tried to drown in the warmth that lay in his nightly glass of whiskey.

The children knew the limits of his patience. They recognised the edge that came into his voice when they'd reached the boundary. He hoped the security of knowing that warning sign took the harshness from his strict rules.

But he was aware of how much they missed Johanna. After she married she'd continued looking after them until Hannah was born and then he'd had to make other arrangements. Apart from Hughie, she had mothered the children even longer than Margaret, so he tried to take this into account when admonishing them. The fact that she was no longer in the house to be a leveller and comfort them with her cuddles was something that was missing. He had envied her that ability, wished he could have shown them more empathy but it didn't come naturally. Too late to change his ways now. He had tried in small ways but it felt forced to him, something the children must surely have picked up on. No, they didn't feel comfortable with anything more than a pat on the head from him, of that he was sure.

If he were honest, he missed the warmth of his sister's company himself. Gina, the girl who looked after the children in his absence was good and the children liked her, but it wasn't the same, and she was certainly no company for him. He hadn't appreciated just how comfortable his sister's companionship had been until she was gone.

Now that they were older Hugh had begun to enlighten the children on the ways of the business world, speaking to them as if they were equals, not like he was teaching. Explaining things like how the stock markets worked and encouraging them to read from the newspaper to him in the evenings.

"Do I have to?" Patrick hated it. Reading wasn't his thing. Not one who enjoyed even children's books, except when being read to, columns and columns of the dull black print of the newspaper filled him with dread. No pictures to give him a clue and to him the words and figures were utterly meaningless anyway.

"You just do the first bit and Hughie will take over." His father sat back with his whiskey and relaxed as they read, aware of the nudges that Patrick gave his older brother when he needed a prompt. He was aware that most of it went over their heads so he didn't wish to prolong their agony more than a few minutes. Its purpose was just to give them an introduction to the ways of the world. He was pleased when the day came that Hughie asked him simple questions about the content and he gave as uncomplicated an explanation as he could.

They were aware he was watching but something in his eyes reassured them as he corrected them gently when they stumbled over the unfamiliar words. Had they been asked to describe it they could not. It was years later before they recognised that all these 'somethings' added up to one big unspecified certainty. It confirmed that somewhere inside him, harsh and all that he might have seemed, their father loved them deeply.

Occasionally there was a rebellion – now that they were that bit older. It puzzled them that he insisted they do Saturday chores when he employed staff. It was a failure to recognise their father's aversion to allowing them grow up incompetent in the basics of life that put a sudden end to young Hughie's appetite for mutiny.

That Saturday had started off well. Pleasant enough until a minor difference of opinion at the breakfast table turned the morning sour.

"Don't forget the grass needs mowing."

"Why do I always have to do it?"

"The others aren't big enough."

Hughie's eyes turned dark as he glowered across at his father. "I have other plans."

"You do, do you? Well, it might surprise you to know that so have I. And mine involve earning a living. To keep you in the style you're obviously taking for granted."

Hughie was aware that Patrick's eyes were widening in alarm, as were Gina's as she removed the porridge bowls from the table.

The chair made a scraping noise on the tiles as his father stood up from the table.

"I'm sure your plans can wait 'til you have the mowing finished."

"We should have a gardener anyway."

The sulking tone was a mistake. His father relished a challenge and his son's obstinacy ensured the argument wasn't finished.

"We could. But we don't." He paused and glared at his son. "And just so you're not in any doubt, we won't." He watched his son's bullish expression. "Unless, of course, you'd like to train under him as his apprentice."

Hughie leaned back in his chair, tipping it until it balanced on two legs. He crossed his arms and, avoiding his father's eye, gave the clear impression of one who believed that the world was there to serve him.

"Have a think about that, young man, and let me know when I get home," Hugh pressed on. No harm to stamp out that attitude permanently. "It might be a good idea to learn a trade."

The morning grew hotter. Hughie smouldered as he bashed the lawnmower out of the shed and hoped the wheels would fall off. The argument with his father burned around his head as he circumnavigated the garden. He fried his brain with it until, hot and sweaty, what seemed like a good idea had formed in his head, one that would 'teach' his father.

Dumping the mower in the middle of the lawn, he walked out through the gates, setting off for somewhere he knew not where, nor did he care.

He could hear young Michael shouting after him.

"Where are you going, Hughie?"

"Anywhere but here."

The child put down his toy bus and ran into the house to tell Gina.

Hughie plodded on until he arrived five miles away, hungry and with no money. He sat on the wall in the strange district until he tired of looking up and down a road where nothing much was happening. For twenty minutes he mooched around, straddling the wall for a while before turning his back on the road and, with legs dangling, threw stones into the stream below. He stood up and began kicking at the weeds growing from a crack at the base. The pale dust coated his shoes as he struck each one and blamed everyone for his predicament.

As he sat back on the wall a dog came out of a house opposite and barked at him before lying down on the doorstep. They eyed each other for a while, the dog only taking his eyes off Hughie to wander over to drink from his water bowl. As he lay down again Hughie knew he had to get a drink, not something he felt inclined to do, necessitating as it did a move in the lethargy of the afternoon heat.

As he watched the careless snooze of the mongrel it dawned on him that this might not have been the best of plans. It was his father's fault but Gina would be worried.

He quashed the pang of guilt. It wasn't her fault but she hadn't stood up for him. Johanna would have. Gina had been there and had heard his father but stayed silent.

While he wallowed in the thought that they deserved to worry, to not know where he had disappeared to, he realised that only he alone knew what he had done, unless Michael had told them. And he wouldn't have known why and no-one else was aware. They probably hadn't even missed him. He glanced again at the dog. The eyes were closed. Even he had fallen asleep. No one cared.

He checked his pockets for the third time just in case there were a few coins lurking in the corners but he knew even before he put his hand in that it was hopeless. The police station opposite seemed his only choice.

"I'll put him on to you, sir, and he can explain more fully himself."

Hughie felt very grown up making the phone call from the police station. The glass of water had wakened him up somewhat.

"I want to come home." He stole a glance at the officer to see if he was impressed but the man continued writing in the large book on the desk before him. Hughie's mind refocused on the telephone. The silence at the other end wasn't promising.

"And what's your plan for that?"

"Em . . ."

"*Em* is not an answer. You obviously had a plan when you were setting out?"

"But how will I get home?" He heard the hint of a whine enter his voice and glanced over at the officer who didn't appear to be taking any notice.

"The same way as you got there, I suppose. I don't have a plan either."

His heart sank at the calm response. It was a long walk.

"And by the way, son, the lawn isn't finished. It'll be waiting for you when you arrive."

He heard the click at the other end.

Chapter 26

"Why not give them a start?"

Johanna had been the one to come up with the idea. She had her reasons for suggesting Hugh provide opportunities for the relatives to get experience in the grocery trade. Having a few of them nearby would take the burden of being the only family support from her shoulders. She glanced across at him and could see from the set of his face that he was intent on ignoring her. It wasn't the first time she'd broached the subject.

"You're always saying you're looking for good staff."

"How would I know they were any good?" He had already toyed with the idea himself but had dismissed the notion. It had been so long since he'd left home that those left behind were all but strangers. Some of them he remembered as no more than children.

"You wouldn't. Not until they got here. But you could give them a go." It worried her that apart from his business socialising he was becoming a hermit. And it would be good to have some of the folk from home around – nice for herself as well as for him, even if he was reluctant.

"Ah, I'm not sure, Jo. They might be happy enough at home in Ireland."

She could see in the tired way he shook his head that it was more likely that he hadn't the energy to rise to the challenge rather than having a disinterest in the idea.

"It would be nice to see them. Come on, Hugh, it would give us all a boost. Why not try it?" She lightened her tone as she saw the glimmer of uncertainty. "Sure, can't you ship them back across the Atlantic if they're no use?"

"*Mmm*, I suppose." He gazed across the room in a way that said the cogs in his brain were turning over the idea. "Leave it with me. I'll have a think about it."

Hugh remembered the slack jaw that confirmed that his brother James had never given a thought to what lay beyond the embarking on his great adventure. It made him wonder if he himself had looked as gormless when he'd first arrived.

"Don't think because we're related that you'll have an easy time here, James. You're going to have to work twice as hard to prove there is no favouritism."

While he was prepared to give him a start he had no intention of allowing his brother to think he might be a pushover. James had worked out fairly well once Hugh had knocked the corners off him. Wasn't afraid of hard work and surprisingly enough after that first impression turned out to be pretty smart on the uptake. So much so that when he'd gained enough confidence he'd seen a wider world open up to him and had taken off to find his own way in it. Hugh had been disappointed to lose his brother but had to acknowledge that it was for all the right reasons. Yes, James had worked out well, so maybe he'd take the chance again.

Each relative or neighbour was met with the same advice on arrival, their raw Irishness stamped all over them with their battered brown cases and tweed jackets. He'd soon smarten them up. But if they didn't, as Jo had said, he could ship them out.

"Once you understand that, you'll get a good training," was the only soft comment in his harsh warning.

By the time he'd exhausted the expansion of his chain of stores around the city and environs Hugh was beginning to get itchy again. Once the previous venture was up on its feet and running efficiently and profitably it was always only a matter of time before he began to look for a new challenge and it was in the summer rental of a family beach house, suggested by Johanna, that he found it.

"It would do the children good and it'll give you a rest. You never take a break." She looked at the grey face of her brother as he came out of the church after Sunday Mass. "At least will you think about it?"

"I will." Hugh looked at the ground. Suddenly, his head shot up. "I've thought about it. I'll do it, Jo."

"That was quick." She laughed. "Not at all like you."

"Well, you're always a great one with the ideas and so far you haven't let me down. They've nearly all worked out well." He smiled at her. "But on one condition."

"What's that?"

"Only if you and Matthew and the children come also."

"But sure there'd be too many of us." Johanna tried not to look too delighted. "How would we fit?"

"I'll book two places beside each other. My treat."

Hugh left no room for an excuse, not that she was looking for one.

"It would be better for the children if your lot came. They might find it a bit dull with only me."

"Never." She grinned back at him.

"And anyway it'd be handy with you around in case I have to come back to Boston for a meeting."

"I don't like that bit about coming back to Boston –

you're taking a holiday, remember? But how could I refuse. Mind, I'm only doing it for the children so I'd better get home and break the news to them."

A crisp May sun filtered through the clouds as she made her way home. A double success, the second of which she hadn't anticipated adding a spring to her step.

JOHANNA

Chapter 27

Cape Cod, Massachusetts, USA
1888

The sun was beginning to scorch her face as she lay on the rug. She had draped her cotton scarf across it but it was now burning through, at least that was what it felt like.

She sat up and as she opened her eyes everything around dazzled her. It took several moments before things settled and she could see Mattie in the sea, pulling Hannah along by the arms, telling her to kick harder. Bridget was holding Mary by the waist, trying to keep her cousin in a horizontal position in the water, while encouraging her to keep moving forward.

"I'm holding you, Mary! I promise I won't let you go under."

Johanna could hear her reassurance but had a fair idea that her efforts at teaching the terrified child to swim were not going to meet with much success.

"No, Mary, you'll have to take your feet off the bottom. You'll never learn if you keep trying to put them down." She had worked for most of the week on it but it was beginning to look like Mary was not going to be a natural in the water. "You have to trust me."

Maggie Mae was still asleep beside her on the rug. The position of the sun had moved so she shifted the parasol slightly and checked her forehead, hoping she wouldn't waken.

Hugh had left them as soon as they'd finished the picnic. He had come to the beach without any swimming gear so she wasn't surprised.

"Business to attend to."

"Holidays, remember? You can never leave it behind, can you?" she'd said, laughing at him.

She put on her sunhat, jamming it firmly on her head in the hope the breeze wouldn't take it off down the beach. She knew she was lucky. Had always known it. From the time they married. Indeed, she knew even before they married that he would be the love of her life. There had been something about him, something she couldn't quite put a finger on. Knew she could trust him with anything. There were no hidden agendas with Mattie. He was straightforward – what you saw was what you got. Simple, kind and funny. As she watched him now, splashing about in the water with the girls, she was glad he was not like her brother. No problem ever in relaxing and having a bit of fun. He knew how to enjoy his children.

She thought back to their births. No-one had told her how awful it was going to be. How excruciatingly painful. Maybe that had been for the best. Something she had to discover for herself. They only confessed afterwards when she brought up the subject.

The doctor had been worried about her blood pressure and had insisted on a hospital birth for Hannah. For weeks beforehand Mattie had fussed about her, checking as soon as he came home from work that she hadn't yet had any twinges. So anxious to get her to the hospital in time they had been sent home on the first occasion and told to wait a bit longer. She'd suspected it herself but he couldn't be convinced so she went along with him, couldn't have coped with his waking her up every hour to check. She remembered how he'd cried when he first held Hannah in his arms. She'd loved that. And the way she'd found him lying on the hospital bed, totally worn out from anxiety when she returned from a visit to the toilet. She'd made the most of the teasing he'd let himself in for there.

The memory of Hugh's Margaret worried her though. How she had watched her fade away after the twins. Not really sure why. During her own pregnancy, the fact that she was a big strapping country girl reassured her, something that the lovely ethereal Margaret had not been. She hoped it would stand to her in what lay ahead.

Mary's birth, despite the agony, went smoothly but she didn't reckon on how much energy she would need to look after a toddler while nursing a newborn. Fortunately Hugh had got a girl, Gina, to live in to look after his own family – a niece of Miss Doyle in the shop so she came with a reliable pedigree. It was a great help that she sometimes called around when she was herding her charges to the Common.

"One more won't make any difference, Johanna." She smiled at Hannah. "Get your coat, missy, and come and join your cousins."

"Thanks, Gina. You've no idea what a relief it is to get her off my hands." She threw her eyes to heaven. "Even an hour of freedom is wonderful. Especially when Mattie is working late."

By the time Maggie Mae was born Johanna had learned to juggle. Hannah was five so she was delighted to be given little jobs to do. Bringing the baby cream and nappies and helping to feed Mary. Johanna would hear her boasting to Mattie when he came home in the evenings.

"What would your mother do without you, Hannah? You're a great little helper." He turned to hug Mary. "And what about you, little Mary? What did you do?"

"She wet the floor and I had to clean it up, Daddy." Hannah threw her sister an accusing look.

"Sure isn't that what big sisters are for?"

He always knew how to divert a situation. Johanna had watched the trio and seen how the threatened wobble in Mary's lip ceased as he spread his smile between them.

She roused herself as a murmur came from under the parasol. Her daughter was beginning to stir.

"Yes, indeed." She whispered to Maggie Mae. "There's no doubt about it, I'm one of the luckiest women in the world."

Hugh's boys were further up the beach kicking a light ball. She watched for a while as the breeze blew it towards the water. Young Michael was the one sent to retrieve it each time as it blew further and further down the seashore as he chased it. She noted how Hughie and Patrick stood waiting and smiled, wondering how long it would take the youngster to get wise to their tricks.

Chapter 28

By the end of the first week in Cape Cod he'd spotted the gap. A new world opened up in the discovery of the numbers of families who decamped to the coastal areas for summer holidays once the schools closed. Retail facilities around the beach areas were sparse – enough for the basic needs of families, but something more might be needed. An opportunity waiting to be grasped. He'd buried himself too long in the city.

By the end of the holiday he'd already started taking walks around the vicinity. Unlike his earlier strolls, these had a purpose. He hadn't said anything yet, it was too early and it might come to nothing, but he had started looking around for suitable premises. It might take a while but the possibilities looked good.

"This place is lovely but it could do with a shop a bit nearer. And with a wider range," said Johanna.

It was the day she came back with the shopping bag full, mopping her brow that the time felt right to share his thoughts.

"I was thinking that myself."

"Thinking?" She looked at him in the armchair where he sat gazing out at the ocean. "I might send you hoofing down there when we run out of milk the next time."

"How about I do something better?"

"What do you mean 'better'?"

"Well, I was thinking myself there may be an opening for a decent store here." He looked at her. "What would you think? Just for the summer months."

"Are you serious?" She raised her eyebrows. "Do you not have enough on your plate already?"

"I wouldn't be running it myself on a day-to-day basis. I'll appoint a manager. I've the very person in mind." He grinned.

"You needn't be looking at me."

He laughed at the alarmed look on his sister's face.

"Oh, you needn't worry, it's not you. I'm only teasing. No, there's a good manager in one of the Boston branches that I'm sure would love to come here for the summer months with his family and run it." Hugh looked thoughtful. "Say nothing yet to anyone until I have a word with him."

She nodded. "My lips are sealed. Not a word to anyone."

"And, anyway, we can't have you puffing yourself up and down for the shopping next summer if we're back here on holiday."

"Well, a good grocery store is needed. I can't argue with that." She looked a bit dubious. "But I hope you wouldn't be taking on too much."

"Leave me to worry about that." He paused. "So you think it might be a good idea then. Maybe you'll come with me for a walk this evening and I'll show you a few sites."

"So that's what you were at when you've been going off all secretive in the evenings."

"You're on for it then?" He grinned at her, hoping by the time he was back in Boston he'd have everything sorted and that negotiations might be under way with the possibilities for expansion this new venture offered. This was going to occupy him fully and he couldn't wait to get started.

With Hugh not being one for looking back, it was Johanna who could see the lift in his spirits, like he had stepped over an invisible line that propelled him into a brighter phase, as they all headed back to Boston.

Chapter 29

1892

She loved her new Saturday job. One of Hugh's better ideas – that she consider working in his original Boston store. Just on Saturdays, one of his busiest times.

"I'd love to, Hugh, but it's just not practical, what with Mattie out working too." She looked disappointed. "Sure we couldn't afford to pay someone to look after the children. It wouldn't make sense."

"You didn't think I'd have thought of that?" He raised his eyebrow, a smile playing around his mouth. "How about Gina takes the twins over to your place and keeps an eye on your brood at the same time?"

"Have you run this by her?" Johanna looked doubtful. "The children would love it but she mightn't be so keen."

"Oh, she's happy to, you needn't worry." His satisfied look was that of a man for whom it has been arranged and satisfactory to all parties already. "I'll be financing a treat each Saturday and she'll look after the practicalities. Something that will widen their horizons and maybe even strengthen family bonds."

"Well, then, you seem to have it all in hand." She grinned at him. "When do I start?"

* * *

She ran the cloth over the glass of the flip-up lid of the cabinet that sat on the wooden counter holding the display of cigars and tobacco. Lots of finger-marks today. Good for business. Hugh would be pleased. It took some vigour to remove them but she persisted until she could see her face in it. Going behind the counter, she opened the drawer underneath. A smell of polish wafted out as she returned the cloth to its holding place.

Moving next to the shop window she gave the inside a rub with the damp chamois leather and a final polish of the week with a page of scrunched-up newspaper before standing back and focusing on the finish. There was always one smear that escaped every time and she spotted it. Hoping it wasn't on the outside she gave it a firm rub. Good, it cleared. No need to go out in the cold.

Even in the distance he stood out in the crowd. It was the jutting forward of the head with each step that caught her attention. She could see him on the far side of the street as she admired her handiwork. He stopped every now and then to look around as if to get his bearings.

It was Saturday and trade had quietened down coming up to closing time. The other assistants were busy in the back, finishing the evening's chores. Johanna had volunteered to keep an eye on things in the shop – she had never got used to calling it a 'store'. She needed to keep a lookout for Declan and with a clear view now she could watch the comings and goings as dusk began to fall outside.

The roadway was busy with people making their way home from work. A young man arrived at the kerb opposite and even though there wasn't much vehicular traffic, his head, thrust forward, was swivelling nervously from left to right and back again. She watched him step onto the road and poke his way across the wide street

"Mind your head doesn't arrive first!" She could hear the

163

teasing he must have got at school and felt sorry for him. They would most probably have followed him around the yard, mimicking his gait.

As he passed the shop window she continued to scan the crowd and wondered if she would recognise her nephew when he appeared. He'd be due soon. She hoped he would arrive before they closed for the evening. The sound of the silence was a bit creepy when the staff went home, so she would prefer not to be left alone there waiting.

Art's two boys were still young children when she left Ireland. The image in her head was of dawny-looking twin boys, sandy-haired youngsters. Their physical resemblance was the only thing the twins shared. Luke was an affectionate little fellow, always wanting to sit on your knee, but her memory of Declan was of a strange cold boy who only made eye contact in moments of defiance.

When the letter arrived Mattie hadn't been too keen on the idea.

"If Art can't manage him, why do you think we'd be able?"

"Well, we have to give it a go. I can hardly say no to my own brother, now can I, without giving it a try?"

"I suppose." Mattie sounded doubtful. "But, have him staying here? I dunno."

"Imagine if Hugh had said no to me coming? We'd never have met." Johanna recognised the need for more persuasion. "Sure maybe they thought I was hard to handle at home too?"

"And weren't they right?" Mattie dodged the swat she made with the letter. "Oh, alright. Maybe Ireland's too small for him. The challenge here might do him good."

"We could give it a few weeks and see how it goes. The lad deserves a chance and sure if it doesn't work out I'll tell him to sling his hook and fend for himself. How about that?"

"I've no doubt you'd be well able to do that." Mattie grinned at her.

"That's settled then. I'll write to Art tonight."

Johanna's first impression of her adult nephew was not a good one. It was only when he doubled back after passing the shop window that she suspected it might be him. Hadn't recognised the snakelike head-movement, a development since she'd last seen him but then he'd only been a child.

He stood for a moment, letting the door close behind him. Despite the fact that she was alone in the shop, she watched his head rotate as if he was looking for someone else to approach, before strutting over towards her. The swing with which he carried the small brown suitcase made it look as if there was nothing other than a single change of clothing in it.

"I'm looking for Mrs. Coyne."

"Well, look no further. You must be Declan. Welcome to America."

She extended her hand over the counter. His arms remained straight down by his sides as he looked at her.

"You're Aunt Johanna?" His eyebrow raised slightly.

"I am indeed."

The way he looked at her made her wonder if he was pleased or disappointed in what he saw. Placing his case on the floor, he jabbed his hand forward and then made to pull it back, like he was afraid she might draw hers away first. She caught it on the second thrust and with a bit of a fumble gave it a shake.

"You've changed since I last saw you," she said, "and I daresay you don't remember me at all. You were very young."

"Not really. Well, vaguely. You've changed too."

He stood there, his eyes twitching around the shop. Johanna waited for him to finish surveying his surroundings, giving him a chance to take in his first sight of what was to be his new workplace.

The job of persuading Hugh had been difficult but her perseverance had paid off – the reminders that everyone needed a leg-up sometimes and at least he'd help Art out if he were to give the nephew a few months of a trial. He could take it from there, depending on how it worked out.

She was surprised Declan had turned into quite a good-looking young man from the pasty-faced child she remembered. Pity about his gaucheness. At close quarters now she could see that he'd somehow grown into his face. It proved her theory that everyone had their 'good' period at some stage of their lives. She wished she'd been aware of this when it mattered, when she'd been in her own 'plain' adolescent phase. It was watching her daughters develop that she had noticed the changes in each of them.

"I wish I looked like Susie in my class." Hannah examined her face in the mirror. "She has lovely smooth skin. All the one colour. I've every shade of freckles. I hate them."

"That's the Irish in you."

"I'd like a bit of American."

"Don't worry, you'll grow into your skin."

Johanna remembered the children at school, the ones she'd considered pretty, the way they had often taken on an unremarkable look as they matured, while the plain ones had become attractive. Everyone had their moment. She was still waiting for her own to arrive. But there was no point in expecting Hannah to believe her theory.

"Isn't old Molly beautiful? Reminds me of a painting of a Madonna."

She could hear her mother's voice, remembering how she had thought her daft at the time. Wondered how she could ever think that their elderly neighbour was anything but ancient. She could still picture Molly sitting on the granite windowsill outside her cottage door, drinking in the last of the evening sunshine. Only now that she thought about it did she understand how that elderly beauty radiated from Molly's smile, something to do with the peace in her. Maybe there was hope for her too.

Style or beauty was not something considered important at home, but here in Boston it had a place. At work the tea-break argument amused her. None of the young women could agree on what ingredients were required for beauty in a woman. It seemed it was something different for everyone. She'd told them about Molly and they thought it was hilarious.

The experiment started off as fun. To describe what impression they each gave.

"It's your eyes that you'd notice first. They're nearly turquoise."

"Your smile. You knock them out with the dazzle of it."

The observations ranged from hair styles to perfect symmetrical features to the way a girl held herself.

Her turn. The moment she dreaded. To hear what she knew to be true, what she most certainly didn't want confirmed.

The young girl opposite her studied her features, cocking her head to one side.

"A kind face. That's what I see when I look at you, Johanna." Her serious face was of one approaching the task like she was asked to comment on a portrait in a gallery. "Yes, that's what I see. Kind."

"So I'm the sort of person that strangers would stop and ask the way to somewhere?" The girl was right – that's what always happened, had been happening since she first came to Boston, even when she was lost herself. If there were ten people available to ask directions of in the street – who would they head for? Yes. Good old Johanna.

"But I don't want to look kind, I want to look beautiful."

They all laughed. She joined in herself at the ridiculousness of it.

"You should be happy, Jo. When all the rest of us are old and wrinkly and have faces like lemons, all bitter and twisted, you'll still look kind."

She studied Declan now, leaning her back against the dark wooden shelving behind her, as he continued to take in the shop. Suddenly, realising how long it had been since his attention had been on her, she awoke to the possibility that he was waiting for her to lead the way.

"Well, we'll head on home so. Wait there 'til I let the others know I'm off."

She went into the back and returned with her coat, her arm already in one sleeve as she came out from behind the counter.

"It's only a short walk from here. You'll get your bearings soon enough. It's a nice evening so we'll go through the Common. Every place you'll be needing for the moment radiates from the Boston Common so let me introduce you to it. That was one of the first pieces of advice I got when I came and it served me well, I can tell you."

Declan picked up his case and in silence followed her to the door. She stood aside to allow him open it for her, but the two arms by his side suggested he was either lacking in social graces or was simply not going to oblige. She hoped it was the former. At least something could be done about that. She would start the way she intended to continue.

"Door, please?"

Eyeballing him, she noted the impenetrable expression on his face. This was going to be hard work. Without looking at her he reached forward and gripped the brass door handle then stood back to allow her pass through as he opened it.

"Thank you, Declan."

Chapter 30

Mattie arrived into the kitchen with the bucket of coal and she could hear muffled noises from upstairs and the sound of someone straggling down the stairs just as she was ready to leave for first Mass.

"Foiled again." Johanna looked at Mattie. "I thought I'd escaped."

Spotting her mother dressed in outdoor clothes, the blue eyes of her youngest daughter looked up at her, chubby hands gripping the edges of Johanna's coat. "I want to come with you, Mama."

"But you're not dressed, Baba."

"Put my shoes on. I want to come."

"I'm late already, Maggie. You can't come like that. It's very cold outside and I can't wait." Johanna gently prised the little hands from her coat as a whine threatened.

"I need you here, Babs." Mattie put down his bucket and, washing his hands at the sink, glanced over his shoulder at his daughter. "Your mam will be back soon and you can help me in the meantime. Me and my little Maggie Mae, always left to do the work. Isn't that right, Babs? Here, bring me over that towel."

As Maggie trailed the towel towards him he cocked his head.

"Now, who's that I hear coming down the stairs?"

He nodded his head at Johanna. Thankful for the distraction she slipped into the hall just as Hannah and Mary were yawning their way downstairs. Their arrival into the kitchen would help put an end to the whine.

"Morning, girls." Johanna pulled on her gloves. "I'll see you when I get back. You can go to Mass later with your father."

"Mornin', Ma."

She took her hat from its hook on the hallstand as the girls made their way into the kitchen.

"What's for breakfast?" Hannah's usual question.

"Hold on there, madam, and I'll bring you the menu. Just take a seat and I'll take your order in a moment."

Johanna listened to Mattie's banter with the girls. She could hear the scrape of the chair and imagined him pulling it back for his eldest daughter as she rubbed the sleep out of her eyes.

"Sorry for the delay, madam. And you too, Miss Mary. Make yourselves comfortable there."

Opening the front door the sharp early morning air hit her face. It would be nice to just close the door again and go back to the kitchen, into the warmth created by her husband.

Since the start of the New Year she'd checked the trough that stood outside on the windowsill whenever she remembered. Still a bit early in the year. She could understand why no flower would want to poke its head through the soil in this cold.

A week ago, when she'd knocked off the snow that had collected she was rewarded by the first signs of green shoots poking through the dark brown soil. Excited by the prospect of the advancing spring, she watched them daily. The first small white swelling of the flower heads appeared but seemed hesitant to expand and with their progress slow she forgot about them.

The morning had warmed up a little as she returned from Mass. A weak sun penetrated her coat and heated her back as she approached the house. She paused at the door, enjoying the moment before delving into her bag for the keys. She fished around for a few seconds without success before leaning across and resting her newspaper on the trough while she searched.

"Ah, there you are!" She whipped them out and as she reached across to pick up the newspaper she spotted the white heads of the snowdrops nodding at her.

Removing her glove, she reached out to touch one of the little bellflowers. She could hardly feel the weight in its fairy lightness as it danced along her fingertips. She played with the satiny heads and wondered how in their delicacy they managed to hide such strength that allowed them to bloom in these Arctic conditions.

A long-ago white carpet under the old chestnut tree in front of the farmhouse drifted through her mind. They bobbed about as if to say they were brave enough not to need the shelter of its leafy canopy. She could hear the wind that set them dancing under the bare branches. No-one had planted them – not that she could remember anyway. The carpeted area increased each year, appearing from under the frosted grass like a secret army of fairies, until it covered the lawn under the full spread of the ancient tree.

A long forgotten act. She doubted if Declan would remember it. She hadn't until this moment. The child running across the lawn, trampling the delicate white flowers with his heavy leather boots as she watched, horrified, from the window. She saw him look down at the grass and, expecting him to head for the gravel when he saw his error, she was appalled to see him, arms outstretched like a whirling dervish, start to run in ever widening circles around the thick tree trunk. She'd hammered on the window and saw him glance up. As he looked at her, his face froze into a mutinous mask and turning away he continued with his destruction.

She ran to the door but was too late. He had already flattened the entire area of snowdrops.

"What are you doing, Declan? Can't you see you're trampling the snowdrops?"

"So what? They were in the way."

"*Get off the grass, you little brat!*" She made a run at him, intent on giving him a wallop but he dodged her outstretched arm.

"*I'll tell me da on you!*" He ran off, laughing. "*I'll tell him you hit me!*"

"*Not before I get to him, you little upstart!*" Her face flushed with rage. "Oh, that I *had* hit you!"

"You needn't worry, Johanna – he'll get a wallop from me. I saw all of that." Ellen had stepped out of the house.

Unknown to Johanna, his mother had been watching them from the window.

"I thought you had the situation under control and left you to it. I thought that maybe he might listen to you because he doesn't pay any heed to what I say." She shook her head. "I'd better go after him before he does any more damage." Leaving Johanna, she set off to find her son.

Bending down to survey the damage, Johanna put her hand under the flattened heads as if she could help them stand upright again. Her eyes flooded. Stupid to get so upset over the flowers. His lack of appreciation of their perfection horrified her more than the loss. A soulless creature.

It came back to her now. The cruel thought that had gone through her head that day. He was only a child. A thoughtless one. But still a child.

That was then. Now the adult, probably still lying upstairs in his bed in her house on his day off.

DECLAN

Chapter 31

It was the screeching sound of the metal wheel-rim of the trolley that did it. It shot right through Declan's head, setting his teeth on edge as he worked alone in the storeroom. No other noise to take the edge off the shrillness. A sound he'd forgotten until this moment.

The icy classroom with its damp turf that sat in a bucket beside the sputtering fire. The snotty-nosed pupils, their constant winter colds dripping, until a furtive wipe transferred the evidence onto their sleeves. He thought he'd left the sounds and smells of those schooldays behind, the door firmly shut on them.

All the other children talked to each other. Even if it was mostly stupid stuff. He didn't always feel like conversation and that was the start of the trouble. It wasn't that he didn't want to talk, it was often simply because he didn't know what to say. He noticed how words just seemed to spill out of the mouths of the others. They didn't seem to worry about where to start – they just leapt straight into the middle of the story or even sometimes to the end. It didn't seem to matter to them.

"Did you see the way that fella kicked the ball? Right into his own goal? The eejit!"

The other boys would just pick it up and continue the commentary. By the time he'd decided where to start, the conversation had moved on and he knew he'd missed his opportunity.

"Where was the match?" It seemed more logical that it should start at the beginning, but when he tried to join in they just talked over him. *Who was playing?* He shouted it this time and still nobody heard. It happened all the time. They just ignored him, not even noticing his efforts to get involved. As if the question hadn't even been asked.

And then there was the incident in the classroom. The one that led to the discovery. The teacher had picked him to hand out the primers. He didn't mind that. It was only when he was asked to hand out the slates and pencils that he could feel his whole inside tightening into knots. It wasn't the giving out of them that was the problem. It was the screeching sound of the pencils on the slate when they started to do the sums, going right through his teeth and piercing his eardrums.

"What did he say?" The orange-haired boy beside him gave a nod in the Master's direction, not having understood the long division sum the teacher had spent ten minutes explaining.

Declan was good at his arithmetic. Probably the best in the class.

"Let's see how you're doing it," the child said, leaning over, jostling Declan's elbow as he strained to get a look at how his neighbour was working out the magic formula.

The high-pitched squeaking, like a set of sharp needles set Declan's nerves jangling. No room for this dunce beside him adding to the noise inside his head. He whipped his slate away, covering it with his arm as he presented his back to the surprised boy. Bending his head over the sum, he ignored the boy's whining voice.

"What's wrong with you? I only wanted to see how you done it. You're mean!"

"*I said – quiet – boys!*" the Master's voice boomed out. "Put down the slates now. You've had enough time to do that sum. Come on now or we'll be here until next week."

An end to the shrill scraping. Relief coursed through his body. He put down the slate, still covering his work, and glanced at the boy beside him. A puzzlement, directed at Declan, was written all over the screwed-up face. He might have felt sorry for the boy had it not been for the discovery of a weapon. The power of revenge. To pay no heed to someone. To ignore just like they did to him. This boy wasn't the worst. But now that he'd made his discovery he could try out his newfound skill on the others and that would give him control and pay them all back.

It was difficult to get to know people in Boston. They all seemed to dash off to their own lives at closing time each day. No-one ever said where they were going, just seemed to have a destination. Unlike him. Going back to Aunt Johanna's after work each evening was beginning to wear thin. How does anyone make a life? Where to start?

"Do you want to join us for a drink, Declan?"

The invitation took him by surprise.

"We're going to the saloon to celebrate. Young Davy – you know, Davy from Deliveries – is getting married next week."

"Sure. Give me a shout when you're going." Maybe things were changing.

It was easy once you got started and now he was over that barrier. The first drink was the most difficult. Who was buying? He held back, watching until the order of business was established. Only when that happened could he settle down. With each drink he could feel an increasing effortlessness in his attempts to fit in. He could get to enjoy this.

Settled in his relaxation, he hadn't noticed the others disappearing. It had happened gradually and fairly early on. One by one they each melted off to their other life, until he found himself alone on a barstool, staring at his own mirrored image swimming back at him from behind the lined-up bottles.

"Haven't seen you in here before?" A dark, slick-haired man, about his own age, slid onto the stool beside him.

Without turning his head, Declan observed him in the mirror.

"Dewey . . . Dewey Burke."

Declan continued to watch him. Watched as Dewey turned his head towards him and waited a few seconds before answering, just long enough for the smile on Dewey's face to begin to fade.

"Declan. Declan McNamara."

He turned and looked at Dewey, whose grin widened, narrowing his already thin lips to a slash.

"Not from here then, Declan."

"How very astute of you, Dewey. I take it you're a detective?"

"Not quite."

It was a couple of hours later that Dewey linked him home. He helped him up the steps to Johanna's hall door and rapped on the knocker.

"I'll leave you to it then, Declan." He propped Declan against the doorframe and headed down the steps. He had no wish to meet the aunt under these circumstances, the one he'd listened to Declan droning on about for the last hour. "See you around."

JOHANNA

Chapter 32

"What's the big deal anyway?" Declan shrugged as he walked away from her. It hadn't taken long for the Americanisms to drop into his speech. The shrug was different. He'd brought that with him from Ireland.

"The big deal is, Declan," Johanna paused, glaring at him, "that you could have told me you wouldn't be wanting your dinner. Save me the bother of making it."

By the time she'd completed the sentence she found herself talking to his back. He had already gone through the door, leaving it open behind him.

"I'm speaking to you. You might at least show me the courtesy of facing me and listening."

Another shrug before he turned around, eyes trained on the floor.

"You know I'm not trying to spoil your fun. I'm just asking for a bit of consideration." Johanna hoped a more conciliatory tone might get the message through. She looked at him, waiting to see if the different approach had any success.

Suddenly he looked up and from the steel in his stare she knew that the silence between them had not been used for thoughtful reflection. It had done nothing but inflame the situation.

"You mightn't have to put up with me much longer." The cockiness of his tone was clearly intended to taunt her. "I have plans."

"Great." Johanna, surprised, felt the wind drop out of her sails. But it felt good and she knew Mattie would be pleased to be rid of him if that was what he meant. The defiance on his face rendered her unable to resist a final dig. "Any chance you might share them with me or would that be too much to ask?"

"When I have them sorted you'll be the first to know."

He slammed the door behind him.

Standing on the top step, he turned up the collar of his coat and, poking his head forward, paused to look up and down the road. The wet street glistened with the drizzle that had been falling all evening. Pushing his hands into his pockets, he hunched his shoulders and, with an irritation churning around in his head, headed into the damp wind.

She's on my back again. This time it's the dinner. Bloody bacon and cabbage. You'd think it was a banquet she was after laying out. And such a fuss. I've had enough of her. And I wouldn't mind but I'm paying for the privilege of staying there. You'd think she was doing me a favour.

He removed his right hand from the comfort of his pocket and gripped the corners of his coat collar where the wind was creeping in through the gap.

Not going to sour my card game. I'll show her. I'll just have another talk with Dewey about moving in with him and Abe.

Johanna always had a nose for 'a bad one'. *Evil* or *wicked* would have been too strong a word for it. He hadn't done anything terribly wrong. Was just generally unpleasant. Would rarely throw a word to the girls. If he happened to meet one of them in the hallway or the kitchen the most they'd get would be a grunt, if even that. Like they didn't exist or had no right to be there. Even they had given up the effort of communicating with him. They had asked him questions in the beginning but in the way of children seemed to sense his disinterest in them and now kept out of his way.

It wasn't just his lack of social skills, no, it wasn't just that. That he might be unscrupulous given the chance was a possibility. He emanated something more than simple selfishness. She just couldn't put a finger on it. Not yet. It was just an instinct.

There was the situation at work. She didn't notice anything strange at first. Had just seen the young man standing smoking a cigarette at the open door of the warehouse. Not a familiar face. She presumed he was one of the casual workers or perhaps a delivery man. Of so little consequence that at first she didn't give it a thought. It was only after she'd seen him on a few subsequent occasions with Declan that she begin to wonder about him. Might never have asked had it not been for the shifty way Declan glanced at her when he saw her looking at them. It was that glance alone that alerted her to the fact that they might have been up to no good.

"Who is that young man I saw you with in the stockroom, Declan?"

"A friend of mine."

"Does he work here?"

The frown on his face told her he didn't see it was any of her business.

"Well?"

"What do you want to know for?"

"I asked you, does he work here?"

"No." He turned away.

179

"I didn't think so. I don't imagine your Uncle Hugh would be too happy for you to be encouraging people onto the premises."

"He wasn't on the premises. He was only at the door."

"Well, I'm just saying if he doesn't have business here, he shouldn't be hanging around. You know the rule. Strictly no-one other than staff near the stockroom."

"*Huh*, ridiculous rule." Under his breath but loud enough for Johanna to hear.

"Ridiculous or not – it's not up to you to judge that. Not if you want to keep your job."

"He's not doing any harm. We were only talking."

"Well, don't be encouraging him. Meet him somewhere else. Away from here."

"Who are you anyway? The boss? And there was I thinking you were only a part-timer." He glared at her, challenge leaping from his eyes. Then, as sudden as a door slamming his expression turned to stone, blocking her out.

Johanna shook her head slowly and walked away. There was no getting through to him when he was like that. Something was coming back to her, something she'd noticed soon after his arrival. At that stage she thought she might be imagining it. Had anyone asked she couldn't have put a finger on what exactly it was. She could now. The attitude. His belief that the world and everyone in it was there for his convenience. All was for the taking. Always seemed to be wanting something. Like wanting to come to America. Or maybe that had simply been his father's wish. She could see now how Art had been able to do nothing with him. But no, she could remember him saying that he wanted to experience life outside Ireland. Found that stultifying, the way that everyone knew your business. That information was shared early on when he was finding his feet. Needed to communicate with her.

And once his needs were satisfied he'd spat her out. Of no further use to him.

It had been gradual. Each unpleasant incident had heralded the end of a particular need. She could see now that enough time had elapsed for his 'know it all' arrogance to manifest itself in all its glory. No need for anyone anymore.

The job didn't seem to satisfy him, even as a stepping-stone to greater things. Not a trace of gratitude in him, no sense that he might be expected to pull his weight or that he could repay his uncle for the opportunity afforded him, handed to him on a plate as it was. No, in Declan's mind, from the way he treated it, it was only right that he should be set up. At least that was the impression he gave off. All take and no give. Evidence enough that he didn't know his Uncle Hugh. If he didn't pull up his socks and drop the swagger he was in for a rude awakening. She had tried to warn him. The rest was up to himself.

His inability to empathise was a worry. No people skills was one thing, but the incident with the cat was something else. On a completely different level.

He hadn't realised she was watching through the window the morning it happened. Out smoking a cigarette in the garden. That annoyed him. No smoking in the house. She knew he did it when she was out. Could smell it in the drapes. Refused to accept that she had a right to make the rule in her own home.

Quietly crouched over the bread and milk she had left out for him earlier, the cat ate in silence while Declan leaned against the wall watching. The mangy stray jerked his head up between mouthfuls, checking for predators. Declan uncrossed his legs and heaved himself away from his prop. Hand cupped, he took a last pull from the butt. Johanna watched as he eyed the cat and aimed the lighted butt at the animal. It hit its target with surprising accuracy, right between the two eyes. She didn't want to imagine how he had perfected that skill. The cat darted off, not waiting to check from where the missile came, the remainder of his breakfast left behind in his fright.

"Why did you have to do that?" She tackled him as he came in through the door.

"Do what?" The query on his face confirmed that he had no idea what she was referring to. Doubly worrying.

"The cat."

"For the fun of it." With a smirk and a puff of his lips at her concern he passed through the kitchen, leaving her staring after him.

Chapter 33

She knocked on the office door. She hated having to bring this to her brother's attention. It sounded childish. Like tittle-tattle. But she didn't want to wait, only to be proved correct in her suspicions. It might be nothing at all. That would be the best outcome, but she doubted it.

None of the incidents were connected or bore any relationship or resemblance to each other but there were enough of them to no longer be able to ignore Declan's strange behaviour. A stop had to be put to whatever it was went on in his head and she had failed.

"Come in." Hugh's voice came through the dark wood.

She turned the brass knob and, opening the door, swivelled her head around to check if he was alone.

"Are you busy, Hugh?"

"Always. But come in anyway."

Johanna closed the door behind her. Seated behind his large mahogany desk he continued writing and without looking up pointed to the seat opposite. She glanced at it but remained standing.

"I have something to say and you're not going to like it."

He stopped writing and, raising his eyebrows, looked up at her.

"I don't like the sound of this but take the chance, Jo. If you've a complaint about me just say it."

"It's not about you, Hugh. It's worse than that. But I'm not sure about it." She hesitated. "I feel bad even saying it – I might have it all wrong. I could be taking away someone's character and they might be innocent."

"Would you just get on with it, woman. Not like you, Jo, to beat around the bush. Would you just spit it out and get it over with."

"It's Declan."

"Why am I not surprised?" Hugh put the cap on his pen and laid it down on the leather insert of his desk. He sat back, making himself comfortable in the chair.

She knew he was waiting for her to continue, the way he folded his arms like he had been expecting this. "Go on. I'm waiting. I know you've been having problems with him giving guff to you. Has it got worse?"

"No, no, that's not it. Well, he is difficult in that respect but I'm well capable of dealing with him there. No, that's not what I'm here about." She hesitated. "Well, I have a feeling, but it's only a feeling. I have no proof."

"A feeling about what?"

"I'm not sure how honest he is." There it was. Laid on the desk. The words bald. She looked straight at her brother and the lack of surprise on his face made her wonder if she had spoken his thoughts. "I know he's family and he would have been brought up to know better but there's something shifty about him. There. I've said it."

Hugh nodded. "I've had my doubts about him too."

"Well, thank God it's not just me. I was beginning to think I might just be getting cynical and suspicious about people." She pulled over the chair and sat down. "What is it that makes you doubt him, Hugh?"

"It was a few months after he started in the stockroom.

The books weren't tallying. Nothing major, a few shortfalls. I thought at first it might be just a couple of minor errors and I didn't pull him up on it. Wanted to give him time to get the hang of it."

"But now you're not so sure?" Johanna sighed, disappointed that she hadn't been wrong. "And why do you think it was him?"

"Well, the head fellow is the same stockkeeper I've had for years and he's as sound as a bell. Never so much as a biscuit went astray. It's only recently that discrepancies have shown up. Cigarettes, cigars and other stuff missing. Not big quantities, but regular. And the only other person with easy access is our Declan."

"Do you think he'd be so foolish as to bite the hand that feeds him? His family?" It had progressed further than she imagined. "Stealing from his own?"

"I've no proof yet either, but I'm watching him. There's something I don't trust and he's only here because of Art." Hugh paused. "He'd have been out on his ear long ago if it wasn't for that."

"Well, you couldn't meet straighter than his father." She shook her head slowly and sighed. "Art would give you his last farthing."

"I'll ask you the same question, Jo." He looked at her sharply. "What is it makes you suspicious?"

"Like yourself I can't be sure. But it's who he's hanging around with that makes me uneasy."

"I didn't think he'd any friends."

"Well, I don't know if it's a friend but there's been a lad hanging around the warehouse – a bit too often for my liking. I don't go down there much but whenever I have occasion to he seems to be loitering."

"Not staff?"

"No. I don't know who he is. Looks like a bit of a low

life. Not what you'd want anyone belonging to you mixing with. Declan knows him though. That's what worries me."

"I'm glad you came to me, Johanna. Keep an eye on him, will you, and in the meantime I'll have a quiet word with the stockman."

"Do that because I'm only here on Saturdays. I don't know if he appears during the week."

A closer inspection of the friend was needed. Not too obvious. She didn't have a lot of business in the warehouse herself so she'd have to work out a plan. Her nephew might be devious but she too was well capable of learning that skill now that the need had arisen.

As it turned out she didn't have to. An opportunity presented itself sooner than expected without the need for subterfuge. It was a Saturday evening after the tea. Mattie was upstairs reading the bedtime story to the children. Johanna was sitting by the fire with her knitting, listening to the soft giggles filtering down the stairs. Declan was in his room. Whether he was staying in or going out was not something she would ask by way of conversation. The suspicious "Why?" in his response to such a query was not something she was prepared to draw on herself anymore. What he did was none of her business. At least in his mind. He'd made that clear.

A knock sounded on the hall door. She pushed back the stitches on the needles before sticking the sharp points into the ball of wool on her knee. Standing up, she laid the half-finished sleeve of the child's cardigan on the seat of the armchair and went to the door. She wasn't expecting anyone at this hour.

The bowler hat took her by surprise when she opened the door. She didn't recognise the face at first, half hidden as it was, in the shadow cast by the brim. It sat low on his head, a size too large, forcing the ears to stick out like jug-handles.

"Am I at the right house?"

It was the thin-lipped smile she identified first. She'd seen it before. Without the hat. Before she had a chance to respond he continued.

"For Declan?"

"And you are?"

"Burke. Dewey Burke. At your service, ma'am." He bowed with a full flourish, brandishing his hat. "And this must be the lovely Johanna."

Returning his hat to his head, he shone a beam at her before extending his gloved hand. She looked at it, hesitating a second before stretching out and shaking it. Might be better to lull him into thinking he was welcome.

"Mrs. Coyne." She couldn't resist setting the boundary. She paused before returning his smile. "Mr. Burke. Come in and I'll give Declan a shout."

She heard his footsteps on the stairs before she turned.

"Don't wait up for me. I'll be late." Declan brushed past her and out the door without looking back. "C'mon, Dewey. We don't want to be late."

"I'll bid you goodnight then, Mrs. Coyne." Dewey tipped his hat and, turning, followed Declan down the steps.

She stood in the doorway, watching them silhouetted by the light from the gas lamps. His smarminess souring her mouth was enough to confirm her first impression but it was the confidence and over-familiarity bordering on insolence that made her most uncomfortable. Declan might think himself clever, but he wouldn't be smart enough to be able for this Dewey boyo. He was in a different league altogether. She watched the darkness swallow the two men as they headed up the street.

Chapter 34

She put the last of the meat from yesterday's dinner into the sandwich, covering it with a leaf of lettuce before placing the top slice on. She pressed down to secure the contents and cut it in half, straight across the middle. Mattie preferred his sandwiches cut that way.

"Don't be giving me those triangles. They're too big to fit into me mouth," he always said.

"Big and all as it is?" she'd respond.

Monday mornings were leisurely for Mattie. He didn't have to meet Hugh until half past ten for the cash round after the weekend. He loved the routine of the Monday fry. While Johanna delivered the children to school he tucked a tea-towel around his waist and had the rashers ready and the eggs cracked onto a saucer waiting to be dropped onto the frying pan as soon as he heard her key in the door. The only uninterrupted hour in the week when they could sit down together without children.

He heard the signal for the eggs and by the time she had removed her coat and arrived into the kitchen the breakfast was almost ready to be slipped onto her hot plate.

"Ah, great. I love that smell."

As she sat down he placed the breakfast before her and

poured her tea. He replaced the cosy on the pot before taking his seat opposite her.

"Well, how are you?" He smiled across at her, and changing his face into a scrunched-up question mark asked. "Who are you?"

"Do you never get tired of that old joke?" She laughed. "Isn't it time you came up with a new one?"

"Ah, I leave that clever stuff to you." He dug into his breakfast, dipping his fried bread into the egg yoke.

They ate in silent companionship except for the occasional indications of satisfaction from Mattie.

"*Mmmm*, that's good, that is, even if I say so myself."

Johanna laid down her knife and fork and, taking a deep breath of relaxation, rested her elbows on the table. Propping her chin on cupped hands she looked across at her husband and watched as he munched away on the last of his rasher.

"Are you not eating that rind?" He eyed her plate.

"Here, you can have it." Picking it up, she landed it over.

"What more could a man ask for?"

The tranquil smile of a satisfied man gazed back at her. As he swallowed the last mouthful she could see a glimmer of mischief reach his eyes.

"Another one maybe?" He winked and waved the empty fork in the direction of her plate.

"Don't even think about it." She laughed, picking up her rasher in her fingers and taking a bite. "Come on. It's time you were off." She finished the last mouthful and wiped her fingers in the towel. By the way, your day might be getting even better."

"Not possible."

"That's what you think. Declan might be leaving us."

"Oh, there is a God! *Thank you!*" He joined his hands in prayer and looked at her. "When?"

"Well, maybe not that soon."

"And how did it come about? Did you give him a warning or what?"

"No, I didn't have to. I think he got fed up with my nagging."

"So it worked then." Mattie poured the last of the tea and stood up, facing her.

"Very funny, aren't you? Hasn't worked with you yet." She picked up the plates and began stacking them on the drainer. "No, I'm not quite sure what brought it on. I didn't want to ask too many questions in case he changed his mind."

"Wise woman. Where's he going to live? Or is he going back to Ireland?"

"Seems he's thinking of moving in with that Dewey fellow. Remember, he called here the other night. Doesn't seem to be a date on the move yet. I'm not sure if it's all in Declan's head. Anyway, if it comes up be sure and give him every encouragement."

"I thought you didn't like that Dewey?"

"I don't, but it'll solve one of my problems. I'm not sure how much longer I can put up with Declan."

"I'd like him gone out of here too, but what sort of influence is that ne'er-do-well going to have on him?" Mattie frowned as he put his cup on the drainer.

"Now you're making me feel bad." She paused – a flicker of annoyance at having to look in on herself. "You're right. But he's going to have to move out at some stage. It would be better if it was with some of the young Irish lads in the store."

"Someone like me, you mean?" Mattie grinned.

"I'm serious, Mattie. Would you talk to him? Maybe suggest that Dewey mightn't be the best one to live with. There's no point in me saying anything. There's not a chance he'd want my opinion on the matter."

She slipped a couple of tomatoes into the lunch bag. He hated the way the liquid seeped through the bread if she put it into the sandwich. Much better keep them separate. And whole.

"Here, now don't sit on them." She handed them over.

"D'ye think I'm an eejit or what?"

"Don't have me answer that."

He put the pack into his jacket pocket with exaggerated care. "Sit on them? Why would I do that?"

"I've no idea. But you did last week and I'd an awful job picking the tomato seeds out of the lining."

Chapter 35

Johanna didn't know she had a dream. Not alone did she not know she had a dream, she didn't even realise she had been living it for years.

Occasionally Hugh varied the route, but it usually started and ended with the main store. The first one he'd opened near the Common. The one that Margaret had encouraged him to go ahead with when he'd had moments of doubt that he was getting in too deep. He'd never admit to the sentimental attachment but it was the one he saw as his 'headquarters'. His pride and joy. The one that had started him on his journey. He'd always leave that store as his last collection point, located as it was closest to the bank.

Mattie normally arrived ten minutes early on a Monday and today was no exception. He went upstairs and knocked on the dark wooden door and stood studying the classy script of the black lettering on the brass plate – **Hugh McNamara Managing Director** – as he waited for the voice inside to shout 'Enter'. The 'Enter' always had a slight inflection at the end of the word as if the Managing Director wasn't sure who it was knocking at twenty minutes past ten each Monday.

Mattie turned the brass knob and stuck his head around the door.

"Your carriage awaits, boss." Announcing himself as he did each week, deliberately keeping the playful tone out of his voice. He knew from previous experience that Hugh did not appreciate jokes in the workplace. He liked to keep things formal at work.

"Be with you in a moment."

"I'll wait for you at the front then." Mattie headed down to where the horse and buggy were parked at the door and climbed up onto the driving seat.

Within five minutes, as always, Hugh appeared in his coat and hat, carrying his briefcase. The tan leather of the satchel had his initials embossed on the front in curlicued lettering. He stepped up into the buggy and, taking his seat beside Mattie, opened the bag and took out the revolver, laying it carefully on his knee. Hugh was aware that his reputation as a businessman-not-to-be-messed-with preceded him, but as a precaution he always carried the gun on his lap. Not loaded. Only he and Mattie knew that. There was no point. Apart from the fact that he knew little about firearms he knew he could never actually use it. Simply there as a deterrent.

The Monday promotion was an excuse to pay Mattie a higher rate than the other workers. Hugh knew that he handed over his wages each week to Johanna to manage the money so there was no chance it would be wasted. Workwise he was still a bit of a lightweight, but Hugh hid his lack of respect for Mattie's performance and lack of ambition behind the small promotion he'd given him. He bore him no ill-will. He was a likeable chap and he had to admit that he had his redeeming points, the main one being his good heart and there was no doubt but he made Johanna happy.

Mattie gave a little flip to the reins and talked softly to the horse as they made their way to the first store on their round. He sat in the buggy as Hugh entered and waited until he could see him through the shop window make his way towards the door. At that point, as always, Mattie jumped down and walked to the door of the store, the gun in his coat pocket. A quick glance up and down the pavement to ensure they weren't being stalked, a nod to Hugh who waited inside for the signal, and they both walked over to the buggy and boarded. Before they headed on to the next store Mattie passed the gun to Hugh to keep hidden under the money satchel.

When he talked to Johanna, Mattie admitted that he thought this safety routine a bit excessive, but it was what Hugh wanted and what the boss asked for the boss got. If the truth be told, he thought it an obvious advertisement that there was money exchanging hands but was wise enough to know his opinion on the matter would not have been considered appropriate, much less welcomed.

Neither of them saw it coming. It happened after the last collection, between the headquarters and the bank. They had slowed down on the approach to the bank when the men appeared from nowhere, dark woollen scarves wrapped around their heads and faces. Gloved hands reached for the satchel on Hugh's knee. A silent muffled tussle, Hugh fighting him off, holding tight to the bag.

"Get off, you blackguard!" Mattie leaned across to push the man off. Trying to halt the horse at the same time, he could feel the animal's anxiety travel up the reins.

"*Mattie, Mattie, watch out! The gun!*"

Mattie, misunderstanding, made a grab for the gun on Hugh's lap as the second man, with his two hands free, beat him off. In the scuffle a shot rang out and in seconds it was over.

It wasn't loaded, the gun wasn't loaded – where did that shot come from? was Mattie's last thought before he lost consciousness.

The leather satchel, the only thing keeping the blood from seeping into Hugh's camel coat, remained clutched to his chest, as Mattie lay on top of him. Their assailants had fled empty-handed as Hugh's unloaded revolver lay futile on his lap.

"I tried to warn him, Johanna. About the gun."

"But it's never loaded, Hugh."

"I know. It wasn't my gun that shot him. It was the one the robbers had. He didn't see it but I did. That gun was the one that shot him. I tried to warn him."

It didn't make it any easier, knowing that it wasn't her brother who'd shot him. It changed nothing. Her Mattie was dead. Maybe knowing that made it even harder. If it had been Hugh who'd shot him it would have been an accident. But to think it was in cold blood . . .

And all the while Hugh had held onto the satchel. That was the worst of it. She didn't want to direct her anger and grief at him but she knew, in time, that might change. She looked at him, his head buried in his hands. Maybe not now but eventually she knew she would blame him, wouldn't be able to help herself. If the roles had been reversed, without a shadow of a doubt, Mattie would have let go of the briefcase, maybe even flung it at the thieves and none of this would have happened. She knew there would be no rest if she didn't give voice to that thought. But now was not the time.

When they eventually returned his clothes she kept thinking back to that last conversation. About his packed lunch. The bullet had gone right through his pocket, exploding the tomato. She couldn't bring herself to wash the jacket. A mixture of horror and the precious connection to him. She couldn't admit it to anyone. It sounded so foolish, but she didn't want to wash this connection down the sink.

DECLAN

Chapter 36

Declan sat in the armchair staring out into the night. The curtains were open, the blackness held outside only by the glass panes of the window. If there were stars he couldn't see them. He sat there and stared at the nothingness of it all.

Minutes passed. Nothing to break the stillness except the tick-tock of the grandfather clock in the hallway. The sound travelled in through the keyhole getting louder and louder, blotting out all other sounds that might have come from the road outside. The more he tried to smother it the more pronounced it became, like an elderly relative clicking his tongue in displeasure. It was getting on his nerves. His head felt ready to explode.

The children were asleep upstairs and Johanna had gone to bed early. He was aware it was to avoid sitting with him. He couldn't blame her. He found it hard to sit with himself.

A faint mirage appeared in the window, like someone looking in at him. The apparition formed more clearly as he stared. No body. Just a head and shoulders. He blinked. The image blurred, threatening to disappear. He stared again, willed himself not to blink, holding the gaze until his eyelids hurt and his eyeballs threatened to burst. Held it until the edges sharpened and he could see the face looking back at him. The face of Mattie.

He sat rigid, halfway between shock and amazement. He blinked, unable to hold it any longer. Mattie was gone. He found himself gripping the wooden armrests of the chair and all he could see in the glass was a wild pop-eyed image of himself looking back at him. He raised his hand to his face. He watched the mirrored image reflect back his action and he breathed again.

He turned his chair around, away from the window. Nothing to look at now. Without his noticing, the images had blotted out the tick-tocking of the clock.

As he stared at the wall he could feel his head begin to swell as it filled to bursting point with the realisation of what he had got himself into. He had been warned and he hadn't listened. And the worst part was he'd had a few doubts himself and he wouldn't give in to them. Ignored them for no reason other than they mirrored his aunt's concerns.

He'd been used. That much was clear. All the plans to move in with the boys. All the delays, the excuses. The waiting for the other lodger to move out, the visitor to go home. Dewey always brushing aside his anxiety, his rush to move out of Johanna's home, holding the carrot of lodging with him always an arm's length ahead. He could see it now. Next week, next month, what's the rush. But it'll be great when you move in.

It wasn't my fault. He could hear his own familiar mantra although it wasn't said this time. Not to anyone. It was inside his head. *Not my fault. I wasn't even there.* He tried it out loud on himself. "*Not my fault. I wasn't even there.*" It didn't work. There was no escaping the fact that it was his fault. All his fault. Could blame no-one else. He hadn't pulled the trigger, but he'd given the information that led to it. Only told him the schedule, the collections and drop-off of the cash. Exciting to be part of Dewey's big plan, to have the vital information and release it bit by bit as he wished. To pretend he only had a little, to pass that over and say he needed time to research the next bit. Make out that he was Mister Big, the one who held the key to the whole operation. Make them dependent on him. The power of it. That was all. A game to him. Didn't want to have anything more to do with it than that. He couldn't. He was family. All he wanted was to feel important. No-one was to get hurt. That was never the plan. It was only money. That's what Dewey and Abe promised him. He never imagined it would have gone this far.

"Jesus! What have I got myself into? Oh, Christ!" He ran his hands through his hair, grasping it between his spread fingers as if to tear it out. Realising he'd spoken aloud he listened, not sure whether he'd shouted it out or not. No sound from upstairs. Maybe it hadn't been as loud as the roar in his head.

He'd never have got involved if he'd known this was going to happen. But that was no excuse either. For the moment no-one other than Dewey and his mates knew anything about the tip-off but would they keep that to themselves or would they drop him in it? He was trapped. Worse than trapped. Mattie was dead. A harmless poor devil who'd only do you a good turn. Going nowhere, no ambition, but a decent fella. And now he was dead. He was out of his depth. It was all out of control. His stomach hadn't stopped churning since it happened. Everything was out of control. He grabbed the newspaper and threw up, catching it before it spewed out all over the floor.

The stores were open again. They only closed for two days after the incident. Hugh wanted to keep things as normal as possible for the staff and customers. And the family.

They would close again on the day of the funeral but that wouldn't be immediately. Not under the circumstances. It was all in the hands of the police now.

Declan was glad to get back working, trying to act as normally as possible. Glad to get out of the house. Couldn't bear to be around Johanna with the burden of guilt weighing him down, afraid it would show. Wanting to ask Dewey questions but afraid to go in search of him. Terrified too that he might turn up at the door of the stockroom, he jittered his way through the day, glad to get home in the evenings. Until he got home. And then there was the agitation of the silent dark evenings to put in with nothing to break the endless cycle of thoughts going around in his head. He wandered the streets to try and distract himself, going out after the tea, walking for hours without seeing or hearing anything except the pounding torment, lashing at his head in waves.

JOHANNA

Chapter 37

Hugh stared out the carriage window. Johanna sat opposite. Neither spoke on the way home, each deep in their own thoughts. Her children sat on either side of her, their white-faced whispers, as if afraid to disturb the silence, were oddly comforting.

"The Claddagh. That's what it was." A sense of wonder accompanied the thought as it came from his lips.

"What?" Johanna, surprised at the interruption to her thoughts, swung her head towards him. "What are you talking about?"

"I saw it. It was the Claddagh. On the glove. On his glove. The one with . . ."

Johanna's blood ran cold. She shot him a warning look.

"Hugh, can this wait until we're inside?" She clenched her expression, indicating the pale faces looking up at him.

"Oh, yes. Are you alright there, children? We're nearly home now."

The horses drew to a halt outside the house. Hugh lifted the younger ones down from the carriage before holding his hand up to Johanna. The children ran ahead and up the steps. They stopped at the door and looked back.

When she looked back on that day she felt a pang of

guilt at how frightening it must have been for them. And she had been beyond making it any easier. What must they have made of a mother with the life gone out of her? The grey-faced stranger who'd stepped down from that carriage with Hugh holding the door open for her, concern written all over his face. Not the mother and uncle they were used to. Maybe it would have been better to have left them at home. She remembered how they had waited and watched her walk, eyes downcast, from the carriage and up to the front door with not a word. She remembered the uncertainty on their faces, each one of them unsure what to do.

Hugh's children had arrived to the house first. All had been assigned chores, something that had probably been a relief to them. Patrick opened the door, nodding to his father that all was ready. Hughie appeared and stepping forward enveloped Johanna in a hug. As he released her she saw him look at his young red-eyed cousins on the doorstep and wondered if it brought back to him the hollowness of a similar bewildering time of his own long ago.

"Come on, girls. Come on in." Patrick put his arm around Hannah and ushered the younger girls ahead. "Take your coats off and I'll hang them up for you."

Johanna was grateful that Hugh had organised a meal to be prepared in his house after the funeral. She wouldn't have been able to think about domestic things. Wouldn't have cared if she never ate again. But it was necessary. For the children.

"Go down to the kitchen and tell Kathleen we're here and the others are following. They'll be arriving any minute, so whenever she's ready to serve the meal to go ahead, make a start." Hugh waved to his son. "Girls, you go with Hughie and Patrick, I'll send the twins down to you when they arrive. I just want to talk to your mother for a moment."

Johanna took off her hat and placed it on one of the big wooden knobs on the hallstand. Hugh waited as she removed her coat and hung it up before taking off his own.

"Go ahead into the parlour, Jo. There's something we need to talk about."

Johanna rubbed her hands together, not realising how cold they were until she saw the fire lit in the grate. Going over she held her palms to the flame and tried to block thoughts that were forming in her head. She was too drained to deal with things now. Everything could wait. Except whatever it was that her brother was determined to tell her. Whatever it was that he remembered.

Hugh followed in, shutting the door behind him.

She turned to face him. The raw pain was evident in the strained skin around his eyes.

"Jo, I remembered something I saw. I know it's hard but I have to tell you and I'll have to make it quick before the others arrive. The fellow with the gun. I saw the heart in the clasped hands, like a Claddagh ring, on the stud on the edge of the glove, like a cufflink." Hugh pinched his cuff and held it towards her as if to make it more real. "I never saw one like that before. It's something we have to tell the police." He paused. "We have to, Jo. We can't just ignore this. It'll be important."

"I knew, Hugh. The minute you said about the glove."

"What do you mean, you knew?"

"I've seen it before."

"*Where?*"

"I only caught a glimpse of it but I thought it strange at the time. Reminded me of Mama's wedding ring. Couldn't understand how an American fellow like him would have that symbol."

"Who are you talking about?"

"That Dewey fellow that I told you about. The evening he came round to the house looking for Declan. The one

202

who was hanging around the storeroom." Her eyes filled.

Hugh took her by the shoulders as she began to shake.

"Hugh, this is a nightmare. There couldn't be a connection. Surely not with Declan?" She pulled away from him and gazed into the fire. "This just gets worse."

Hugh moved towards her and with his head to one side looked into her face.

"Johanna. Jo, look at me."

She didn't even hear him, couldn't process the thoughts that swirled around her mind.

"He shook hands with me. He kept his gloves on." She continued to stare into the fire, as if was talking to herself. "I saw it then. But only for a second. It mightn't have been that but it reminded me of it, like he'd made the stud himself out of a ring." She looked up at her brother. "I don't want to believe that Declan had anything to do with this. He just can't have. Hugh, he can't."

"Johanna, you're jumping ahead. It's very unlikely." His face suggested that even to himself his words sounded false. "We don't know anything yet. Say nothing today. We'll have to mention it to the police though. I'll deal with that – let them follow up on it. Let's talk again about this later but for God's sake just keep away from Declan when he arrives. Don't say a word to him."

"How easy do you think I'm going to find that?"

"I'm not going to find it easy to hold my tongue either, Johanna, but we've got to." He paused. "Not in front of anyone here. You've got to think of the children. They're bewildered enough as it is."

He watched Johanna's set face as she headed towards the door.

"*I mean it, Jo.* Don't say a word to him. God forbid that there is a connection but if there is we don't want him tipping them off."

DECLAN

Chapter 38

His stomach turned over as soon as soon as he saw them. It happened each time they arrived. He knew he should have kept sweeping. Was aware that by leaning on his brush and watching as they looked around for the stock manager, he was drawing attention to himself. But he wanted it to finish, an end to all this.

"What are they doing here again?"

"I don't know. They must think some of us know something."

He could hear the voices of the lads as they worked, filling the shelves with a new consignment of stock. Little did they know. He knew it all but this time it didn't feel good to have one up on them.

He brushed a few bits of straw, adding them to the pile of dust as he watched the policeman talking to the stock manager. It was only when he stopped nodding and turned his head, pointing a finger in Declan's direction that he knew what the questions had been about. They had come for him and despite the thumping in his chest it was a relief. They'd called around several times before the funeral but this time they had asked for him by name.

* * *

The days waiting for Mattie's body to be released for the funeral had been punctuated by nights full of horror for Declan, wishing for the morning, which when it came was no relief. Another day of torment to be faced.

The porridge, like a bowl of sick in front of him on the breakfast table, rendered him unable to bring himself to stick the spoon in, much less eat it. He worried that Johanna would notice. As he sneaked a furtive glance he realised that he needn't have. She sat there in silence picking at her own breakfast, too deep inside herself to be bothered by his lack of appetite.

Her red-rimmed eyes were downcast, the dark shadows under them accused him from across the table. He watched her staring down at the crack in the wood of the table. The enormity of the situation, the consequences for his aunt written all over her slack face. He didn't know what to say. He preferred the strong version that normally annoyed him, not this broken woman who sat opposite him.

"What's wrong with you? Why is it you're never satisfied?" His father's words came back to him as he supped his tea. *"Why can't you just want what you have instead of always thinking you can have what you want? It's a bad world that works that way."*

Why hadn't he listened? The security of being able to kick against her rules was suddenly more comforting than the freedom he'd craved. Now it was gone. He wanted to blame her but he couldn't deny it. She was what his father would have called 'a decent woman'. Annoying maybe, but for his own good. Easy see that now. Maybe if she hadn't cared, hadn't given him the chance he wouldn't be in the situation he was now in. He twisted it around in every direction but there was no getting away from the truth. It had been he, and he alone, who was responsible for destroying her. He could argue with that until Kingdom

Come but the end result would remain the same. There was no changing it. It hadn't taken much, just one piece of information, and he himself had wrecked all their lives singlehanded.

A few questions. *"You might be able to help us in our enquiries."* That was the way they put it when they asked him to accompany them to the station. They made it sound like he was doing them a favour. He'd say nothing until they asked the questions. Maybe it wasn't as bad as he thought. They were asking all the staff. Best to assume they knew nothing.

"Where were you at the time it happened?"

"I was working. At the store. My uncle's store. I'm his nephew." Even as he said it he doubted that that fact would hold much sway.

"Do you know a man by the name of Burke? He goes by Dewey, Dewey Burke?"

He knew now for sure that he had been singled out.

"Yes. I know him. We play cards together. Sometimes."

"How well do you know him?"

"Not very well. I met him in a bar after I began to work for my uncle."

It was when they delved into the conversations he might have had with Dewey that he knew they had something.

"Maybe I did mention something. I can't remember. It wouldn't have seemed important at the time. We'd only have been messing about."

"Well, you need to start remembering, sonny. This is murder we're talking about here."

He shifted in the chair. "There was something. I think I may have said something after a few drinks. Something about the gun that my uncle carries on the collection run."

"And what exactly did you say?"

206

"I think I might have said it was only for show. That I didn't think it was loaded. Ya know the way you'd be skitting over a few drinks."

"Well, the skitting ends here, sonny. There's a man dead as a result of your loose tongue. So you better start talking, giving us a bit more information on this Dewey boy."

"What makes you think it was Dewey who was involved?"

"We're the ones asking the questions here."

Declan could feel the screws tightening as he looked at the pocked face of the police officer leaning forward, eyeballing him.

"So?" He placed his thick beefy arms on the desk that stood between them and waited while Declan digested the situation. "If you want my advice, sonny, you'll tell the truth and face the consequences."

He imagined Johanna's sensible voice in his head advising him to take the advice, not to dig himself in deeper and, in that moment, before he could change his mind, he made his decision.

JOHANNA

Chapter 39

In that quiet time before dawn, between slumber and the slow awakening to meet the day, the day she no longer cared to enter, sometimes the sun-baked fields that bordered the lake leading to the abbey drifted into her head.

In those semi-dreams the sun always shone on the bodies that rested in the cemetery there. Not just on those buried inside the roofless ruin of the old church where the important people were – it was the same sun that warmed those who lay outside in the walled grounds. The flat limestone slabs, their inscriptions washed away, grain by grain, with the centuries of raindrops that fell on them. The stroke of a hand on the surface could feel their presence, maybe forgotten by some, but not gone. The misty grey drizzle of an Irish day never encroached on her slumbers, just the yellow sun and the flaking seed-heads of the wild quaking grasses. That was the place where Mattie should have been laid to rest.

A letter had arrived from Ireland. From Art and Ellen. It contained the promise of having a special Mass said in the local church. She wished she could have attended and sat in the candlelit chapel surrounded by the comfort of family and old neighbours. The ease of kneeling amidst those who knew her, who would have understood without explanation. She wanted to smell the candlewax and the burning incense and hear the soft Clare accent of the priest droning on in Latin, not knowing what he was saying but it wouldn't matter. All she wanted was for the lulling sound of it to absorb her grief.

They didn't know Mattie but she could have told them and they would get a feel for him. She knew they'd have loved him. A part of her life now that they could never share with her. Now that it was fractured and gone there was to be no opportunity, no hope for the future.

The letter had arrived shortly after his death. Sent as soon as they had received the telegram. In total innocence of their own son's involvement. Sent before Johanna herself suspected. But now that she knew she couldn't bring herself to respond. Simply didn't know what to say.

Hugh blamed himself for what had happened. It was largely his fault. The detached sternness that had made him successful in business did not go deep enough to allow him to shift that blame. He wouldn't have done that anyway. It just wasn't his way. Face up to your mistakes and learn from them. The advice he always gave others and adhered to himself. But this one was not an error he could fix. All he could do was to try and help out financially. To cushion the hard life she had been left with. On top of the monthly envelope which she never mentioned and neither did he, something he was glad about. His initial fear was that it might have been thrown back in his face but her silence confirmed that she knew why the money arrived each week. He used any excuse he could conjure up to have hampers and treats delivered. Addressed them to the children. *From Uncle Hugh*. Easter, Thanksgiving, Christmas, their birthdays – any opportunity to make her life easier. The reaction of the children when he called after they'd opened the boxes told him that she hadn't allowed the blame she might rightfully dump on him to spoil the anticipation. Instead she appeared to have managed to push aside some margin of grievance she might have held against him and join in the children's enjoyment of the surprises.

Hugh kept a keen eye on her in the months following the funeral, partly to assuage the guilt over not having rated Mattie, but largely because of her strength. It was only now in its absence that he'd noticed her missing element, realised the power of it and its disappearance frightened him. The rippling out of that silent force she possessed, a quality she was possibly not even aware of, was only matched by her ability to draw them all in, like strong arms keeping each of them secure. How often had he been the recipient of that strength and taken it for granted. Her loss now echoed a desolation inside himself and she wasn't there to fill the hole. It worried him that the old strong Johanna might be gone for good. The selfishness of the thought, of the need for that reassurance, was not lost on him.

It was Sunday afternoon. They had just arrived back to the house after lunch out. Hugh had hoped the treat for her birthday might help shake her out of her lethargy.

"Do you want me to help you with the letters?" He remembered the way she'd taken control of the correspondence after Margaret died. He hadn't wanted to know then. Didn't care if they were never answered. People meant well but it was only another pressure, having to respond. He might never have done it if she hadn't encouraged him.

"What letters?" Johanna hung her coat on the hallstand.

"The condolences. You need to get them done."

"I'm sure people don't expect a response. Anyway I'm not able, Hugh." She moved towards the kitchen.

"They don't expect a response – but it might do you good. Give you something to focus on, help you get back to normality."

"There'll never be any such thing as normality." She paused. "Not for me anyway."

He said nothing, knowing it would only result in an argument.

"Anyway I've no envelopes or writing pad."

The sullen tone told him the mood wasn't good.

"I have. I brought them with me and there are some stamps in with them." He put the paper bag down on the table. "Will you make a start? Do you want me to stay and give you a hand? I could address some of the envelopes?"

"No. I'll do it myself." Johanna picked the bag up and emptied it onto the table. "Thanks." She flicked through the pages of the cream pad. "Maybe I'll make a start on them. Get a few done this evening."

"That would be a good idea." He was glad he'd had the foresight to pick up the writing paper before he left the house. "I'll be off then."

He looked towards her for a response but with none forthcoming he went into the hall and let himself out the door.

Normally she dreaded the long empty evenings that stretched ahead after the children went to bed but tonight felt different.

She wiped the table with a damp cloth to remove traces of jam and butter they'd left after their supper and dried it off with the towel. Taking the bundle of letters and cards from the dresser where they were propped behind the large milk jug she took them to the table and began reading.

She'd only given a cursory glance as they'd arrived, unable to take anything in. As soon as she'd read a name it immediately went out of her head. If anyone had asked if she'd had heard from any particular person she could honestly have said she'd no idea. The names and faces had all passed over her in a blur. Now she was ready to concentrate.

Fanning them out, she selected a couple of envelopes with postage stamps from Ireland and put them to one side. The familiar writing on the envelope from Art was like a beacon in the middle of the bundle. She picked it up. Her name was written in black ink in a childlike scrawl, the unsure hand of a farmer unused to putting pen to paper. The address in pencil, like he'd completed the address at a later time, having had to search in some box of old documents for the information. This letter was going to be the most difficult. Best get it dealt with first.

Dear Art and Ellen,

I am sorry it has taken me so long to respond to your kind letter of condolence. I really appreciated your warm words and wished you could have been here with me to help in my time of need. Not that there was anything you could have done to lessen the pain but just to have you beside me would have been a comfort.

Hugh has been a tower of strength and makes me realise how important family is. He doesn't say much but I know he understands as he has been through the death of dear Margaret and although I can't talk to him about my grief he helps out in very practical ways without my ever having to ask him.

I am sorry I cannot talk about Declan. When you wrote, none of us knew of his involvement in my dear Mattie's – she hesitated, the pen poised over the paper. She took a deep breath, knowing she couldn't do it. The word she wanted to write was 'murder'. But it would be very unkind. Not their fault. She continued – *death.*

Now we all know the truth and we cannot pretend it is otherwise. Please do not blame yourselves. He is your son, but he and he alone is responsible for bringing this terrible tragedy upon the family. I appreciate it is your tragedy as well as mine and your hearts must be broken as mine is.

I really miss Mattie so much now, so it is even more important that you continue to write to me. I look forward to seeing the stamps arriving from Ireland. Something that has always given my heart a lift when they drop through the letterbox and I'm sure you understand that I need that more than anything now.

Johanna paused and tapped the end of the pen against her lip. She knew she had to ask it, something they might consider harsh. But what had been done to her was worse than that. Worse than harsh. She couldn't be on edge every time a letter arrived from them, afraid to open it for fear there would be a mention. She wouldn't allow him that power over her life.

But please forgive me, because I must ask something of you and it is this, that you never mention Declan's name to me again. I feel bad about this, saying it to you about your own son, but I cannot cope with hearing his name. Not yet anyway, and maybe never. I hope you understand. Give me news of Kate and how she is surviving convent life and also Luke. How is he doing?

All my good wishes to you both and to Kate and Luke also

Your loving sister,
Johanna

213

DECLAN

Chapter 40

He was surprised that first time when the warder told him he had a visitor. Why would anyone want to come after what he'd done? Especially family.

The hollow echoes of the shouting, like he was encased in a metal barrel, bounced around the insides of his head, coming as they did from around and above him. He felt eyes boring into him as he was marched from his cell.

The fluttering in his stomach increased as he walked alongside the officer. How was this going to go? The anxiety threatened to overwhelm the welcome break in the monotony, where every day, every week ran into the next with little or nothing to differentiate between them.

Like the first day he'd arrived when he'd kept his gaze downcast after his first look around and saw the wild stares measure him. He had hoped the warder wouldn't leave him alone. Every thing, every sound different to what he was used to. The vibration of the metal stairs as they ascended. The jangle of the bunch of keys as his jailer selected one to fit the cell lock. The sound of the door as he threw it open. And worse still the clang as he banged it shut and turned the key, having told him the basics of survival in his new home.

As the prison warder walked him into the room, he found it hard to look at his uncle. In furtive glances he could see him stony-faced as he sat rigid, looking neither right nor left, his eyes firmly focused straight ahead on the wall facing him. He wished Hugh would look at him as he approached. Not sure why he wished it. Maybe to dispel some of the hatred his uncle must feel towards him, give it time to dissipate before he sat down in front of him. He slowed his pace. Give it time. But Hugh did not adjust his gaze. Like he could read his nephew's thoughts and was not prepared to budge. Holding his stare, it was as if he was forcing Declan to walk into his eyeline.

Declan took his seat opposite the grey unmoving statue whose eyes now seemed to bore through him. He wished it would speak. He opened his mouth. Nothing came out. Hard to know what to say. Nothing seemed appropriate.

Despite the power of his stern silence his uncle looked much smaller than the authoritative man he was used to seeing strutting around his grocery store.

"Hello, Uncle Hugh." He closed his mouth and dropped his eyes. He waited, wishing his uncle would say something.

"Well . . . now." The words came out slowly.

He knew even without looking up that Hugh was taking a long hard look at him.

"And how have we come to this?"

In the silence that followed he looked up. He knew his uncle was waiting. To his horror he could feel tears welling up. And this time it was not sorrow for himself but regret that it was he who had caused all this, landed them all in this situation. He blinked, but his efforts to absorb the tears only resulted in squeezing them out and over his lower eyelids.

For the first time ever with clarity he knew that the world hadn't been against him. He had been against the world. And he hated himself for that. For not having being able to see that, to recognise it in time.

Hugh had no idea what to expect when he'd entered the gates. It was the first time he had ever been inside the boundaries of any sort of a correctional institution.

The frightened boy he saw before him surprised and startled him. He could scarcely recognise his nephew as the same defiant upstart who resented every instruction in the storeroom. The young man who saw every request as an order to be resisted.

He had considered telling Johanna that he was thinking of making a trip to see Declan. The visit was something he'd decided on after thinking long and hard about it. A duty he knew he had to perform. He'd also thought about asking Johanna to accompany him but it was definitely too soon. Maybe it would always be. Leave well enough alone for the moment. Trust his instinct. Best to do it himself and see how it worked out. If things went badly there would be no need to mention it.

From the moment the tears spilled down the boy's cheeks Hugh knew he'd done the right thing. What he saw before him held a glimmer of hope, the possibility of a new start. An opportunity maybe to rebuild a half decent person. He was glad he'd come. But there would be a whole lot more work to be done first. There was no rush, it was going to take time and Declan was going nowhere, not for a long time.

JOHANNA

Chapter 41

Hugh waited until after the third visit before mentioning it to his sister.

"How could you? How could you after what he's done?"

He wasn't surprised by her reaction.

"I know, Johanna, I know. But I had to. I didn't do it for Declan. I did it for Art." He put his hand on her shoulder but she shrugged him off. "He is his father. Our brother. I did it for him, Jo, not for Declan."

Batting him away with her hand, she walked to the pile of clothes and prepared to start ironing.

"You never did think much of Mattie anyway, so why am I surprised that there's no loyalty?" It came out like a spoilt child's reaction but she was beyond caring.

"I did like him. In fact, I'd grown very fond of him." He paused, realising how true that was. He propped himself against the table. "I know it took a while but I did. His heart was in the right place."

Johanna pounded the iron onto the table and began smoothing the sheet.

"A very good man. No doubt about that." He sighed. "It's a pity Declan didn't learn a thing or two from Mattie and we wouldn't be where we are now. That's for certain."

Had he read Johanna's expression properly it would have told him that this realisation had come far too late. Too little, too late. What was clear to him, watching the set look on her face, was that this definitely was not a good time to suggest she might accompany him to the prison. That he read without a shadow of doubt.

The soothing motion of the iron eased the silence that fell between them as he watched her smooth and fold one item after another.

"*Are you going again?*" Her tone, as sharp as the look she threw in his direction, punctured the silence.

"Well, yes, I'll go again." He spoke gently. "I know you won't be happy about it, Jo, but I have to try and turn this thing around."

"*That'll be hard!*" She spat the words at him. "*What are you now, a miracle worker?*"

"I didn't mean it that way." He rubbed his forehead. "Look, I'm sorry, that came out all wrong."

"You can bet your life it did." She glared at him. "Unless it's Lazarus you're talking about."

The slapping sound of the linen tablecloth came between them as she shook it into folds.

"You needn't think I'll be going with you, Hugh. In case you're thinking of asking." She'd read his mind. "The answer is no. Even before you ask. I don't need to think about it. I won't go now . . . *nor ever*."

She added the tablecloth to the pile.

"I won't ever forgive him. We gave him a home here, me and Mattie, couldn't have been better to him and he does this?" She picked a pair of trousers from the pile and, smoothing them on the table, resumed ironing.

He could hear the wobble in her voice.

"He robbed me. He robbed my children. He deprived us of the best man in the world *and you want me to visit* him?" Her voice went up an octave. "*And what?* I suppose you'll be asking me to forgive him? Never, Hugh. *Never, never, never!*"

"Alright, Jo. Stop. Don't upset yourself. Look, I'm sorry, I shouldn't have . . ."

"You're dead right, you shouldn't have. And I don't want his name mentioned here again. *Do you understand?* Never again. He's dead to me. He's not my nephew."

"I understand. But before we end this I have to let you know . . . he asked me to tell you that he is sorry. Very sorry."

He paused, long enough to allow it sink in. To have her hear the words, just a few seconds before she rejected them. They might be some consolation if she were to remember them somewhere down the road. Some time in the future when maybe she might be more receptive.

"I know it's no consolation but he is and he was genuine. He's learned a very hard lesson."

"At *our* expense, at *my* expense. Well, don't expect me to feel sorry for him."

"I don't and I'm sure he doesn't. But . . ."

"And when he gets out, and he didn't get half long enough in there, I don't want to see him ever again. He's not to come here. Make sure he knows that. Make sure he's clear. The further he gets away from Boston the better as far as I'm concerned." Her face was red. "He can go to Hell for all I care."

It was only after Hugh left that the dark spot on her conscience bothered her. It followed her up the stairs as she carried the bundle of ironing up to the linen cupboard. She swatted it away but it kept returning. It entered through the cracks between the chores and the demands of the children to niggle away all evening.

"Would you just learn to forgive and forget?" Her mother's exasperated voice kept poking into her head. *"You can never let a thing go."*

Even Mary Ann would hardly expect her to let this go. It was just too big a 'thing'. No question of forgetting. She didn't have to wrestle with her conscience over that. Forgetting was not something that was ever, ever going to happen. But forgiving? It was the forgiving bit that was the problem.

She pushed in the half-open door of the girls' bedroom. The outlines of the slumbering bodies were visible in the white moonglow that made its way through the gap where the night curtains didn't quite meet. The sound of their gentle breathing reassured her that they at least would have a peaceful sleep. Closing the door quietly, she made her way along the landing. Maybe it was time to let Hannah move into the spare room. The time for lodgers was over.

Her anger at Hugh from earlier had passed. An empty disappointment had replaced it, sucking the life out of her. She sat on the edge of the bed. She was tired. No energy to shift, to change into her nightclothes. Everyone else seemed able to move on. Why not she?

The quiet sounds of the street filtered into the room through the open window. Never able to sleep without some fresh air, even now despite the cold she had to have it open an inch.

"What are you trying to do, woman? Freeze me knobs off?"

She smiled at the memory. She could hear his voice. But how long before it receded and she could no longer remember how it sounded.

Standing up, she began to remove her clothes. She slipped into her nightgown and threw a cardigan around her shoulders against the chill. Kneeling down beside her bed, her propped elbows sank into the softness of the eiderdown. As she gazed across at the shimmer of the lace curtain on the window, the drapes not yet drawn, she gave a deep sigh and shifted her focus to her night prayers, and went with the automatic drone of the Lord's Prayer.

" . . . *forgive us our trespasses . . . as we forgive those who trespass against us.*"

As soon as the words were out she halted. For the first time ever she realised how little thought she'd ever really given them. Burying her face in her hands she tried again.

"*. . . as we forgive those . . .*" They stuck in her throat. She could go no further. She never could. Never would. Forgive him.

Massaging her head as she knelt there, she knew for certain that she would never be able to say the words again. Not now, even after Hugh's visit. They would choke her. She would just have to drop the second part of the sentence and go straight to the next bit.

"*. . . and lead us not into temptation but deliver us from evil. Amen.*"

Deliver us from evil was right. What Declan had done, the betrayal, the evil, was just too great to forgive. She could only hope the Lord would see His way to forgive her her sin.

With each passing night the difficulty with the line became worse. Even before she went upstairs she'd begin to think about it in the armchair. It started to spill back earlier and earlier, stealing her evenings. By the time she knelt down beside her bed it had grown into a monster, halting her thoughts, the unsaid words accusing her.

Her resentment towards her nephew increased for having put her in the position of having to face her own intolerant, unforgiving nature. That dark spot that the Lord would judge. She could see the scales weighing her sin on one side and her nephew's on the other. With her strong faith shaken to the core, she wondered if she should abandon the nightly prayers. Why not? Just as everyone seemed to be abandoning her. Let her be judged. So what?

"*Forgive? Never, never, never. Amen.*" This was the last prayer she would ever say. She'd made her decision on that.

One uneasy week passed before the habit of a lifetime wormed its way back into her life. Seven days of discomfort. The itching started about ten o'clock. Not something she could scratch. It sat between her ears, nagging away until it formed a tense bridge spanning the inside of her head. Would she, wouldn't she?

She wouldn't. The Lord had not provided. She told herself this and, adjusting the cushion, settled back to reading the newspaper.

She held out. But on the seventh day she gave in. The comfort of the ritual. She missed it.

She made her way up the stairs. Lighter. The torment of the week subsided now that the decision had been reversed, even if the Lord wasn't listening.

As she lay on the bed, her prayers said, something began to nudge its way into her mind. It started like a gentle prodding but an instinct told her that it was not a thought she was going to be happy to entertain.

She rolled over onto her back and stared at the ceiling. The soft pushing at her brain persisted, reluctant to admit defeat. Not sure if she was too tired or relaxed to fight it she allowed her natural curiosity to permit it entry. As soon as it was in she knew why her brain had tried to deny it access. Maybe she had been blaming the wrong people. It had been she herself who had put pressure on her brother to take on Declan, to give him a job. She too who had persuaded Mattie to allow her nephew live with them. There had been times when she had even felt anger at her beloved Mattie for having tried to save Hugh's money. Maybe it was time to question her own judgement. Always so confident that it was the best. Always so definite. She could no longer deny that some of that blame must rest with her.

Even if her prayers were futile, she had to believe that something might change. Maybe not now, but sometime in the future. Had to hang on to that hope. If she didn't it might all unravel.

Chapter 42

It was a topic seldom discussed. No-one ever mentioned how difficult widowhood was. It hadn't yet touched her friends and, apart from a few acquaintances who had lost their spouses who weren't people she knew well enough to confide in, she had no-one to talk to, to compare experiences.

Hugh had been the only widower whose grief she'd been close to. Only now she knew that she hadn't understood her brother at all. Too young and inexperienced at the time and too busy trying to keep the household going to realise the depth of the gulf inside him where his heart had been torn out. Even had she been inclined to unburden herself to him now, the circumstances of Mattie's death made it impossible. They were all too ensnared in the complexities of it, each coming from a different angle and going through their own torment.

Most widows she knew were elderly. At a different stage of their lives when they lost their partners. Maybe that was why she hadn't thought about it much. They all seemed to accept their lot and their loss as the normal progression of life. Once the wake and burial had passed they just appeared to slip into the part without complaint, as if it were the mantle they were expected to accept. To consent to this as their natural role, without having any say in the matter, and just get on with it.

She didn't want to be associated with white-faced old ladies dressed in black, the ones she saw at Mass every Sunday who seemed to be happy to wear their widow's weeds for the rest of their lives. The widow that a younger member of the family would be assigned to look after on social occasions to make sure they felt included. It had always looked easy for them but now she knew different. They too had to face being dropped off at their cold dark houses where they had to enter the silence alone. Age had nothing to do with it, nor had appearances.

Her heart yearned to take Mattie home to Ireland where he belonged. It wasn't even that she associated him with their homeland, never having shared a life together there. It didn't make any sense why she felt the pull. It just seemed like the proper place for him to rest, somewhere he wouldn't be anonymous. A little corner of the earth with permanent links.

The very word 'home' had disquieted her of late. Like a magnet pulling her towards somewhere she knew she couldn't go. The children were in bed. The only sound in the kitchen was the tapping of her fingers on the tabletop as she picked out the notes of 'Abide With Me' with her right hand while she hummed along quietly to herself. The words of the hymn drifted into her head but they were hard to catch. The first few were easy but they began to trail off towards the end of each line. She started the hymn again in the hope that they would come to her but the more she searched about the more they eluded her.

"Why am I tormenting myself?" She shook her head slowly and picking up the teapot she topped up her cup and watched the pale scum separate. She pushed the cold tea aside and propped her head on her hand as she tried to work it out.

225

She had a life. Had had a life, and a home. She didn't want any of it now without her husband. The home she'd made here in Boston for herself, Mattie and their children, the very essence of it gone now, no longer feeling like the cosy family unit it had been. The building still kept them protected from the elements but what had happened had changed everything. It had her stuck here, bound to a foreign place for eternity. *"Your life is over there in America now. You've got to make it your home and content yourself."* Her mother's voice came to her from one of the early letters. *"You've only been there a couple of months. Have some patience and give it a chance."*

And that is what she thought she had done – that rebuke to another Johanna, a young girl who was having difficulty settling. Patience was not going to solve her problem this time. How easy it had been to fool herself into believing a life and a home combined together added up to the same thing. It had never struck her before. A life. The thing that kept her going forward, moving along, lulling her into thinking she belonged. Its changing nature had fooled her, kept her from realising that she didn't belong. Not really. At least not now. A home was the opposite. Herself and Mattie. Somewhere solid and safe that she'd never gone looking for but that they had built without realising. And now one of the key elements was no more. She couldn't sustain it on her own.

She wondered if others knew these things or did they go along, blissfully unaware, as she had until something huge happened. She had a life, in turmoil now, but she no longer knew where home was. All she knew was that she needed somewhere to retreat to, a place to burrow into and lick her wounds. Somewhere she belonged.

The two things were once linked but had little connection now. It was somewhere between these two words that Johanna got lost.

DECLAN

Chapter 43

1907

This last month, so many years waiting for it, looking forward to getting out and then it was on top of him. Not at all what he'd imagined. The thought of fending for himself terrified him. It was the last thing he'd expected to have to worry about. So much time to fantasize and now the daydreams were over. So much to be thought about and the reality was frightening.

"You sent for me, Declan?" The chaplain unbuttoned his black coat as he sat down opposite. He knew why a visit had been requested. He'd seen it all before. The distracted look of a prisoner made vulnerable by the prospect of their liberty, of their release from captivity. Different to the anger or resignation they had coming in.

"I'm not ready for this!" Declan held his head in his hands, scratching his scalp as he ran his fingers through his hair, unable to look at the chaplain.

"Not ready for what? Freedom?" Father Larry watched the man before him. "Is that not what you've been working towards? What did you expect? That they'd keep you here forever?"

"I don't know." Declan's head jerked up. His eyes darted around the walls. "I don't know."

Father Larry could hear the sound of Declan's foot tapping rapidly on the floor. He waited in silence for the calm.

"What is it you're afraid of?" The question was asked gently. "That you're going to have to look after yourself?"

"I suppose." Declan picked at a bit of loose skin on his index finger. "Yeah, probably that's part of it."

"I suppose with everything being done for you in here any of us might think we've lost our survival skills. But the truth of it is that if we managed before we'll manage again."

"Maybe."

Father Larry sat and watched Declan picking at his fingernails, allowing time for whatever thoughts were going through his head to be processed. He could image the confusion. Jail had become home, much as all prisoners hated it. He could see how rattled he would be with that security about to be taken away. Not knowing whether to turn right or left when they let him out the gates. Nowhere to go. No-one to go to. He knew all the details of Declan's situation. The man could hardly ask his uncle for a second chance even though he visited occasionally. He probably couldn't even understand why his uncle did that, came to see him. After what he'd done, sure what did his Uncle Hugh owe him? The jumble of thoughts must be frightening. He could imagine them swirling around inside Declan's head and felt sorry for him.

He sat and waited until Declan looked up. He had some of the answers but nothing would be learned if he jumped in too soon with solutions. This was something Declan would have to consider, to work out himself.

"We talked about a lot of things over the years, Declan, and I know you thought most of them were stupid. At the time." He paused. "But maybe now some of them might make sense."

"Nothing makes sense. Nothing ever did. But now I'm getting out. I've nowhere to go and nobody wants me." There was no belligerence in the comments, just an acceptance.

Father Larry looked at the miserable face before him, the eyes downcast. He couldn't disagree. There was truth in what he said.

"So what's your plan?" He had to shake him out of the defeatism he saw approaching. Now was not the time for sympathy and understanding. That ship had sailed.

"Well, I don't have one. I'm sure no-one will employ me. Not when they find out where I've been for the past few years." He paused before shooting an angry look at the priest. "What's your plan for that?"

"I don't have an answer, Declan. That's up to you. God knows you've had plenty of time in here to work out a plan for yourself." He was aware of the edge to his tone but he couldn't back down, couldn't allow despondency to creep in. "So what do you intend to do? Just give up?"

"It's fine for you with your nice respectable priest's life."

The goading had obviously stirred something. The chaplain could see that the words had spilled out before Declan could stop them, as if they'd flown out of their own accord. Probably now wished he could take them back. He took a deep breath, could see Declan watching him, unsure where this might go.

"I'll ignore that." The words came out in a tired sigh.

He watched Declan release his breath, relief that there was no damage done. Probably feared that he might just get up and leave him to his own devices.

"You won't conquer the world in one go, Declan. You didn't do it before and you'll not do it now. In fact none of us will ever conquer the world. We can only try and make sense of it and hope to build some sort of a life for ourselves. Survive the best way we can and, maybe if we're lucky and put the right type of effort into it, we do some bit of good along the way."

"I'm not sure I know how to survive. Don't know where to begin."

Father Larry propped his head on his hand and looked across at Declan in silence.

"And as for doing a bit of good? I haven't exactly excelled at that now, have I?" Declan gave a weak grin.

"You're right there." The priest smiled back. "But it's not too late. We can all change. It's up to yourself whether you want to or not. I can't make that decision for you."

Declan surveyed the grey wall before him, his eyes roaming over the expanse of it, examining the stains, as if the answer was going to appear on its surface.

"You have talents, Declan. Maybe untapped as yet but they're there. Don't leave them buried."

He watched as the eyes suddenly stopped roaming. That had obviously rung a bell ... remembering the parable from those Bible lessons he'd got him to read. The simple ones that had trickled back from his schooldays, a time when all of that stuff had been of another era, another way of life, for another type of people who wandered around in robes in the desert. People who gathered in sand-coloured colonnaded buildings and listened. The ones who made the rules, the ones who followed them, people who betrayed each other, the takers and the givers and the wasters. Not situations that made sense to any child and certainly not something that would ever have appeared to apply to himself. Not even when Father Larry had produced them. Now bits of it might mean something, perhaps be of some use when he went outside the gates.

"Maybe you're right. I need to think. I just need time to think."

The chaplain stood up and buttoned his coat.

"Will you come back before I get out?" The note of anxiety was confirmation enough. A message or two might have hit their target.

"I will. I'll come back in a few days, but in the meantime make a few decisions about what direction you want your life to take." He walked towards the door. "That'll be the hard part. We can work out the logistics once you do that."

Father Larry brushed his hand over the shoulders of his coat. The droplets of water sprayed off onto the floor. The rain had only started so it hadn't had time to seep through the wool. As he sat down to wait, he glanced around the room and noted the dirty marks on the wall, most of them about boot-high. A few chunks of plaster gouged out here and there gave a hint as to the frustrations of such a place.

A shuffle at the door alerted him to Declan's arrival and the determined look as he came through the door reassured him.

Declan sat down opposite him, his face alive. "I've been thinking. Thinking about what you said."

"Good. I'm glad to hear it."

"I want to pay back something."

Things had been thought through, at long last. There was now a solid starting point. He resisted the urge to smile at the lack of small talk, the absence of a greeting. Straight in like he was bursting to tell someone.

"And how do you propose to do that, Declan?"

"I've no idea. Haven't worked that out yet." He took a deep breath. "I know I can't do it with my family. It's too late

231

for that. The damage can't be undone there."

"Well, there are other ways to make restitution if you are prepared to."

Declan's direct look, eyebrows slightly raised, looking for guidance was all he needed.

"I have a suggestion that will give you a new start if you want one. It's not glamorous and it won't be easy." He paused.

"Well, are you going to tell me or what?" Declan leaned forward, forearms flat on the table.

"Working with the homeless." He waited to see how this proposition was received and watched the flicker of uncertainty cross Declan's face. "How does that sound to you?"

"I'll be homeless myself when I get out of here. How could I help them? Sure I won't be able to help anyone."

"You'll be told what to do. Although you mightn't like the sound of that." Father Larry smiled. "I can arrange accommodation to go with the job. Caretaking and generally helping out in the kitchen. What do you think?"

"*Mmm . . .*"

The chaplain waited.

"Unless you've a better plan of course."

"Me? Sure I'm full of plans." Declan laughed. "When can I start?"

"As soon as they let you out." The priest studied him. "Now, you're sure this is what you want because I don't want to be wasting my time? It's going to take a bit of organising."

"I've had no better offers, so yes, I'm willing to give it a go."

"I'd need something better than that. A bit more conviction that you'll stick at it. I don't want to hear in a month that you don't like it because I can tell you there isn't a lot to like about it."

"Yes, I told you I want to pay back."

"Well, there's very little money in it so it won't be in cash that you'll be making restitution. No, payback will take another form." He paused. "I'll talk to them here about it and sort you out with what you'll need initially." He stood up. "By the way, it's in San Francisco."

"San Francisco?" A shadow of uncertainty passed over his face and the faint trace of a whine entered his voice. "Sure I don't know anyone there."

"Sure that's the very idea. A clean slate – away from your past." Some growing up still needed there. "An opportunity for a fresh start. It's best that you move a long way from Boston. I'll give you your first introduction and it's up to you after that." He watched the worry spread over his face.

"I suppose . . ."

"It'll be tough so be prepared for that. There's plenty of work to be done there that might help keep you out of trouble." He looked down at Declan. "I can assure you there are people worse off than you there. They've more to be worrying about than you and your past." He began to move towards the door. "I'll be back at the end of the week with everything you'll need to start your new life and to see you off on your journey. A fresh start, eh?"

Declan watched the priest's black coat disappear as the door clanged shut. His stomach lifted in an excitement that had not altogether been doused by anxiety. A new beginning. This time he wouldn't mess up.

Chapter 44

San Francisco

1907

It hadn't been easy. Life itself wasn't easy. That's what he'd discovered. Why he'd ever expected it to be he couldn't quite work out. The only simple part had been making a mess of it. That hadn't taken too much effort.

That nobody else's had been easy either was something that might not have eluded him had he ever taken the time to look outside of himself and his own miserable little life. Why had things always appeared simple and straightforward for others? At least that was how it seemed from the cursory glance he'd given. Big mistake that. It had taken a disaster to teach him that particular lesson.

He'd learned a lot since he came to the Centre. His own petty discontentments had been nothing. Of no importance whatsoever when measured against what he was seeing here. It had taken a while to rid himself of that creeping little worm of a thought that he hadn't quite banished from his mind. The attitude that they'd brought a lot of their misfortune on themselves. The difference now was that he recognised the little worm – God knows, Father Larry had worked hard on ridding him of it. These people certainly didn't have it easy. But none of them appeared to be expecting miracles or fairy-tale endings. Just glad of the bowl of soup and to be indoors out of the weather.

Declan sat on the plank that rested on the blocks outside the kitchen door. A short break in the air to enjoy his own cup of tea and slice of toast after the breakfasts. The early-morning sun had taken the chill out of the wall behind him. The gentle warmth eased the ache in his back as he leaned against it. Ten minutes' rest before the lunch preparations.

The spell in prison had straightened his thinking. To say it hadn't been a pleasant experience was putting it mildly. The violence that permeated the very air in there had frightened him witless. Only for Father Larry he wouldn't have survived. He came at just the right time. Had to give him credit for recognising a fool when he saw one. That's what made the difference.

He couldn't blame her. She had tried. He couldn't hold his aunt responsible. She saw the fool early on and had tried to advise him and failed. Not Johanna's fault that she now saw him as evil. If that's how it was. Simple as that. And after what she'd been through it was no wonder. He'd had plenty of time to mull that one over.

Not a lot else to do there but look at the walls and think. When he had a change of scenery it was corridors with rows of metal doors and bars. That was mostly what he remembered. Not a hint of the lush greenery he'd taken so much for granted. Bars, bars and more bars. And not the sort he'd become used to in Boston either. Here it was all hollow sounds – not a lot to stimulate you.

It was that life that ran round and round in his head. Not all the time but it was like when that period came back into his head it managed to drive all the rest out. Try as he did to remember the before, the before in Ireland, to swell it up big enough to keep the prison out, wasn't enough. Nor was the after, the now, here in San Francisco. That wasn't strong enough either. The horror and boredom always managed to displace the better bits of his life, pushing them further and further away until they dropped over the edge and out of sight.

All that thinking and hopping from one side of his brain to the other. All those conversations in his head where he was always right, always the winner. He hadn't worked it out overnight. It hadn't happened in the first year or even two. Took a few. Time passed slowly so it was hard to remember when the realisation dawned that he despised that person. Strange how for somebody who was always right he'd managed to end up inside, looking out through the bars of a prison cell . . . and the rest of them, the ones he'd considered didn't have a clue, had their freedom outside. Hadn't met too many winners in the jailhouse. Every last one of them a know-all like himself.

Father Larry was a saint. Must have been to stick with it. All the guff directed at him and in return he still hung in there, still gave him a chance, and all the others too. Helped him recognise himself as nothing more than a dope, a misguided idiot. Immature. Plain stupid. Not evil. Not through and through bad. Just a thicko. Had to laugh now at the way he'd bucked at those descriptions of himself. That had been part of the problem. He didn't know himself. Not at all. It took the patience of the chaplain to show him that being a fool with no sense of judgement was preferable to the vast selection of other things that might have described him.

It bothered him sometimes that Johanna might have been right, that there must have been a bit of evil. At the very least there had been a fair amount of bitter and twisted thinking. No idea where it came from but it had been there. Would still be if Father Larry hadn't tried to help him unravel some of it. Showed him ways to spot the 'hard-done-by' little kernel that was planted deep inside him. To recognise the little hard nut each time it threatened to sprout. Not give it a chance to grow. How to turn it on its head and break off the growing shoot.

"You could start with being polite and co-operative with the warders." Father Larry had ignored the puff of air from Declan's lips. "Alright, make it harder for yourself if you like." He paused a moment before standing up.

"Are you going already?" Declan looked up at him.

"They have a job to do, Declan." He sat down again on the edge of the bench. "Even if you don't like what they do or their tone or anything else about them, remember they've a lot to put up with in here and they mightn't like your attitude either. My advice is that if you want a quiet life just go along with the system, because believe me you're not going to change it. Harder men than you have tried. And failed."

The temptation to resist it was more his way but he remembered having bitten back the smart answer at the time.

"You might think you know better but you need to get something into your head – they don't need your approval." Father Larry raised an eyebrow, shaking his head slowly. "Just remember this. They're not interested in your opinion. They're just here to do a job and . . . they're the ones in charge."

He could still see how the priest had cocked his head to one side and looked straight into his face as if watching the message sink home. And he could still remember the faint smile of the chaplain as he said 'Amen' and stood up.

The growing-up didn't happen quickly, nor did learning a few basic social skills. It didn't need to. He was in for a long stretch. Time was something he had plenty of.

Probably no bad thing. For an otherwise bright boy, when it came to some things, he was a bit of a slow learner.

"Just be civil and keep the head down."

"Don't get involved with the other prisoners unless it is absolutely necessary."

Advice not taken on board the first time. The message that an Irish bog-trotter would be no match for some of them eventually sank home, but not before the guidance had been ignored, resulting in a split lip and an arm almost wrenched from its socket. Those painful lessons ensured he paid more heed after that.

Looking back, he wondered at Father Larry's persistence. How he had tolerated him doing the big fellow every visit. The very thing that had him where he was.

The priest just sat there each time and ignored it. Had waited until he'd blown himself out and then changed the subject as if the storm had never raged. Why he didn't just give up on him was a mystery. Had he been in the priest's situation he would have admitted defeat. But not Father Larry. The unruffled demeanour, the passive look on the face was an irritant sometimes as he sat opposite on each visit. A man in no hurry, someone with nothing better to do than sit there and listen and wait. Not that he'd worked out the waiting bit. Not then.

Some days he couldn't stop himself. Saw it as a competition, where he'd sit obstinate and bullish, arguing, pushing the limit until he felt the little niggle of fear inside. Afraid sometimes that his tongue might cause the chaplain to snap, to drive him to a point where he might not return, and he wasn't exactly inundated with visitors. Eventually it was this fear that helped the lesson register. He found himself, just when he arrived at the brink, that maybe it would be wiser to button his lip. It was all becoming clearer now. All part of the plan to allow enough time for him to master the basics. No rush. He was going nowhere. The priest could afford to wait. It would take as long as it took.

When he considered the time was right, when he had arrived at a more receptive stage, Father Larry set him a few challenges. Put no pressure on him. No hard sell. Just suggested things and left him to take it or leave it. They hadn't all come out in a list. More a drip-feeding over the years. A new one every few visits, whether or not he'd accepted or rejected the previous one. Had waited until he was fairly certain that the old Declan sneer had been absent for a while before he suggesting reading a little from the Bible he always carried with him.

"Well, what did you think of it?"

"Made no sense. A child saying to his ma that he was going off to tell people how to live and she could hump off if she didn't like it? Sure I know what I'd have got from my mother if I'd tried that one."

"Here, try this one then. You might find it more relevant." He leafed through the dog-eared pages. "The Prodigal Son."

"What's the point?" Declan turned sideways in his seat, crossing his legs away from the priest. "The last one was fairly boring."

The chaplain stood up.

"It's up to yourself but maybe you'd find this one more interesting. A fellow who took a foolish road and was given a second chance." He held the book out and saw the flick sideways of Declan's eye.

"Here, give us it." He uncrossed his legs and reached out for the book that the priest held between them. "I suppose I've nothing better to read anyway."

Chapter 45

Half the population of the city were homeless after the fires that followed the earthquake. Not sure if he could still detect it in his nostrils, he sniffed the air to see if the residue of the smoke still lingered.

"Have you a cold or something?" Father Eugene's Kerry accent was as strong as if he'd left Ireland yesterday instead of the thirty years it had been.

"No, no, I'm fine," Declan reassured him.

The sniffing was in danger of turning into a habit. Father Eugene wasn't the first to have asked the question. He found himself doing it each time he went out into the air. He would have to rein that in, not let it become like an uncontrollable tic that he couldn't let go of.

"Funny, but I sometimes think I can smell the smoke." Explaining might help to put an end to it. Reduce the danger of coming across as a bit of an oddity. "You were here at the time. Can you still get the whiff or is it just me?"

"Sometimes I think I can but I'm not sure if I'm imagining it."

Declan glanced down at his shoes as they walked along the dusty pavement in silence. His uncle had bought them for him along with a few clothes to start him off in his new life. They had been walking for half an hour and by now a coating of grey hid the brown leather. Maybe he should have worn his old ones.

The priest was easy to be with even though he'd had to slow his pace to allow for the limp. He didn't seem to expect much conversation from him. He wasn't sure if it was because of the old man's heavy breathing as they headed up the slopes of the steeper streets, but it suited. There was so much to take in and he needed space in his head to accommodate it after so many years of nothing but sameness day after day.

He could never have imagined it. He'd heard of natural disasters occasionally happening around the world but they'd always seemed like something that struck a different planet, another world, and without consequences for real people. At least not the sort of people he knew. Like it happened to people who were made of sterner stuff, who didn't feel what ordinary folk might, a different species built to withstand such hardships.

They were on their way to visit a refugee camp.

"We're nearly there."

Father Eugene had eased him in gently, had already taken him to various shelters to give him some idea of the problem. The rows and rows of temporary huts in the last one were impressive. Must have taken a lot of organisation. How did anyone even know where to begin?

"Prepare yourself for this one. It's in a different league to the others. This one is on a whole different scale."

They walked past what remained of the walls of buildings and turned the corner, Declan watching the pavement for stray rubble. He was a couple of yards ahead before he realised that Father Eugene had stopped. He looked behind him to check. The priest seemed to have forgotten him, his attention directed at something in the distance.

Declan followed his gaze.

"What . . . ?" He stopped in his tracks. His jaw fell open as he gawped at the vast expanse of tents and makeshift shelters spread over acres. "Look at that. Sure our food centre is only a drop in the ocean, we can't sort this."

He hadn't been aware he'd said it aloud until he heard the sharpness in the old priest's voice when he said, "I hope you're not suggesting we shouldn't try?"

"No, no . . . I'm only saying there's thousands of them."

"Well, every little bit helps." Father Eugene sounded resigned. "We can only do what we can do. We can't save the world. But it doesn't mean we shouldn't try."

They stood watching the activity below.

"The Army, they're doing their best too. Could you imagine if they gave up? Where would the people be then?"

Declan was only half listening, unable to take in the vista before him.

"They can't sort it out either but the people didn't know where to start when it happened. They needed someone to show them how. That's when the Army came in."

"And where did they start? Sure you wouldn't know where to begin with all that devastation."

"Well, they had to work it out too. But they provided a sense of order and that was important. They behaved as if they knew what they were doing, even if they didn't and that was what the people needed in the beginning. When they were in shock. To feel somebody was in charge. That someone somehow had a plan." He paused, as if waiting for Declan to digest what he was seeing.

"I wouldn't know what to do."

"We all thought that. Sure nobody had any experience of something on this scale. There's a bit of a system in place now but it didn't start out like that. Just grew gradually. One thing led to another."

Declan breathed out, his shoulders relaxing slightly.

"Yes, the Army was a great help," said the priest. "Someone taking control. It motivated some of the people to get going again and establish some sort of a routine in their lives. Even if it isn't home. None of these people have a choice, for the moment anyway."

The vacant faces distracted Declan. The man in the grey jumper, his back bent forward, his head resting on his hands. His wife sat on the plank beside him. She stared into space, her neck sunk into her sagging shoulders, scarcely able to hold her head up. Their very reason for living gone up in smoke. He stared at them, wondering what that might have been. What sort of a life they had lost. Whatever it was, didn't matter. It had been theirs and now it was gone, never to be restored as it had been, despite the reconstruction efforts of the city.

He was glad the priest remained silent. Nothing he could have said would have as much impact. For the first time in his life he could see how the little story in front of him told a much bigger picture. In this pair he could see what the future held for so many. And for himself.

"I'd say some of them will be here long enough." The priest spoke quietly. "There'd be a lot that'll never manage to move on. They're the ones we'll be left dealing with, I daresay, in the years to come."

Declan couldn't take his eyes off them. They were near enough to make out how the shock of it all was embedded in their very being. Nothing remained of the people they must have been. Dried-out shells with the life sucked out of them and too old to start again. For the first time he could see a purpose. Something to justify his existence.

Father Larry had been right. It was rough those first weeks. Declan's nose curled at the unwashed stench of hopelessness as they filed in and queued.

"Don't worry, you'll soon get used to it," the volunteer working alongside him at the soup cauldron assured him in a voice that would have sounded overly cheery only that it matched his rosy cheeks.

Ashamed he'd noticed his distaste, Declan tightened the muscles in his face, hoping to discipline it to maintain a bland unreadable expression. He ladled the soup into the bowl, added a slice of bread and handed it into the outstretched hands of the waiting woman.

"Would you try serving it with a smile? All part of the service. It costs nothing extra." Ruddy winked at the woman, one of the regulars, and put his hand to his mouth as he whispered the loud aside to Declan.

She laughed and walked away with her lunch.

"See. We've made her day now. Might be the only bit of entertainment she gets."

Declan scowled at him, trying to suppress a grin.

"We could all be in the same boat if we hadn't been the lucky ones to be somewhere else at the time." Ruddy kept up the chat as the line snaked along. "It didn't matter if you were rich or poor, you hadn't a chance. If anything good came of it, it was that for once everyone was equal."

Declan wished he'd stop his nattering. He just wanted to serve these people as fast as he could until he could see the end of the line. It stretched back to the door of the church, four or five abreast. Some of the family groupings added a lightness. The playful squabbles of siblings broke through the dejected air that hung over the singles and silent couples in the queue. Here and there children's chatter forced the odd smile from a mother or father.

"I think we might need to give smaller portions?" Declan could see people through the door and shadows of a queue continuing down the steps.

"Maybe I'll slip out and make a rough count." Ruddy

hung his ladle on the side of the cauldron and as he did Father Eugene arrived up to the table.

"Where are you going? You can't leave now. It's all hands on deck. They're way up the street. I went to the corner and I could see the queue disappearing around the next one. There seems to be no end to it."

"What'll we do if the soup runs out?" Declan speeded up the service. "I'm already giving smaller helpings."

"They're making more in the kitchen and it's nearly ready. You keep the lines moving here while I get a few more to come out and serve."

"I suppose when it runs out, it runs out?"

"Will you stop that? You'll start a riot if they hear you."

The edge in the priest's tone cut him – he was doing his best.

"When the others come out, maybe you'd go and clear some of the tables. Give you a bit of a break."

Chapter 46

"What are you saying? That I shouldn't have ambition?"

"No. That's not what I mean. I want you to think about where your ambition led you last time."

"I've changed." He didn't need a reminder from the tight-lipped priest who stood at the sink, washing the cutlery and crockery after the lunch.

"Perhaps." He looked at Declan. "But we all need to consider things sometimes. Check ourselves and why we are doing things and look at the way we might be doing things."

Declan was annoyed with himself for his earlier carelessness, something that would handicap him for days. The turnip had been tough, tougher than he'd expected and the blade had slipped. Father Eugene had had to take over the preparation of the vegetables for the soup while he tried to stem the flow of blood. And now he was only fit for drying-up.

He stood there, impatient for him to pass over the last of the bowls. He would show him how he'd changed. It felt better when he could work hard. Harder than everyone else.

"I'm just saying there's ambition and ambition. And there's also how you go about achieving it. You're in too much of a rush. There aren't any short cuts to getting there."

He stopped the retort that was rushing up, about to be spat out at the elderly priest. He was already losing some of the lessons he'd learned from Father Larry. It hadn't taken much for the old impatience to return. Maybe it was the gash in his hand that had him narky. A few deep breaths to calm the irritation. He knew the man was right but he didn't want a halter put on him, now that he was beginning to learn the ropes.

"It's not all about getting them in and out. Your ideas are good. But not for this place. It may just be a job to you but to them it's an anchor. It doesn't need to be a more efficient operation."

Declan drew back his waiting hand and leaned against the drainer. What was the rush? He watched in silence as the priest turned back to washing the last of the dishes.

"I'm just asking you to think about that when you're tempted to take the fast route. And I'm not only talking about this place." He passed the last handful of cutlery to Declan. "There's a rhythm to life. Just go with it. That's all I saying, Declan."

He turned and looked around in search of a towel. Picking up a damp one from the drainer he leaned his back against the sink and dried his hands slowly.

"I may be old and while you mightn't think it I do know what I'm talking about." He hung the towel from the edge of the drainer and heaving himself upright gave Declan a pat on the arm before limping away.

Declan looked after him. Dot and Carry One. He smiled at the old schoolboy joke. The Master back home never knew his own nickname even though he was a stickler for the decimal sums.

The cut on his finger stung. He was glad to be finished

the cleaning-up for the day so he could dry the wound and put a fresh bandage on it. He welcomed the pain. Another small instalment off his debt. He peeled the damp fabric from his finger and examined the cut. The skin, now soft and spongy, was in danger of starting to bleed again. If it did he'd be useless again tomorrow. He'd let the air at it for a while. Just like his mother used to recommend.

Walking the streets in the evenings helped with the geography of the place. He looked forward to the day's work being finished when he was free of responsibility and could go off wandering into his own time.

He pulled the crumpled sheet of paper from his pocket. Not so much need to use it now as the streets were becoming more familiar, but he liked the security of the rough map he'd drawn for himself. In the early days with so many buildings gone there were few landmarks to memorise and he'd had difficulty identifying the unsupported walls of empty-eyed windows and the chimneystack pillars that spiked up into the sky with no buildings attached.

He stood at the corner of Union Square and looked around. He couldn't get his head around how fast the restoration of the city was progressing. By the time he'd arrived most of the rubble in the main areas had been cleared and rebuilding had commenced.

He'd watched the changes from week to week as work advanced until the dereliction had almost been blotted out. It was beyond him how it was beginning to look as if the earthquake had never happened.

Faces became recognisable. Some of them users of the facilities at the Centre – the ones lying under shrubs in green areas for shelter or shade. If they were asleep it made things easier. Then he hadn't the worry of wondering whether he should acknowledge them or not.

"Just put yourself in their shoes," Father Eugene had advised him. "If you do that you'll know what to do. There's no right or wrong way. No need to agonise over it."

"I'm not sure if they'll be embarrassed that I see them sleeping out."

"Don't worry about it. If they look at you just respond with a nod or a smile and if they ignore you they either don't recognise you or don't want to. You'll get the feel of it in time."

Declan looked doubtful.

"How would you like to collect some of the food donations this week? Father Tom is off on retreat for a few days."

"If you tell me where to go. It'll make a change from stirring the pot." He grinned.

This was the stuff that magically appeared after the shops closed. In some cases it was left anonymously and randomly, in others it was a regular donation – like the crate of fruit and vegetables that arrived on the step on Saturday evenings. This came after the food kitchen closed and it was Declan's responsibility to wait for it and see that it was taken in before being stolen. One evening he had bumped into a burly man with a woolly cap, yellowed strands of curly hair escaping from under it, laying it down on the steps. As he straightened Declan tried to make conversation but the man just turned his bulk away, without making eye contact, and waddled off down the street.

"I was just going to ask him to leave it around the side. Put it in the shed if he was going to be late with it," Declan grumbled to Father Eugene as he heaved the crate onto the table. "I don't think that's too much to ask."

"Look, we're hardly in a position to complain, now are we? If he's good enough to give us the stuff for free, the least you can do is wait and take it in. You might ask yourself if that's too much to ask?"

The priest's response had silenced him. He'd been tempted to argue but he knew this led nowhere. One of the things Father Larry had instilled into him. This had been one of the hardest things to put a lid on, but he knew the priest's way worked, made life easier. Every time it happened again he was disappointed at how little he'd changed. The old resentments were still there. He wanted them extinguished completely but there were still traces, hidden deep but still capable of bobbing to the surface. Times when he felt like giving up. Maybe he wasn't able to change. Not really, not fully. The one thing kept him from allowing his doubts to drown him, from giving up the effort was Father Larry's advice. It was like a crutch that he'd come to rely on. *"Just write it off as a bad day and start again tomorrow. Nothing feels as bad after a good night's sleep."* The words echoed from the prison. *"And, anyway, the only bad day you'll have is one where you don't learn something new."*

What had changed, what he'd learned and it worked most times, was to listen to the rebukes, button his lip and filter the truth. Buttoning his lip was the difficult bit. The thing he had to work hardest on, knowing it was the key to achieving a bit of progress. On good days he could see the truth in that. Harder to do it on days when he didn't think before objecting to some petty inconvenience.

"Anyway, he's deaf and dumb so you'd be wasting your time."

"Who?" Declan's thoughts had strayed.

"The fruit-and-veg man."

"Oh, I didn't realise."

"A lot of things you don't realise, Declan. Just so you know. His name is Johnnie. He was one of our first people to come here for a feed when we opened. Everyone has their story. It was a supplier who gave him a chance." Father Eugene glanced at Declan. "Just like you've been given." A slight pause – just long enough for the dig to sink in. "And sure look at Johnnie – he's never looked back since."

"I suppose." Declan picked up an orange and began to peel it. "Makes you think, doesn't it?"

"Indeed it does."

Chapter 47

The Centre was almost empty. Most people just had their food and left. But there were always a few regulars who hung around well into the afternoon, nowhere to go and with nothing to do. They'd usually come late when the rush was over, so that they wouldn't be put under pressure to give up their space at the bench table. Glad to be under cover and out of the weather, to have a place to rest instead of wandering aimlessly around the city. They'd spin it out as long as they could inside, a few hours respite from the chill of the breeze and the misty damp of the streets.

Declan cleared the last of the pots and ladles from the serving table and poured a mug of tea for himself. He noticed the man walking towards him, his pace slow. He hoped he wasn't going to ask for something he'd already packed away.

"Don't suppose there's a chance there's a sup of tea left in that?" He nodded towards the big kettle and held out his mug to Declan for a top-up.

"You're lucky. The last drop." Declan handed it back to him. "Just check if there's some milk left in that jug."

The man shuffled to the side table and emptied the last of the milk into his mug.

"Here, it's empty now." He handed the jug to Declan.

"Thanks. That's the last of the tea anyway. There'll be nobody else needing milk and I take mine black." Declan picked up his own mug. "Where are you sitting? Mind if I join you?"

Pointing with his free hand to a table in the corner, the man turned and strolled towards it.

Declan came out from behind the serving counter and followed the stooped back. Swinging his leg over the bench, he pushed the debris on the table to one side out of the way with his forearm.

He'd seen the man over the weeks coming in clutching a frayed shopping hold-all. He always sat on his own if there was a bench free. Otherwise he'd sit at the end of a table, leaving a couple of spaces between himself and the other occupants. Sometimes he might exchange a few words with others but more often than not he sat looking into space after he'd eaten, with the faraway look of one unaware of his surroundings. There were moments when he returned to the present, like a man coming out the other side of a fog. Declan had seen him glance around at others, in puzzlement, like he was unsure how he'd arrived here.

"I'm Declan." He stretched his hand across the table.

"I know. I've heard them calling you." He took the outstretched hand. "Bernard. Bernie."

He opened the buttons of his coat, revealing a grey waistcoat underneath, the trace of an old soup stain on the front. The brown overcoat was old but the quality, the ghost of a more affluent time, could still be detected under the grubbiness that had matted the weave. Not something Declan would ordinarily have recognised except that it reminded him of a similar coat worn by his uncle on occasions when he visited the prison.

"Pleased to meet you, Bernie."

It was the absence of his normal vague air that Declan noticed first. Sipping his tea he waited for Bernie to speak. Now that they were seated, facing one another, introductions over, Declan didn't quite know how to continue. Maybe Bernie felt his presence at the table an intrusion. The thought made him want to stand up and get busy again, already regretting the offer to join him. He pushed away the doubts, the old awkwardness that threatened to drown him. Wait, just wait. The quiet chatter of the few groups left in the room amplified the lack of conversation between them. He drummed his fingers lightly on the table top and as he did so could feel Bernie's mind slide away to somewhere else.

When they came, the words were so quietly spoken that it took a few moments before he realised the old man was talking to him.

"The rest of the world asleep in their beds or going about their normal business and us rocking around like a ship on a stormy sea not knowing what was happening."

Coming from the silence as they did, Bernie's words riveted him to the seat. He stopped his drumming now that conversation had started. It took a few seconds before he realised what the old man was talking about.

"Where were you at the time?" He looked straight at Declan.

"Me? I was in Boston." He hoped Bernie wasn't going to ask too many questions.

"So you knew nothing about it then?"

"I heard talk ... and read a bit about it in the papers."

"Not the same. You can't begin to imagine what it was like." Bernie shook his head slowly.

"What about you? Where were you when it happened?" Declan steered the conversation away from his own history.

"At home in my bed. What woke me up was when the bed rocked so hard my head started hitting the wall. I didn't know what was happening. Books started falling and then the whole bookcase keeled over." He paused. "I jumped out of the bed and went to the window and I could see people appearing like ghosts out of the smoke and dust, still in their nightgowns."

"Did you guess it was an earthquake?"

"Only when I saw the buildings gone, nothing but rubble left. I knew then and I knew mine might be the next one to go."

"What did you do?"

"I froze. I'd never seen anything like it before. I'd no idea what to do. I could see a child running down the middle of the road with her little dog under her arm. Her mouth was open screaming, but I couldn't hear what she was shouting." He looked into the distance as if seeing her again.

"What happened then?" Declan was impatient for him to continue. He'd heard stories before from some who wanted to talk about it. Everyone's version was different. And there were others who came in who never mentioned the earthquake, like it had never happened. Or more likely they wanted to forget that it had.

"I knew then I had to move. I jumped into my trousers and shirt and grabbed my coat and ran into the street."

Declan watched the pale scum form on the tea as it grew cold in Bernie's mug. Resisting the urge to tell him to drink it up, he could see the man was no longer there at the table with him but in the middle of the chaos again.

"It was like the end of the world. All the people shouting and crying as the buildings toppled around us." His voice rose. "We were trying to run to the empty spaces where they had already collapsed and we were all turning grey from the dust. And then the pipes burst." The horror surged from his eyes. "And there were fountains shooting

255

up in the street and then the fires started."

His eyes darted around as if watching it all before him and then he paused as the faraway look settled again, wiping away the scene.

"It was a miracle any of us survived."

The signs were all there. Bernie was one of the many unable to get a life together again after the disaster, just as Father Eugene had predicted.

Declan lay on his side in the bed, the faint smell still in his nostrils. He thought of the casual farm workers at home, their coats tied with bits of rope, the ones who came every season to help with the harvest. Earthy bodies that wouldn't have seen a bath too often either, but he couldn't remember that same smell of hopelessness as they trooped into the kitchen for the feed of bacon and cabbage. Although dependent on the seasonal labour for survival they lacked the aura of deprivation that these shells of men carried in through the door of the charity kitchen.

He lay there trying to figure it out, trying to find what it was that made the difference. The ruddy Irish faces danced before his eyes. The work, more than just money to feed their children, was a social event. The laughter, the banter and the opportunity to exchange news sat lightly on the communal pride in their usefulness. Being part of something where they shared the unspoken knowledge that the farmers were as dependent on them as they were on the work. The constancy of it. Decades, if not centuries of knowing their place was there, unchanged. Waiting for them when the season came around. Somewhere mixed up in all that lay the difference. Unlike Bernie. Nothing now to go back to and, worse still, no energy to start again. His place, his people had all gone.

He'd never have been interested in working things out

before, things that didn't directly affect him. Strange to admit his spell in prison had helped. He could smile about it now. Could have done without that experience maybe, but perhaps there had been a reason, a purpose in it.

He turned over onto his back and stared at the ceiling. The tiny black spores of mould on the ceiling, dozens of them in the corner, evidence of a window closed too long. A crane fly buzzed, struggling to escape the web that trapped him. The web had been there for weeks without any activity. He'd meant to remove it, the spider who'd woven it long gone.

Where might he have ended up had what happened not happened? No point in thinking about that now. It had churned around his head long enough in the cell. Unaware at the time it was anything other than passing the time.

The buzzing started to get into his brain. He got up from the bed. His jacket, hanging on the back of the bedroom chair, fell to the floor as he moved the chair into position underneath the cobweb. Stepping up on it he steadied himself and, cupping his hands, rescued the crane fly. He picked off as much of the sticky web from its long legs as he could without tearing its limbs off. Using his elbow he pressed on the handle of the window. It was stiff, reluctant to yield to the pressure. With both hands occupied he wasn't sure how he would manage to open it if it didn't give. As he pressed harder a pain shot up his arm and at the same time he felt the handle move. With the knob of his elbow he pushed it open wide enough to allow his hands fit through. He laid the fly, its body still partially encased in threads, on the windowsill. It would have to work on freeing itself further. He could do no more for it.

* * *

The queue snaked around the block three times a week. They didn't have the funds to open the centre every day but the odd stray caller was never sent away empty-handed on the in-between days.

His cup of tea after the lunch before doing the final clearing was more to give them time to vacate the place. Jumping into action as soon as the last soup was served made it seem like you were anxious to finish up, to rush them. He'd learned that. You might have plans, you might be in a hurry, but remember they had nowhere to rush to.

It had taken a long time, to find his place and understand his purpose, for Father Eugene's advice to sink home, to become part of him until he hardly remembered from where it had come. It wasn't until he met the hairy man that he knew he'd arrived.

He's spotted him quietly humming to himself at the next table, a tune that Declan didn't recognise. He was leaning back in the chair, his dirty overcoat hanging open to reveal another thin beige one underneath. The chair creaked under the weight of him, his tuneful humming taking him into some half-forgotten world.

Declan listened, watching and wondering.

"What you looking at?" The voice was thick.

"I was just listening . . . enjoying the tune."

"Name it."

The suddenness of the challenge startled him.

"I can't. That's why I was . . . to see if I could recognise it."

"*Ha.* Ya see. Ya can't." The twinkle of the blue eyes in the bulbous face surprised him. "Tchaikovsky."

"I'll take your word for it. Can't argue with that." Declan grinned. "I wouldn't be that well up."

"I played the horn in orchestra for years. Europe. America. Played all over world, in all the big cities in

America." He nailed Declan with a look as if expecting to be contradicted. "Yes, I did. I wasn't always like this, ya know." The challenge back again.

Declan didn't know whether to believe him. "Do you play at all now?"

"Can't. Earthquake. Injured. Look ..." He opened his mouth.

It was hard to see anything under the wild beard that covered most of his face.

"What am I looking at?"

He bared his teeth.

"Look. No front teeth. Building fall, big rocks knocked me over. Bashed face, and shoulder no good anymore too. Can't play."

"God, that's awful."

"You'd never think I was classical musician now, would you?" The man gazed into the middle distance. "Well, I suppose I'm not . . . not now anyway. Not anymore."

His accented way of speaking suggested eastern European. Declan didn't ask. There must be a story there. He had been advised not to ask too many questions. If someone seemed inclined to want to talk, just listen. Look interested but no probing. Some just wanted the food and too many questions might frighten them into not returning. No problem with that. He himself wouldn't want anyone asking him questions. Particularly the Irish. They were the ones who always asked the most. He'd never noticed before but they always wanted to know where you were from, what brought you to America and what you'd been doing there. Wanting to see if they knew any of your kith or kin, always looking for connections. Always with this curiosity about them and while it might have its uses if you'd nothing to hide, in his case it had its drawbacks. That had been the easiest bit for him, to understand and remember why some of the users of the Centre might not welcome too much delving.

Some of the more reticent sometimes had a way of drip-feeding their story to you. A little bit one week. How they'd come to the States after the Famine. Nothing the next week and then if you just listened and asked nothing of them they might come to entrust you with a big chunk of their life. How their lives began falling apart slowly over fifty years since. Drink. Lonesomeness. The bad luck that had followed them across the Atlantic Ocean and no family to fall back on here.

Some were so wrapped up in their own story that they didn't notice how little Declan revealed of himself. He wanted to but the fear of their knowing someone who knew someone never left. He wasn't that person now.

The slow unravelling of the stories was his education. If only they knew. He owed them. They were what kept him going, attached to the squalor of their lives, unable to leave this new family. He could never admit to any of them that he'd had it all. Had thrown it all away without recognising its value. Only now realising when it was too late. Could never tell them in case it was the story of their life too.

MARIA

Chapter 48

Halifax, Nova Scotia, Canada
1912

He worried that he mightn't recognise her. Little more than a baby when he left Ireland, they'd only met a few times since.

The awfulness of the task ahead turned round and round in his head. Based in New York as she was, with all the travelling a lady's companion was expected to do, he hadn't seen her in years. He regretted that now, his lack of effort. No bond between them. Brother and sister but little more than strangers.

He rested his head on the seat back and gazed out at the dark evening. The rain ran down the carriage windows in rivulets and into the void inside him. The loss now, as he sat on the cold train had hollowed out a cavity, a hole that could never be filled if she was amongst the drowned. His own flesh and blood and he hadn't made the effort. It had been up to him. The big brother, the successful businessman. But she had never asked for help, never looked to him for a job. And so she'd been forgotten by him. It said a lot about her. But even more about himself and what it told him was not good.

Johanna returned to the carriage, sat down and opened her travel bag.

"Would you like a sandwich?" She pulled out the package and began to unwrap it. "It might be a while before we have an opportunity to get something to eat."

He was glad that she hadn't been in a talkative mood throughout the journey. She spoke only when it had been required and then only about practicalities. Both had avoided talking about their sister as if it wasn't necessary, as if by some miracle she was going to be alive when they arrived.

Doubt began to creep in as the train neared Halifax. He was the obvious one to make the journey but he knew he couldn't have done it on his own. Maybe he wouldn't even recognise her. The last time they'd met was when she accompanied her employer on a trip to Boston and he had taken them to dine in a hotel. That had been five years ago. He was glad that Johanna had agreed to come with him. She had written regularly to Maria and they'd exchanged photos. He was ashamed that he'd only ever looked at them in a cursory way.

He tried to picture Maria now. Tall, slim, stylish and with the self-assuredness of a well-travelled woman. Couldn't have described her individual features in any great detail, although he hoped that wouldn't be necessary. Johanna would know.

He was proud of Maria. Of where she came from and where she'd arrived at. At first glance he could see she had turned into a smart independent lady. Obviously clever. He smiled at the thought that she was a little like himself. Her quick wit had left him in no doubt as to why her employer wished to keep hold of her. He had a sense that she was unimpressed by his business empire, probably confident enough in her own success. He wouldn't have minded having her on his staff.

"You need to get out more, Hugh. The world is big." She teased. "Bigger than us."

He felt dull in her company. Something that took him by surprise. After family conversation was exhausted, business topics seemed grey in comparison to her travels.

She'd been right. He needed to see the world and have a bit of fun. Uncomfortable to realise he'd never done that, never tested himself to see if he was capable. Now that she might be gone, the thought that she had enjoyed her life, used her talents to their fullest, might be some comfort. But it was too soon to think about that. Yet. He could still see her smiling face, could hear her laugh. A short visit. It was the warmth of their mother which seeped through her that had left the strongest memory. And now it might be all gone and he hadn't bothered to keep in touch except for the occasional postcard. Not even a full letter.

The subject of every conversation around the world, a disaster no-one ever considered could happen. The *Titanic*. Unsinkable. Its claim to fame. It was like the Lord sent this punishment for such arrogance. But why should the harsh punishment be visited on the passengers? Surely they were blameless, not the ones to be chastised.

Even if she were amongst those recovered following the sinking of the great ship, would she be recognisable? All their hopes lay with himself and Johanna finding her. He couldn't come back and tell the family he wasn't sure.

He pulled his collar up against the cold wind. He was unsure if the smell of death permeated the air or if it was his imagination. He stood back to allow the men carrying the coffins pass, holding out his arm to halt Johanna in her tracks. They waited until the men passed, without a word or a glance exchanged, before heading towards the building that had been set up as a temporary morgue.

A well-dressed woman in black coat and stylish hat exited the building. An older man, too old to be her husband, had his arm around her shoulder. She was weeping quietly. The lace-edged handkerchief she held to her face seemed a futile effort at retaining a semblance of normality in her elegant life. Were her tears for a body identified in the morgue or disappointment at one not found?

He held back a moment, allowing Johanna to enter before him. He closed the door quietly behind them, his mind still on the woman, unsure which result he wanted their own visit to yield. At this stage there was no other possibility. His head told him that, but a glimmer of hope he knew to be foolish still flickered in his heart.

Back at the hotel he drew his chair closer to the fire, trying to warm himself with a whiskey. Johanna had already gone to bed and he was alone. His earlier dread outside the morgue should he find Maria's body no longer lingered. The death of hope no longer a problem. As the whiskey took hold he regretted his earlier anger at the authorities. So many funerals had taken place for those buried at sea, without an attempt to take them to shore.

"You have to understand, sir, they couldn't."

"But why the hell couldn't they? We might have been able to identify them if they'd bothered."

"Hugh, would you calm down!" Johanna gripped his arm. "You can't go attacking people. They're all doing their best."

"Sir, you don't realise, it wasn't possible. You see some of them were so badly damaged they were unrecognisable." The priest spoke softly, the pain evident on his face as he tried to calm Hugh. He'd had to deal with this reaction many times in the last few days.

"But the relatives might have been able to recognise them."

"They wouldn't. Believe me they wouldn't have been

able to." He could see that Hugh was not convinced. "A lot of them were already decomposing, sir. I'm really sorry." He watched as the shoulders of the man before him slumped.

"Your relative?" He looked at Johanna.

She nodded. "Our sister Maria."

Hugh looked at the priest. "Sorry, I shouldn't have shouted at you. It's not your fault."

"You're upset. It's natural. Don't worry about it." He grasped Hugh's elbow and gave it a gentle squeeze. "That's the least of the problems."

Hugh nodded. In the uncomfortable silence that followed, he feared the priest would leave them and was glad when Johanna filled the gap.

"She was accompanying an elderly lady."

"Oh?" The priest waited.

"She survived."

"And could she give you any information about your sister?"

"They got separated," Hugh said. "But she told us she'd spoken to a man who said he tried to revive a woman who lay freezing in the bottom of a lifeboat, but she'd slipped away before the rescue ship arrived. He recognised her because he'd spoken to her on the ship. He'd often seen her walking on deck with an elderly woman." Hugh looked to Johanna for confirmation. "Said she was Irish and that she was living in New York."

"We're thinking it might have been Maria." Johanna looked at the priest hopefully.

"Well, if she was in a lifeboat it's likely the body was picked up. Are you sure you've looked everywhere. In the other section as well?"

"What other section?" Hugh looked at him sharply.

"We didn't realise there was another place." Johanna's face brightened. "No-one told us."

"Behind there." The priest pointed to a gap beyond the last row of bodies. "I'll come with you."

There was still a chance. Hugh's heart lifted as they walked in silence through the gap. They stopped at each body, the priest holding back, leaving a space between them as they looked. The hope and the dread that the next one might be her made Hugh's brain slow to focus. One by one they eliminated them. Too old, too young, wrong hair, too fat, too thin. It was in the second row he stopped, his chest tightening.

"Johanna. It's her."

The third body. Something familiar. One stud earring. He could feel his breathing constrict. An emerald. Similar to those he'd given her on that last visit. His hand reached out to move the lock of hair covering her right eye. A sound escaped as he touched her cold skin. He didn't know it came from himself as he felt the priest's hand on his shoulders.

Maria.

"It is her, isn't it, Jo?" He turned to his sister.

The tears running down her cheeks as she nodded told him all he needed to know. A mixture of relief and sorrow shook his frame. He was glad they'd found her. Too terrible to imagine her still lying alone in the freezing waters.

HUGH

Chapter 49

Boston

1912

Ireland was only a small part of the jigsaw of his life. A very early piece before he knew where he fitted into the world. He recognised it as a solid foundation upon which the bigger picture had been built but not somewhere he would ever fit into again. It wasn't somewhere he could or would ever go back to on a permanent basis. That was not something he'd ever contemplated.

Some of his acquaintances had never quite left their homeland behind. Despite varying degrees of success in America, for them there was still that tug. It showed in their maudlin talk after a few drinks around Christmas or St. Patrick's Day. No matter how long they'd spent in the States they were never able to cut the cord that pulled on their heartstrings. He was never quite sure if he pitied or envied them. Just something that never had a draw for him.

Nothing but the click of her knitting-needles and the odd crackle from the fire had broken the quiet as they sat, he reading his newspaper and she finishing off the back of a waistcoat.

"Do you ever miss it? Home." Johanna hadn't spoken for a while. She gave a cough to clear the hoarseness that had accumulated in her throat.

"No." He was aware of the irritation in his curt answer. She brought it up every so often and he was never sure if she did it deliberately to pile on the guilt or if it was nothing more than nostalgia on her part.

A silence followed as he continued reading his paper and it was the awareness of this hiatus that forced him to look up. She had come to the end of the row and her knitting was resting on her lap. The shadow of disappointment on her face told him she wanted to talk, but not to the back of a newspaper.

"Well, maybe." He felt forced to elaborate. "Sometimes." He hoped he was not opening the door too wide. "But sure I put it to the back of my mind. No point in dwelling on it."

"When something happens it makes you think, doesn't it?"

He folded the paper and put it on the side table.

"Like what? Is there something I don't know?"

"No, I'm just thinking. About poor Maria."

"What brought her into your head now . . . in relation to this?" He was puzzled.

"I don't know. Just thinking how little we knew of her life. She was our sister but she might have been just a friend that we saw occasionally."

"I know what you mean." He thought about it a moment. "I suppose that's the price you pay for leaving home. Going to a different country and building a new life. I should have made a better effort to keep in touch, especially when she came to the States."

"And too late now." Johanna's eyes filled. "A lesson for us all in that."

"Indeed there is. But you were better at it than I was. At least you kept in regular contact with her." He lay back against the headrest and gazed into the fire.

"Maybe I should have gone down to New York more to

visit her. God knows I had plenty of time once the children were grown up but I didn't make the effort." Johanna pondered. "I should have instead of always waiting until she was passing through Boston."

"Well, I was worse. Some of the times I was in New York on business I didn't even let her know. I should have made the time to take her out to dinner."

"But you did – you met her for dinner there."

"I know, but I'm thinking of the number of times I was just too busy and I didn't. Not a lot I can do about that now." His words were barely audible. "Except maybe learn from it."

The ticking of the hall clock muffled by the door soothed them as it penetrated the room, the soft monotonous sound matching their mood.

"I suppose I should think about a visit home at some stage," he said. The words were spoken quietly as if reluctant to disturb the air.

"You don't feel the years passing, sure you don't?" she said.

"I know and I've been meaning to go back and visit but there never seems to be a good time, what with one thing and another."

"Too busy to go home and visit your mother." She deliberately said the words softly to take the sting out of them, so he wouldn't feel it a criticism. She wasn't exactly in a strong position, not having been home herself. "Don't let's leave it until it's too late again."

He knew she was right.

Chapter 50

San Francisco

1912

About halfway through his business trip to the city, he contacted him. Said nothing to Johanna about his intention.

They sat over a drink in the hotel. He was surprised at the change in Declan. The complete turnaround. How he had become the conscience of the world.

"You must have noticed." Declan appeared surprised. "They're all over the city. Lounging around in the parks, nothing to do, nowhere to go."

Hugh was amused at getting a masterclass on social deprivation from his nephew. The first adult conversation that had ever taken place between them. He sat back and listened, allowing him the opportunity to share his newly discovered realities with his socially unaware uncle.

"They'd have bags or bundles with them, stuff wrapped in blankets, not the sort of things you'd be carrying around a city. You can pick them out a mile away."

"And you work with them?"

"Someone has to." He grinned. The pride in his tone belied the comment. "There are some who'll never recover enough to get their old lives back. I used to think it could be fixed but it can't."

"So why do you do it then?" Hugh challenged, interested

in seeing how deep the commitment went.

"I'm not sure." He looked at his uncle, taken aback by the question.

"There must be a reason?" Hugh waited.

"I suppose there must."

He watched the cogs turn as Declan, cupping his chin in his palm, resting his elbow on the table, mulled over it.

"I suppose even if you can't fix it, you can make their lives a bit easier. Even to know that there's someone willing to try, to even care. Yes, I suppose that might be it and because they have no-one else to turn to except us at the Centre." Declan picked up his drink and swirled it around his glass. He took a gulp and laid it back on the table. "That's one thing I've learned." He traced a groove on the glass, avoiding his uncle's eye. "I had the support and I threw it all away. Didn't recognise the value of it at the time."

"Sure didn't we all know everything when we were young? Couldn't be advised." Hugh smiled at him. "It's only as you get older you begin to realise just how little you really know."

"You've seen them huddled in doorways at night." Declan looked at his uncle. "I recognise how easily that could have been me if I hadn't been given that second chance."

It was the final two days of his trip and his meetings had thinned out. He smiled to himself at the thought that Johanna would kill him if he didn't take back some impressions of the city to entertain her with. His business meetings and encounter with Declan would not be the type of conversation she'd want to hear.

He was surprised at the progress made on rebuilding the city and work advanced on bigger projects. Dusk began to fall as he crossed the street and entered the park. It was as he strolled along the geometric paths of Union

Square on his way back to his hotel that he'd noticed her the first time. An elderly woman on her own sitting on one of the park benches, an old worn bag beside her. Now as he waited for traffic to pass before crossing the road from the Square he saw her again. She stood in the doorway of a tea-shop, her face relaxed into a soft smile as she watched the world pass by. He couldn't have explained what exactly it was that made him want to make contact with her. It was nothing more than an instinct, some unidentifiable air about her. It had been there on the other occasions, something familiar, but he'd been in too much of a hurry to concern himself with what it was that drew him to her. He was in no hurry now.

A few yards away from the tea-shop a man stood at the edge of the kerb with his hand out to the pedestrians. Hugh watched as some stepped sideways to avoid him, others ignored the plea and a few passers-by gave him money. What he noticed was that nobody spoke to him.

The woman wasn't with him but every so often her glance wandered in his direction to where he begged. It seemed as if to observe his success. Her bag hung over her arm, hands clasped in front of her. Not putting her hand out, just smiling at the people as they passed, maybe hopeful that if she made eye contact they might offer her something.

As Hugh waited on the kerbside it struck him. A recognition of the familiarity that was drawing him across the road. The hair combed back in a bun, tendrils escaping to frame her face, the way she held her bag and smiled at people who didn't see her. A pang of sadness hit him. An older, sadder version of his mother. Of the mother he remembered. He watched as she nodded to someone who had exchanged a greeting. She too was probably somebody's mother.

He backed away from the kerb and, walking slowly,

moved further along the side of the square. He wanted time to digest the similarity.

He stopped and turning around he watched, knowing she hadn't seen him. Tossing around the idea of approaching and giving her some money he watched her, looking for a clue that might confirm without doubt that she was homeless. He imagined the possibility of doing so, offering her money and finding out that she was just waiting to meet someone. If it happened to his own mother he wondered if she would be insulted or amused. As he considered the notion, a well of loneliness filled his chest, realising it was not a question he could answer. He no longer knew her nor she him. It had been so long since they'd been together that he couldn't be sure. He saw her seated at the kitchen table, imagined her telling the story and her eyes crinkling in amusement. But he couldn't be certain.

He crossed the road, moving at an angle away from the woman, before walking towards the window of a shop. He took a moment, pretending to peruse the array of cigars and pipes as he considered how to approach her.

He turned his head and glanced again with the sudden fear that she might have disappeared. He had to speak to her. He knew that was a certainty. Whatever this instinct was it didn't really matter. He couldn't ignore it, couldn't allow this opportunity to pass.

He walked slowly towards the tea-shop. As he came alongside, she turned, catching his eye and, without parting her lips, she smiled.

"Good evening." Hugh raised his hat slightly.

Her smile widened as she bowed her head in response as he hesitated in front of her.

"Oh, I see it's closed." A good opener, to see if she seemed inclined to talk.

"It is. It closes at seven. But there's another one a bit

further down the street that's open late if it's a cup of tea you're after."

It was the 'you're after' that surprised him, told him all he needed to know.

"Is that an Irish accent I detect?" He couldn't tell why, but he knew he just couldn't leave her.

"It sure is, sir."

Despite the Americanism there was no mistaking it.

"Let me guess. West of Ireland . . . maybe Kerry? Would I be close?"

"Spot on. But can you name the village?" Her eyes twinkled with teasing, the recognition of the invisible tribal bond wiping away all traces of neediness.

"Oh, you have me there. I'm not that good."

They both laughed.

"I'm only visiting here myself. As you've probably guessed." He paused, unsure how to advance the opportunity. "It's getting a bit cold. Maybe I'd better go and have that cup of tea."

He watched the shadow of disappointment pass over her face. He hesitated a moment before making the suggestion.

"Unless you are waiting for somebody, maybe you'd like to join me?" He seized his opportunity. What was the worst that could happen? That she might decline his invitation? Nothing to lose. "It would be nice to have the company." He hoped it didn't sound like a proposition. "And a chat between one Irish and another."

"I'd be delighted." She drew herself up straight and led the way, her step sprightly with the confidence of her local knowledge.

He held the door open for her. Smiling her thanks she led the way to a table in the corner, like someone who had been there before. A quick scan was enough to recognise it would not have been the café of his choice, but he was not going to object.

Noticing the greasy streaks on the table, he sat back on the chair, careful not to rest his elbows on it. The waiter approached and lifting up the salt and pepper pots gave the surface a wipe with a cold damp cloth, only partially removing the fatty film.

The place was quiet. Only one other occupant, an old man at a table in the far corner, away from the draught of the door. He sat reading a tattered newspaper, the cuffs of his jacket torn and as oily as the tabletop he leaned on.

"And what can I get you?"

"A pot of tea for two, please." Hugh looked across at his companion. "Anything to eat?"

"Well, are you having something to eat?"

He wasn't hungry but, not wanting to deter her from eating, he picked up the menu. Her uncertain tone made him wary, sensing she might decline through politeness.

"No, I've just had dinner. But don't let that put you off. You must have something."

Before she could respond he directed his attention to the grubby sheet of paper.

"Now what have we got here? A sandwich or what about a full fry? They have the works here. Bacon, sausages, eggs and a rake of toast. Go on, have that. Remind you of home." He looked across, teasing.

"Don't mind if I do. Thank you."

With a look in both directions she divided her thanks between Hugh and the waiter.

"Coming right up!"

A silence fell as they waited for the waiter to leave.

The loneliness she had stirred in him had disappeared and now that he had her he wasn't quite sure where to go from here. She smiled across at him and he smiled back.

Clearly happy to be in from the cold and basking in the comfort, she smiled again. It took him a while to realise that she had no intention of initiating conversation. As far as she was concerned, she had arrived. She was quite at peace in her silence. If he wanted conversation it was up to him to begin.

"Well, I suppose I'd better introduce myself. I'm Hugh McNamara. From County Clare."

"And I'm Nellie Kenneally."

"Nellie Kenneally. That's some name. A real Kerry one. I'm sure they must think you're joking when you tell them that name here in the States."

"Indeed they do. The policemen would nearly arrest you. They think you're giving cheek when you'd say that Nellie Kenneally is your name. I always have to keep some official documentation on me."

The mention of the police helped confirm his hunch.

"And do you have family here, Nellie?"

"I do." She paused. "I did. A husband and daughter. The earthquake. Before the earthquake."

He waited. As she looked towards the window, he could see her mind drifting off somewhere into the darkness outside, a tenderness descending on her face. He watched her process private memories, reluctant to take her back into the moment. As he waited, his own past drifted through his mind, taking him to a place he'd been reluctant to visit. The thoughts surprised him. Nothing to do with Ireland. Or his mother. He felt the welling under his eyelids.

"And you? Do you have a family?"

The question took him unawares, her direct gaze taking in his red rims.

"Yes, I do. Three boys and a girl."

"And a beautiful wife no doubt?"

He shifted slightly on his seat. This might not have been such a good idea. He glanced across at her, knowing already that she had not averted her gaze. She had noticed his emotion but seemed unperturbed at his embarrassment. He didn't know why, but he felt compelled to talk to her, share it with her. A total stranger. Old enough to be his mother.

"I had. She was beautiful. I never met anyone so lovely."

Reaching across, she patted the back of the hand that lay on the table.

"Like a Madonna she was, if that's not too strange a thing to say?" Surprised at how easy it was to tell her, he hardly recognised his own choice of words.

"Indeed it is not a bit strange. I know the type. Pure and radiant. Inside and out. Would that be it?"

"Exactly." Hugh looked at her, in relief at her understanding. He could never have described his wife so honestly or so accurately to anyone. "And forever young."

"You don't come across them often. You were lucky." She looked at him, nailing him with her eyes. "You do realise that, don't you? Even if you only had her for a short time. It's something you should treasure. Not something to be sad about."

"I do. But I lost her too soon."

"But that's the point. Some people never have that. Even for a short time." She paused, allowing him time. "What happened?"

"When the twins were born. It happened shortly after. She never really pulled up after the births. She had a weak heart."

"What a tragedy! The poor little mites! Growing up never knowing a mother."

"That was the awful thing. And they don't have any memory of her. Her softness. I never gave them a thought.

I was so wrapped up in myself and I feel so guilty now that I ignored them, like it was their fault. I was hard. Very hard."

"Ah, sure you had a terrible loss. It's understandable."

"But how could I have blamed two helpless babies? I'd created them."

"We've all done things we're ashamed of. It's not repeating the mistakes that's important. I'm sure you made up for it in other ways since."

"I tried to, but I think I went about it the wrong way. Tried to toughen them up. Not just the twins but the two older boys as well. Tried to prepare them for a life that mightn't always be easy. I didn't want them growing up soft. But I'm not sure that was the right thing to do. Although they've all turned out alright. And they don't seem to hold it against me."

"I'm sure you did your best and prepared them to face what might be ahead for them."

"I did that alright but maybe I overdid it." He looked at her. "I was lucky though – my sister Johanna had come over from Ireland and she was great with the children. I've always hoped that her ways with them might have diluted my tougher line. I don't know what I'd have done without her, what they'd have done without her."

He paused as the waiter arrived with the meal and waited as he put it down and went back to the counter to collect the teapot.

"Get that into you now and enjoy it." Hugh poured the tea, glad of the interruption.

She picked up her cutlery and cut into her egg as Hugh talked of the sights he'd seen in San Francisco between business meetings. He stretched it to give her a chance to eat in peace but that particular conversation didn't take long. A little uncomfortable as he neared the end, aware that he didn't quite know how to open the conversation on her life. Not even sure if he should.

"Well, how is the fry?" He nodded towards her plate. "It looks good. I'm only sorry now I've already had my dinner."

"Delicious. Fit for a king."

"Or a queen." He smiled at her as she laid down her cutlery. "More tea?"

She nodded as she savoured the last mouthful.

"And what about yourself? What brought you to San Francisco?" He watched her reaction.

"I ask myself that every day." She took a sip of tea before continuing. "I should have stayed at home." She gave a deep sigh. "If I had my life over again and knew all I know now, that's what I'd have done."

He looked at her, unsure if further probing might embarrass her.

"Oh, don't get me wrong. It was great at first." She brightened. "I was only a young one, full of dreams and romance. But sure you don't want to be hearing all that now. It didn't work out like I expected anyway. But sure isn't that the way of life? If we knew how things were going to turn out sure we mightn't be able to face it." She glanced at her almost empty cup and at the teapot.

Lifting the lid, Hugh checked. "There's a drop left."

"No point in wasting it."

"Indeed there's not." With a flourish he refilled her cup.

Before settling back on the chair he reached into his pocket and took out his watch.

"I'm afraid I'm going to have to leave you. I've some work to do for a meeting in the morning." He stood up. As he put his coat on he noticed the drops on the window. "I think it's started to rain. Can I escort you somewhere on the way back to my hotel?"

"Oh, no thank you. I think I'll just stay and finish the tea here if you don't mind and wait for the rain to pass."

He took out his wallet and produced a dollar bill. He made a show of looking for the waiter who was nowhere to be seen before putting the note down on the table.

"Can I leave you to look after the check then? I'm sorry now I have to leave you. A great pleasure talking to you, but I need to get back. It was lovely meeting you, Nellie Kenneally."

"Thank you very much, Mr. McNamara. I enjoyed our chat and the lovely meal. Much appreciated, sir.'

"Think nothing of it. My pleasure."

The big beam that shone up at him obliterated the pretence that both knew hovered between them.

"It was nice to meet someone from home. It can be very lonesome over here. Good to hear an Irish accent." Nellie's slight American accent had all but disappeared.

Picking up his hat from the chair he placed it on his head momentarily and before he turned to leave doffed it in her direction.

"Likewise. Goodnight now, Nellie … *slán agus beannacht.*" He grinned the Gaelic farewell at her and nodded to the waiter who was approaching the table. Out of the corner of his eye he saw Nellie hold out the dollar bill as though it had been her treat, her smiling face a picture of confidence.

The damp air hit him when he stepped out into the rain although it had eased to a light drizzle that was now fizzling out. The night no longer feeling cold he decided to walk back to the hotel, the loneliness having disappeared, left behind to mix with the condensation on the café window.

He nodded to the man at the Reception Desk as he crossed the hotel lobby.

"One – one – two, isn't it?" Turning away, he selected the keys from the hook and handed them to Hugh. "Mr.

McNamara. I think I have something else for you here."

He waited while the man bent down and produced a telegram from under the desk. He mumbled a hasty thanks as he took it, his face freezing in alarm. It was from Johanna. He wasn't expecting anything. Never liked telegrams. They meant only one thing. Taking his gloves off, he began pulling the telegram open as he went up the staircase. Just as he reached his door the words jumped out at him.

BAD NEWS. SORRY. MOTHER PASSED AWAY THURSDAY.

He crushed it in his hand as he fumbled with the keys in the lock, a rush of blood flooding his head. Inside the room he shoved the door shut. He winced as it banged louder than intended. Without removing his hat or coat he sat on the edge of the bed. He placed the telegram on his knee and smoothed it out as if he could wipe away the message. He read it again. The words hadn't changed. A childish impulse coursed through him, an urge to run back down the stairs, out into the night to find Nellie.

JOHANNA

Chapter 51

Boston

1925

It was lovely to get up in the quiet and pad down to the kitchen as dawn was breaking. A sacred time when the world seemed still, like there was nothing happening that might disturb the silence of the early hour. She'd grown used to the empty house. It had taken years but she now quite liked it. To open the window and let the morning in, carrying with it the light tweet of the birds.

Johanna raked the ashes and laid kindling and a few of last night's half-burnt cinders on the crumpled newspaper. She placed two split logs in a pyramid and knelt in front of the fireplace until she was sure the blaze had caught. Leaning on the armchair, she heaved herself up, careful to keep her blackened fingers from rubbing the soot onto the upholstery. She washed her hands before filling the kettle. A cup of tea and a slice of toast. That would be nice after all the rich Christmas food.

Once she'd cut the bread and set it to toast, she rested her hands on the edge of the sink and stood looking out the window. A covering of snow blanketed the back garden. Unblemished as yet by human footprints, the ghost of an early bird had imprinted a pair of skeleton claws to weave their way along the pathway. The shapes of the garden bench and the rubbish bin were visible under cushions of snow.

A robin landed on the fence. His eyes alert, he checked the territory before hopping onto a branch of the pear tree, shaking a light flurry of snowflakes from the bough. He caught sight of her watching him through the glass and cocked his head as if to say "Where's my breakfast?"

She leaned across the sink and raised the window up a few inches. A rush of icy air hit her bare arm. Taking the metal egg-lifter from its hook, she reached out and knocked the frill of snow that had gathered on the windowsill. She could barely hear the gentle plop of it as it hit the ground. She tipped the crumbs from the breadboard into her palm and placed them onto the cleared ledge. All her movements made in a deliberate slow and quiet manner with one eye on the robin. He watched her, the communication calm and acceptable to both sides. He waited until she closed the window before fluttering down onto the sill for his meal. She leaned back against the table and stood observing as he twitched his head from side to side between pecks, checking for competition.

She was still tired, even though she'd slept well. A lot of work. Next year maybe they should think about starting their own traditions. She'd be quite happy to go along to one of their houses. Maybe bake the Christmas pudding and cake and take that much of the work off their shoulders.

She might have to suggest that it was time for a change. It wouldn't go down well. They liked coming over on Christmas Eve, Hannah travelling from New York and Maggie with her two children from the far side of Boston. Mary and her husband and children didn't arrive until Christmas morning. Living locally they met at the Church for Mass and came back to Johanna's for the big fry-up breakfast.

"An Irish custom." She liked to remind them of their

roots. *"Rashers and eggs and the lump of black puddin' came rolling down the lane!"* She still sang the made-up nonsense as she turned them on the pan. Mattie used to do it for Hannah, Mary and Maggie May when they were small and later she'd taken it up with the grandchildren. The sound of their giggling as they all joined in while watching her twiddle away at the pan came back to her. Not the same now. They just indulged her by singing along but it had lost something. Just a pathetic hanging on to a ditty that had grown sad. Something that could never be retrieved.

The middle years had disappeared. Where to she couldn't tell, nor how or why it had happened. They'd just gone, vanished, like they'd never existed. All melted into a perpetual round of domestic chores, work and children.

The world had continued to turn. Things had happened. Happened to other people mainly. A world war had been followed by a flu epidemic that had killed nearly a million in the States alone. She had known several, thankful her own family had escaped the worst. The Russians had had their revolution and so had the Irish. Well, they'd had two. She smiled at the thought. Anyone could have one but it took the Irish to rise up again after the failed first try and then to follow that with a civil war because they couldn't agree with the outcome of their success.

What had happened to her? It seemed there hadn't been a lot to remark on. Just the normal day-to-day events and the usual religious rituals – First Communions, Confirmations, weddings, christenings and funerals. The punctuation marks of a child's broken leg, young relatives coming from Ireland to begin new lives, some of whom had lodged for a time with her, her poor niece Bridie's tangled life, but nothing major that she herself had been the centre of.

All those years and nothing that she could remember of herself. Not since Mattie died. Not died. Was murdered.

No gentle language to assuage the feelings or guilt of others. To diminish what happened. To pretend it was other than what it was. No, she had made that decision long ago, she couldn't allow that.

So much had happened in the first half of her life, but the blandness of her life since bothered her. Only recently she'd begun to think about it. Maybe it was how everyone's life was. Not wasted years exactly, but there had to be more. She wanted more. Time to move things on before it was too late.

IRELAND

Chapter 52

Knocknageeha, County Clare

1926

A sudden sun shower spilled down on them as they approached the turn. Its force slowed Art to a crawl as he strained to see the road ahead through the drenched windscreen. The water seeped in through the loose joints of the car as Johanna moved away from the frame. A real wreck of a farm vehicle but she could see the pride on Art's face when he'd collected them at the station and held the door of his freshly washed vehicle open.

"Probably not up to the standard you're used to but you've no idea how it's changed my life." Art beamed at them.

The cloudburst stopped as suddenly as it started, having washed the dust off the hedgerows. At the top of the lane Johanna asked him to stop and let her out to walk. Her heart thumped as she watched the two men bump along the rutted laneway towards home. Home. She was home at last.

She stood and listened to the sounds all around her and breathed in the damp smells of the earth as she waited for the car to disappear. She could hear the glugging as the earth drank in the recent shower and watched it spilling its excess into the trickle of the roadside ditch. The rich waft of wild clover, a sweetness forgotten, came on the air almost making her sneeze.

When the curve of the driveway had swallowed the two men she relaxed and looked around. She didn't want Hugh in her ear or Art bubbling with excitement in the driving seat. These first few minutes were precious. She had waited so long. She now wanted to have them alone, in peace and at her pace. Not to come upon it suddenly in a rush, but to stroll through the past and into the present, savouring each moment. She wanted, after the wait of a lifetime, to round the corner and see it in the distance, to spot the changes, one at a time, as she walked up the driveway. She had no intention of throwing away the wait of nearly fifty years in one short minute.

Now that she stood on the driveway a lonesomeness washed over her. The isolation of how lives are lived no matter where you spend them. The years in America, her not ever returning until now, paralleled with the years she'd missed at home. The yawning gap where they'd never overlapped, those lives she'd once been a part of. The people she'd known, some of whom were no longer around. She'd missed out and so had they. Back here now a different Johanna, one they never knew. Others she'd never met, come and gone in the space. The yearning took her by surprise, the pity that we can only live one life at a time.

She looked around, hoping they wouldn't come back down the lane to see what was keeping her.

The trees surprised her with their height and thick trunks. Not the scrawny saplings she remembered. The mature canopy of shiny showered leaves replacing the bony winter frames of her youth. Full of innocent hope they'd burst into bud each springtime on so delicate a structure she feared a gale might snap them. She stood under them now, looking up in awe at their early summer freshness, the leaves not yet starting to dry with the advancing season.

For the birth of each child Patrick had allocated a tree in the paddock in front of the farmhouse and along the driveway. Ten of them, well spaced, planted there by her father. Each one of them with their own space to flourish and grow. All different. The huge oak was Art's. So young when she last saw it, now its serrated fresh green leaves new in contrast to its gnarled, majestic eighty-year-old trunk.

She could only remember the last tree he planted, a weeping willow for Maria's birth. Turned out to have been appropriate. Sadly. She could still smell the cow manure as she stood beside her father, watching as he shovelled it from the barrow into the big hole. To give it a good start in life he'd said.

Her own had been an elm. They got that one right. She walked over to it and looked up. Strong and sturdy. She put her handbag on the ground and reached around the trunk. Just as she expected, no longer able to touch her fingertips together, thickened as it had, like herself. Much as she'd have liked it, there was no slender silver birch for her.

She walked on towards the bend, stopping again to look up at their tall stretch as they reached heavenwards to the blue skies. The sun dazzled on the wet drops that had settled on the leaves, shooting bright stars into the air, almost blinding her.

She rounded the bend and walked towards the farmhouse, stopping at the stone pier of the gate. The homeplace hadn't changed. The ivy was still trying to get in through the upper windows, from where it clung, climbing up the sun-warmed stonework on the front of the house. The neat square edges around the window frames, evidence that someone had recently cut back some of the growth in an effort to keep control. She hoped it hadn't been Art, up the tall ladder.

She remembered Art telling her a story about Hugh

rocking a ladder when Art was at the top of it cutting back the ivy. A ladder leaning against the gable wall, a pile of ivy on the ground beneath it. Her father, red-faced, making a run at Hugh. Art at the top, shouting. The first time their father had deemed him old enough to take on the responsibility for the annual ivy-trimming operation.

"Will you quit the trick-acting! D'ye want to kill him or what?"

"Sorry, sorry, Da!" Hugh ran off, dodging him. "I was only messing! I wasn't going to knock him off!"

"You mightn't mean to, but that's what happens when you engage in mischief like that!"

Hugh glanced up at Art and from the distance saw the danger.

"Sorry. I didn't realise it was so high."

"Well, you need to start thinking, son, using the old noggin. If you want to be useful gather up that ivy and take it down to the dump, there's a good lad."

"Alright."

She remembered asking if Hugh got a walloping. All so long ago. Art had told her the story word for word but, although she knew it was true, it didn't fit the Hugh she knew. It had happened before she was born when Hugh was about ten or eleven. She wondered if Hugh would remember the incident. For her, the image was still in her head as if she'd witnessed it herself.

The men had disappeared into the house, the hall door left open. Her parents had rarely used it. Always the back one. A knock on the big brass knocker of the front door meant only one of two things. A stranger or trouble. Or both.

Her first sight of Art at the train station had shocked her. The egg-shaped dome that emerged from under his once-lush hair looked like it should have a knitted cosy on it.

She recognised him immediately. He had turned into her father. An older, slower version of their father before he died when she was only getting to know him. Patrick had never known her beyond five years of age. And now she had lived longer than he himself.

It had troubled her as she grew up that her father was vague and fading, worried that he would disappear altogether. One look at Art and her memory returned in sharp focus. She had never known Art in his childhood. He was an adult by the time her childish self took notice of him. Her replacement father. Never realised that until this moment.

A woman appeared from the darkness within and stepped out into the sun. Johanna guessed it was Ellen and waved. The woman's head jerked a nod of recognition and she raised her hand in greeting. Johanna quickened her step, wondering why Ellen didn't come towards her. Then she saw the cane. Art had said nothing so she hadn't expected it. But then why would he? He was probably used to his wife with a walking stick. She wondered how long she'd had to rely on it. In an effort to take the pressure off, Johanna increased her speed in case her sister-in-law felt she should hobble out to greet her.

Knocknageeha: the windy hillside. Home at last.

Chapter 53

The excitement of catching up on the news of a lifetime had taken up the first few days. Catherine had come over to the farm several times, taking over the running of the kitchen in her own quiet way. Johanna could see that it was all a bit much for Ellen and was glad that her sister was there to help out. They wouldn't hear of her doing any of the work, preferring to have her sit and talk about her life in America.

"I have to say you put me to shame, Ellen. You've the place sparkling." She suspected that it had been Catherine who had done most of the polishing and scrubbing.

"Well, I had great help, Jo." Ellen winked over at Catherine who had just brought in a fresh pot of tea to the parlour. "I can't take all the credit. We've terrific staff around here."

It was now the third day of the visit and the pleasantries were over. Enquiries about locals, most of whom from Johanna's time were long gone, had all but been used up, leaving room for the inevitable question to poke its head into the lulls between topics. It hovered over them now every time they sat at the kitchen table together to eat.

There was no escaping it. The same thing in each mind but no-one brave enough to open up the subject, so the moment she offered to come down the fields with him he knew the time had come.

"Bacon and cabbage. That was the best feed I've had in years." Hugh sat back and patted his stomach. "And nothing like an apple tart with the fruit picked from your own orchard."

"Let's take the cup of tea inside to the fire. We can clear up the dishes later." Ellen stood up from the table and with her hand on the back of her chair eased her way around it. "Art, maybe you'd get the tray and bring it in."

"I'll give you a hand, Art," Johanna said as Ellen left. She began putting the china cups and saucers on the tray. It wouldn't be long before they were moving back to the mugs on the dresser, the novelty of their visit worn off.

"Maybe I'll slip down to the Long Acre," Art said. "The cattle need to be moved."

"Can't you have the tea first and I'll go down with you then?" Johanna couldn't let the opportunity to pass in case she lost her nerve.

"Ah, sure there's no need for you to go out. No, you go in and have the tea with them. I'll have mine later." Art bent down to give the dog's head a rub. "Myself and old Shep here will manage."

"No, I'd like to go." Johanna's voice was firm, blocking all escape routes. She watched him and waited out his hesitation.

"Well, alright then, but you'll need a pair of boots. The ground might be a bit wet still after the rain."

"I'll borrow Ellen's. I'm sure she won't mind." She picked up the tray and headed for the hall. "Come on, let's have the tea then and we can get going."

The early-evening clouds were washed white and the air

refreshed following the afternoon sun-showers. They walked across the fields and through the gates, Art closing each of them as they passed through. The weight of the silence between them hung heavy on the air, pressing down on their heads. She knew he was waiting for her to bring it up. He had never done so since her request and he would not now in case he had misread things. Of that she was sure.

Walking through the Lake Field she reached out and picked a sprig of fuchsia. The purple buds had formed early but had yet to unfurl their crimson and purple ballerinas that would dance along the hedgerows on slender stems. Too early yet to suck the sap from the flowers, fairy nectar, possibly poisonous but as children they'd thought it sweet and most were still alive to remember.

They strolled in a silence that if the circumstances had been different would have been companionable. As it was they both endured the pressure, each knowing that the cloud had to be dispersed sooner or later – preferably sooner so they could get on with enjoying the visit before it was over.

Johanna tossed the question around her head, ready now to ask but unsure how best to word it. She hoped it would come out in a way that wouldn't upset Art, that he wouldn't detect blame or accusation in it, because there was none. Not for him anyway.

As they arrived at the gate into the Long Acre, Art stopped and took out his pipe. He pressed lightly on the tobacco already in it and struck a match. Once it was lit he leaned on the gate and surveyed his cattle.

"A fine herd, don't you think?"

"One of the things I missed." Johanna joined him at the gate, placing her arms to rest on the top. "Not too many of them on the streets of Boston."

293

A waft of damp grass came off the pasture. Breathing in the mix of it with the sweet scent of his tobacco, she was glad of the silence that followed. It was as if he was waiting, leaving sufficient pause after the topic for her to say what was on her mind. Now was the time. If she didn't do it now she'd not be able to later.

"Whatever became of him?"

Art took a draw on the pipe.

"Whatever became of who?" He asked the question without removing the pipe from between his lips.

She knew that he knew exactly who she was referring to. Knew that he was afraid to presume, just in case he was mistaken. Had used the question as a play for time. Had to be sure. She could read his mind. A mistake at this stage would cause an awkwardness on this, her only ever visit home, and she knew he wouldn't want that.

"Declan. Who else?"

A few beats fell between them after she said it. The nerves in her stomach fluttered. It no longer mattered where the conversation might lead. It was out there at last.

Still leaning his elbow on the gate, he turned to face her and as he did she could see in his face the pressure had lifted for him too.

"I'm really glad you asked, Johanna. I thought you never would and I couldn't ever have brought it up." He took a slow puff on his pipe before lowering it. "I'm glad you did." He looked her straight in the eye. "Very glad. We can't have it festering between us."

"You're right, Art. We've both carried the burden for too long. It was time to share it. Time it was aired."

"Did Hugh never tell you?" Art paused. "He knows."

"No, we never spoke about Declan after the trial. I couldn't and Hugh never mentioned him to me again. I wouldn't let him. Although I knew he visited him in prison and that really hurt me, although I know it probably relieved you."

"I can't say I blame you."

Knowing Art was unsure of his ground she held back. They had both waited so long there was no point in rushing it now. She directed her attention back to the cattle in the field and listened to the dull tearing of the lush pasture with each pull of the grass. The mellowness of their brown eyes staring back at her soothing as they raised their heads and chewed the cud.

"It did him good if that's not too strange a thing to say. The years in prison." He drew a deep breath. "No consolation to you, I daresay, but it did. Frightened the wits out of him."

Shep whined gently. Art glanced down at the dog sitting, head tilted up at the pair, a questioning look on his face, impatient to get on with the job.

"Met a priest there, an Irish fellow. Seems he used to visit some of the prisoners on a regular basis." He paused and, removing the pipe from his lips, he checked the contents of it. "He must have been able to see some hope for Declan because he gave him a contact in San Francisco who fixed him up with a job. And that seems to have been a turning point."

"What happened?"

"Well, he got Declan involved in working with homeless people. After the earthquake. I think it was only then that he realised the importance of family and how easily he'd thrown all that away. He's never been home but he writes a couple of times a year. Still working with homeless people. That's his life now." Art adjusted himself, turning around to lean on the gate, unsure if she wanted these details. "He never married."

"Probably just as well." As soon as the words were out she regretted them, glad when Art ignored her comment.

"It's been good for him to learn the hard way. He was

never one to learn any other way." Art gave a jerk of his head. "It's just a shame it came at such a price. Particularly for you. For all of us. We all suffered in different ways, but especially you. A terrible tragedy altogether."

His faraway expression as he looked over the pasture would have told her, had she been facing him, that he had been talking to himself as much as to her. The peace of the evening fell on them as they stood there, each alone with their heartbreak.

Art was the first to speak. "He sent something for you."

"What do you mean? What sort of a something?" Immediately regretting the edge to her voice, she added an extra in an attempt to soften it. "You mean from Declan?"

"A letter."

"A bit late for that now." Muttered half to herself.

Art waited, listening to the munching sounds of the cattle. He was in no hurry now. The letter had lain in the drawer for weeks, since after he'd written to Declan telling him of their planned visit home. Himself and Ellen had ruminated over it, taking the letter out every now and then, as if turning the envelope over in their hands would make the decision for them. Declan had written, asking them to hold it for Johanna until she arrived in Ireland, leaving the decision to them as to whether to give it to her or not. They would know best.

Art turned his head slowly from side to side as if surveying the far perimeter hedges, all the while observing her from the corner of his eye, biding his time until she had digested this information.

"It's at home in the drawer."

"So he took the easy way out again. Got you to do his work for him? Sound me out? After all this time. Not man enough to do it himself." Unable to hold them back, she regretted how her comments might hurt Art.

"I know it's hard for you to think well of him but I don't think he was ducking out of anything." Art took hold of the top rung of the gate and pressed himself upright. "I think he felt you'd a right to a choice. Whether to accept it or not."

Her raised eyebrows were enough to confirm that his son's uncharacteristic consideration was hard for her to believe.

"He knew you didn't want to have anything to do with him so he wasn't going to send it direct to you and cause further upset. For once I think he did the right thing in sending it here."

Johanna looked at Art, trying to keep the disbelief from creeping into her face. It wasn't his fault and, hard as it was for her to accept that Declan might have changed, she could understand how he would want to credit his son for doing something right.

"Think about it anyway. I won't mention it again. I'll leave it up to you. It's in the top drawer of the sideboard in the parlour." He reached into his pocket and took out a crumpled greying handkerchief and blew noisily. "I don't know what's come over me." He folded over the handkerchief and gave a dab at his eyes. "I suppose it's a relief to be able to talk about it at last."

As he fumbled to put it back in his pocket Johanna's heart melted as she looked at the old man who was her brother.

"I'm sure it is." Reaching over, she put both her arms around him. As she hugged him she could feel a shudder escape before a convulsion overtook him. She held him as he wept the sorrow of over thirty years of disappointment and grief into her shoulder.

Johanna patted his back. No tears fell from her eyes, they were spent a long time ago. She had none left. She waited until she was sure he was finished before releasing him. Gripping him firmly by the elbows, she gave him a gentle rock.

"Thanks, Johanna, thanks." It came out in a whisper as he held her gaze, her watery eyes acknowledging her understanding.

Shep whined. Glad of the interruption, Art bent down and rubbed him.

"Maybe we'd better get these cattle moved before the dark falls on us." He opened the gate into the Long Acre and stepped back. "And if you open the gate into the Lake Field and stand there, I'll let them through." He pulled a stick from the hedge and handed it to her. "Here – you'll be needing that if they try to get past you." He smiled. "It'll come back to you once we start. You can't have forgotten what your brother taught you, even after all those years in America."

They walked back to the house in silence, the dew dampening the air as the light faded. In an effort to ward off the chill of the evening Johanna stopped to button up her cardigan while Art strolled ahead. She caught up with him again as they neared home, the only sound as they fell into step the gravel of the driveway crunching underfoot.

"He's not well, Johanna. It doesn't sound good." Art paused and shook his head as they reached the door, a weak pool of light glowing out from the window of the back kitchen. "I think that's why he wrote the letter. In case something happens to him."

"Maybe." She felt a sympathy for her brother but couldn't pretend she cared what happened to his son, other than the grief it would bring Art.

"His lungs are bad. Very bad. They suspect some sort of a growth." Art looked at her. "In the letter to us he said he had to do it just so you'd know that he is truly sorry. I think, Johanna, he doesn't want you to go to your grave not knowing that."

"Let me think about it, Art."

The firmness in her voice as she took the final steps to the back door relieved him. He knew she would, whatever the outcome, consider it fully.

Chapter 54

It had been good to see her sister Maude again. She'd come over for a few days from Wexford with Bridie and Mickie Joe.

Bridie had written to her before the trip. Must have been as soon as she'd heard they were coming home on a visit to Ireland. Probably worried that Johanna might give away her secrets. The ones she'd left behind in America. Those few unhappy years when her life went off the rails. There hadn't been time to write back to reassure her. Probably just as well. No need to make a big thing about it. All too long ago. A big wink had been enough to deliver the message when they arrived up the driveway in the car. Her niece had smiled and responded by pressing her lips together with her fingers.

She was glad that Bridie had found some happiness at last. Mickie Joe was a lot older than she'd expected, but Johanna had taken to him immediately. A lovely warm handshake and a big open smile.

It was four years since Cornelius had died and Maude was still wearing her black widow's weeds. He was a bit of a stiff old stick from what she could remember of him but then she hadn't seen him since she was seventeen. By all accounts from their mother's letters he turned out to be a decent sort and when Bridie had stayed with her in Boston she seemed very fond of her father whenever she spoke of him so he couldn't have been as rigid as he'd come across.

She wasn't sure if she'd been any help to Maude. It had been hard to compare notes on their widowhood, the circumstances having been so different, but when she pointed out how lucky Maude had been to have her family around her, at least in the same country, it seemed to reassure her that it could have been a whole lot worse.

They'd talked about how the gap between them had closed. She hadn't given it much thought but as Maude pointed out she had never known Johanna as a mature adult.

As she hugged her sister before Bridie helped her into the car to return home, she had a moment's regret that they might never meet again. They would have got on so well.

Hugh booked a hire car as a treat for their Sunday trip to Lahinch. It was clear that Art's old jalopy wouldn't have survived the journey.

While the brash Americanness of the gesture irritated Johanna, the luxury overrode that enough for her to put it to one side as they drove along the narrow roads. Having only ever walked or travelled on ass and cart on these same roads, the speed as they passed through the landscape thrilled her as she relaxed back into the leather seat beside Hugh, admiring the patchwork fields.

Art sat in the rear with Ellen settled beside him, commenting on every feature as if seeing it for the first time.

"I think you don't get out often enough, Ellen." Johanna turned back, laughing at her. "Time for you both to start taking it easy and doing less of that backbreaking work."

"I'm getting a taste for this now since you pair came home," Ellen answered. "I could get used to it!"

"Enjoy it while you can then." Art nudged her with a grin. "They'll be gone soon and we'll be back to normal, though it's tempting to hand the work to the youngsters all the same."

Traces of yellow in the fading gorse bushes still remained in the hedgerows where they bordering the fields. Creamy honeysuckle intertwined with the pink of the wild roses, a promise of what was to follow. Nothing escaped Johanna. The magic of nature, as acute to her senses as in childhood. All but forgotten in the intervening years, she saw and smelt it now as they drove along. One of the only constants – most other things had changed to some degree. She had noticed things since she'd come home. How old people looked – people she'd known. It made her wonder how she looked to them. Post-boxes had changed from the British red to a bright green that shouted Irish independence.

"Mind you don't shoot your mouth off, Johanna, and be on the wrong side in that house."

Art's warning to keep her political views to herself had surprised her on the evening she'd planned on going down to visit the neighbours.

"What are you talking about, Art? Sure the Civil War is long over."

"Not in some houses it isn't." He shook his head. "Not everyone's satisfied with the level of independence that's been achieved."

"Sure isn't it a good start?"

"It might be but there are those who think that we should have held out for the whole lot. The six counties in the North that the Brits have held onto, well, that's a festering sore for some I can tell you."

"So you think it's not finished then?"

"Jo, I'm only warning you so you don't start it up again by ploughing in with your clodhoppers." He grinned at her. "Or your American view on the state of the nation. Wouldn't be wise. You'll only be asked what did you do about it in the last fifty years. So keep the lip buttoned."

"We won't be long." Johanna pushed back her plate and got up from the table. "Are you right there, Ellen?"

She picked up Ellen's handbag and passed the walking stick over as Art stood to help his wife pull back her chair.

"Is it far?" Ellen took the stick and shuffled around the table.

"No. Tilly only lives a few houses up on the right. You'll be able to manage it. You can link me."

"Where will we meet you?" Johanna looked at Hugh.

She could see he was happy to be excluded from the visit by the way he relaxed back in his chair. No interest in reminiscing with Johanna's schoolfriend, whose family he knew only vaguely.

"Say in an hour? Here at the hotel. Will that be enough time for you to get through all your gossip?"

"It depends." The dismissiveness of his comment niggled although she knew it was meant light-heartedly. She threw a fake smile at him. His habit of lending an air of importance to his own activities by his choice of words had to be challenged. A meeting, a consultation, a conference. Always something of much more importance than her activities. "I expect an hour will be enough for you pair to sort out world affairs in the meantime. And while you're doing that we'll be chatting, talking, being sociable. What do you think, Ellen?"

"Yes, an hour will be plenty."

The response confirmed that the banter had been wasted on her sister-in-law, concentrating as she had to on her movements.

"Right then, off we go!" Looping Ellen's free hand through her arm she threw a final glance at Hugh. "To our meeting."

Hugh leaned back in his chair and, raising his eyebrow, stifled a smile. "Enjoy it."

Art, still standing, made no move to sit down again. "I'm going to have to go too but I won't be long. Are you alright here on your own, Hugh? I've to go and see a man about a bull. I'll be well back before the women."

"I'll be fine. A breath of air. I'll go for a walk along the sea front. You go ahead and do your business. I'll fix up here." He beckoned to the waitress.

He stood outside the hotel and looked around. With no particular place to go, no business to attend to, he was surprised how good it felt to have no need to rush off anywhere. The slowness of being able to stand there taking in his surroundings, like time was standing still. No racing to keep up. Other people passing with things to do, work to attend to, but for a change it was not him.

Apart from the differences to the shop facades, the rest – the seafront, the beach, the water – all remained unaltered. Only he had changed. Remembering what now seemed as though it had been another life, somewhere in the far distant past. A life here that had been his at one time, something that he'd once been part of, now felt like it had happened to someone else. Nothing at all to do with him.

The crowd thinned as he walked further from the town. He stopped and, placing his hands apart on the sea wall, stood facing into the soft wind. He closed his eyes and listened, allowing his body to take on the rhythm of the sea. The sound of the breaking waves whooshed gently in his ears. A pleasure he had known but had almost forgotten. The childhood memory – holding a seashell against his sister Maude's ear and asking her if she could hear the sea. He'd not stopped long enough since to be aware of the beauty of it as he raced through life. Never even knew he needed it until now. The chat of people passing behind him seemed no more than a murmur, a sound that blended so naturally with the waves as if they were part of it. As he swayed there he felt himself melt into his surroundings, enjoying the gentle breeze blowing in from the Atlantic, caressing his face.

He checked his pocket watch. Half an hour left to explore. Time to move on. Couldn't let Johanna find him like this. Like a sentimental old fool. Slipping it back into his breast pocket, he smiled to himself before turning and joining the life along the promenade. The air of contentment that emanated from the Sunday strollers struck him as the habit of centuries. Unlike himself they allowed themselves to go with the tides, knowing there was a time for everything. Something he was only now beginning to learn.

A row of donkeys and carts were parked on the sea front. A young boy with two buckets of water strolled between them, stopping to give each pair a drink. No hurry on him as he waited until the animals raised their heads, water dripping from their chins, before picking up his buckets and moving on to the next.

Hugh stopped to observe the patience of the animals, their eye movements slow, watching the boy, as they rested after the journey with their passengers, content to wait their turn. The boy patted the head of a grey donkey as he drank. He whispered words to the animal, words that Hugh could not hear. The relaxed stance of the donkey told him a lot about their level of trust.

Further along the promenade, beyond the buildings, the periwinkle seller and the stallholders with their beach toys leaned against the sea wall awaiting customers. They nodded as he passed as if in recognition but it only made him more aware of the stranger he had become. Even if any of them remembered the young man who left Ireland sixty ago there was no possibility that they would recognise him now. For a moment he longed for one person, just one of his own age, someone from a nearby townland, someone he'd gone to school with, to stroll past on their Sunday walk. He searched the faces for one he might identify, yearning for just one single glance to register a moment's uncertainty, a flash of possible recognition that caused them to wonder if it were indeed Hugh McNamara walking towards them. He wished Art was with him. They would know his brother.

Those who'd known him might have been interested. Would have heard of his successes during the early years, but his memory was likely to have faded from their minds over all the years of not returning home, except for one short business trip in the early days. Too short to have made contact with more than one or two of them. His mistake in not finding time to keep in touch since. He thought of Johanna, envying her chat with her old schoolfriend. His own doing.

Stepping his way carefully thought the crowd who had gathered to watch a vested man juggling coloured balls in the air, he positioned himself on the grassy bank. As he watched the entertainer, the Clare accents floated over his head and past his ears but they too seemed as if from a far distant land that he was no longer a part of.

He stepped down onto the beach, wishing now to be alone with his thoughts. He could feel stones and shells pressing on the thin leather soles of his shoes, footwear more suited to the pavements of Boston than a west of Ireland seashore.

The ozone prickled his nostrils as he breathed deeply, the taste of brine on the breeze taking him back to the annual family outing to the beach. Art telling him how to prolong the treat until the following morning by not washing the salt off his five-year-old lips before going to bed.

A bare-topped boy, his shoulders reddened from the sun, ran back from the swooping of a pair of gulls as they descended onto the sand where he had thrown the remains of his picnic crusts. One gull filled his beak and few off with his bounty while another pecked at the morsel on the sand.

The lad turned back to his mother. "Mam! Is there any more bread?"

"Here, that's the last of it." The woman handed the crust to him.

Hugh held back, silent and still, not wanting to frighten the gull into flight. He could see himself in the tentative steps of the sunburnt boy who picked his way towards the gull, on the tips of bare toes, hand outstretched, half hoping, half fearful that the gull would take it from his hand. At the last minute, as the gull waddled in his direction, the boy dropped the crusts and moved back to watch.

The realisation fell upon Hugh. He no longer mattered here. They had all moved on without him. And he without them. Another generation. Two generations. He envied the joy on the lad's face. He remembered it well. Wondered now where had it all gone?

He was tired. Not at this moment. But tired of where he had arrived, the freshness of life gone. To have had it leeched out of him in the years spent working so hard. His choice. But what had it all been about?

As the gull soared he smiled in the direction of the boy who didn't seem to notice him. Moving up the slope and further along he sat on a flat rock. The seaweed covering it had dried to a crisp. He plucked off a piece and rubbed it between his fingers, until the flakes dissolved into nothing. No sounds now but that of the seabirds and the sound of water.

The sunbursts between the puffs of white cloud threw patches of turquoise on the grey-blue surface of the sea. One large wave after another rose before collapsing and slowly rolling in. He could feel the power behind each roller just before it broke into a white foam, its force diminished. Not quite finished, it had a little more to give – in its fanning out to spread a lacy froth on the sand. It stroked the shoreline, leaving its tiny bubbles to burst, before ebbing back out and into the ocean from whence it came.

Chapter 55

Reminiscing with Tilly had disturbed her in a way she hadn't expected. Tilly was still able to name every one of their fellow pupils whose schooldays they had shared from start to finish. The ones who had never reached adulthood, those who had gone on for further education through the priesthood or nunnery, married a 'ne'er-do-well', borne imbecile or genius children. How lives had spun out from childhood, probably not as many of them had anticipated.

It had all seemed so simple. She remembered it. The innocent thinking of them all. That you had control of how your life would be in the future. No understanding of the unexpected or the choices that might be offered. How the decision to take one or the other might be for good or ill and often there was no turning back.

The no turning back. That was what unsettled her.

"Would you not consider coming back here to live?" Tilly tried to persuade her. "There are a few who have done that. They say that America is only for young people."

Johanna was tempted. It was as if Tilly had read her mind. Her friend's words were stirring thoughts that she'd been afraid to give voice to. There had been no tears as they watched her board the ship for Ireland. They had all come to the dock to see herself and Hugh off. A vacation as far as their children were concerned. Hugh also. For him it was simply a holiday. The same for her, but somewhere deep inside her head she knew that for her it was more than that. A reconnaissance mission. A test. Afraid to admit to that, even as Tilly said it. But that's what this trip was about, a holiday certainly, but the other too.

No matter how much she wished them to be otherwise, they were Americans. Her children would never be Irish. They knew nothing of the clean smell of a damp bog, the white bog cotton fluffing up like new-born chicks as it dried in the sun after a shower of rain. They had never, would never experience the satisfaction of collecting potatoes from the field, knowing the miracle of their birth. Her part in that process now had a romance not felt at the time of sowing, at the time of harvesting when her back ached and her fingernails were encrusted with brown soil. Longing for her mother to ring the dinner bell that could be heard carried on the wind across to the Potato Field. It was still called that even though there were years in between when the soil was rested and there were no potatoes planted there.

No turning back. Not for her. Just file away the memories. Take them out every now and then, dust them off and travel back in time and let the evening sun set on them. Another life entirely.

Her father's voice came back to her like it was yesterday. She remembered the phrase, not understanding it at the time. It just sounded funny then. Propped up on the top of the wooden gate into the orchard from where the ground looked very far below.

The knot in the rope had tightened after the rain. It had always been there keeping the gate into the orchard closed. Once opened it had to be knotted firmly again. This was before Da had redesigned it into a loop that didn't have to be opened each time. It would have been more than your life's worth to leave it untied and have cows trampling around. It was the same with the vegetable garden.

Impatient when he couldn't undo the knot, he'd swung his legs over with ease leaving her to climb up. By the time she'd reached the top rung he'd moved away and was already collecting the windfallen apples. It was only when he realised he was working alone that he glanced back and saw her dithering over her descent from her perch atop the gate.

"Don't just sit there! You wanted to come and help, didn't you?"

He was in bad form. Unusual for him. A calf had been born dead. She'd overheard the conversation as he came in from the barn, tired from the night spent tending the labouring cow. A child slowing him up now, unable to get over or down from the gate was an irritation his normally patient self didn't need. Not this morning.

"I can't, I'm stuck."

"Ah, for crying out loud!" He plonked the bucket on the grass and walked back towards the gate. "Come on, just swing your leg over."

"I can't!" Johanna grabbed him, locking him around the neck. "I can't, I'm afraid!"

"What are you afraid of? I'm holding you, you won't fall. Will you let go, you're choking me!"

"Lift me over, Dada!"

"I can't if you won't let go. Let go of the bars, you've them grasped between your legs."

"I can't, I'll fall!"

Patrick prised her hands from around his neck and placed them on the top bar and made to walk away.

"You won't. I'm telling you, you won't fall. But if you want to stay there all day you can. It's up to you."

"Don't leave me here, Dada!" Johanna started to wail. *"I can't get up or down now!"*

"Well, then, would you ever just piss or get off the pot?"

She started to giggle and in two strides he was back, her giggling having loosened her grip, and he whisked her over.

"There, I told you I wouldn't let you fall." Patrick smiled down at her, sorry for his impatience.

His saying now made sense. No straddling anymore. Time now to make up her mind and get off the pot.

Her first seventeen years when Ireland was home. Nothing more than a memory now and lucky to have it. So many more years of her life spent in the States. It all seemed clear. Where was the conflict that she thought existed? He was never part of her Ireland, nor she his. Not one memory of here between them. Time now to go home to where Mattie lay. And to her American children. It had taken this trip to show her what should have been obvious. A lifetime lived on the other side of the Atlantic. America had become home without her ever knowing.

Chapter 56

She had one last job to do before she left.

She had rushed them that morning. "We need to be leaving here by nine o'clock," she insisted.

The men couldn't understand why she wanted an extra hour in the town before the train departed and she wasn't prepared to enlighten them.

"Did you really have to wait 'til the last minute to do this?" Hugh rolled his eyes to heaven.

Ellen had told her where to go, where all the elegant matrons in the town went for their special occasion outfits.

"They're a bit snooty, but you'll manage them fine, Johanna." Ellen grinned at her. "And they do have lovely things."

"There you are and thank you very much, Mrs. Lynch." The young shop assistant finished tying up a hatbox. He came out from behind the counter to escort his customer from the premises. "Enjoy the wedding, I look forward to hearing all about it." He watched her as she walked off down the street before turning to Johanna who was busying herself trying on hats. He approached her, smiling.

"Can I help you? Is it for a special occasion, madam?"

"No, not especially. It's for going to Mass on Sundays." Johanna took a wide-brimmed hat from the stand and, placing it on her head, turned to look in the mirror.

"*Hmmm* . . . I think I might have something more appropriate." He minced away, disappearing behind the counter. Walking along the display, his finger to his lips in concentration, he stopped now and then to consider a possibility.

Johanna, cocking her head, was smiling at her reflection in the mirror when the shop assistant returned brandishing a hat with a matching felt flower on the side. He reached over and catching the red brim of the creation on Johanna's head removed it and with a flourish laid it down on the countertop.

"I think this one will suit you very well, madam. Feel the material, lovely and soft and very stylish." He settled the neat navy hat on her head and stood back to admire his handiwork. "Now, what do you think of that one?"

"No. Dull. Not me at all." Johanna gave a cursory glance in the mirror before whipping it off her head and reaching again for the red hat. "No. This definitely is the one. Much more suitable."

"Are you sure, madam? People around here usually buy hats like that for special occasions."

"Well, I fibbed. It's not really for Mass." Johanna laughed at the young man's earnest face. "It's for when I go to meet my lover."

The shop assistant's eyebrows rose. She could see his training abandon him as she watched his struggle to keep his expression bland.

"You think I'm joking?"

"No, no. Oh, no, madam, not at all. I'll box it up for you. It suits you very well."

She handed him the money and watched the discomfort

sit on his smile as he turned in search of a hatbox and almost felt sorry for him. But she didn't really care. She was never going to see him again. And, anyway, it would give him something to talk about to his colleagues during his tea-break. And maybe teach him not to be so quick to make assumptions.

A couple of customers had arrived by the time Hugh walked in through the doors of the shop. Johanna saw him first, standing tall with his silver-tipped walking cane as he looked around in search of her. From where she stood at the back of the shop she saw him as others must see him. This handsome, elegant figure in his three-piece suit she could hardly believe was her brother. She wondered how she had not observed him in this light before.

She walked forward slowly but as she heard the shop assistant returning she decided to get a little more mileage from the situation.

"Oh, here he is!" She raised her hand to wave at her brother before turning to the shop assistant who was holding the hatbox out to her, dangling it from its red satin ribbon. She watched him try to hide his curiosity as his eyes flicked from her to the distinguished gentleman who was approaching her.

"I'm ready." She twinkled at Hugh, knowing how little patience he had with drapery stores. "Just finished here." She held up her hand, needed to halt him in his tracks before he reached the counter. Couldn't allow him to come any closer in case he gave the game away with the type of comment he could only make to a sister.

"Thank you. I'll enjoy wearing that." Taking the hatbox and her change from the assistant she gave a bright beam.

"Thank you very much, madam."

She turned and smiling up at Hugh, much to his amazement, she slipped her free arm through his, aware

315

that the eyes of the young shop assistant were trained on the frumpy elderly woman heading towards the exit on the arm of her gentleman 'lover'.

The train slowly puffed away from the station. As it began gathering speed, she could see still Art through the carriage window. Pressing her head against it she twisted her eyes to their extreme until they hurt as she watched him grow smaller and smaller. She was unwilling to lose sight of the lonesome figure on the station platform even though he was becoming frailer and more forlorn as the distance between them increased.

Even after Art had disappeared from view she continued to stand looking out, swaying to the rhythm of the chugging, wondering how long he had held his arm up before accepting that he had waved them both goodbye for the very last time.

"Would you sit down, woman? You're blocking my view."

The normality of Hugh's words broke the spell. She knew there was no point in looking any longer. Turning away from the window she checked the bench behind her and, smoothing her coat, sat down. She looked across at her brother and noticed the red rims of his eyes, understanding now why he had sat down so quickly after his cursory wave.

He wasn't inclined for chat and neither was she. Allowing her mind to wander back over the visit she traced the markings in the wood grain of the carriage interior with her eyes.

A visit. That's what it had been. The present and the past. A whole chunk missing from the middle like an elusive will-o'-the- wisp. As she lay her head against the velveteen backrest she turned her eyes towards the window to enjoy her last glimpses of the passing scenery. That missing chunk didn't lie here. Of that she was now certain. It was into the future now.

HOME

Chapter 57

Hugh had been up on deck for the past hour, watching the land approaching, as if he could hurry the ship on. His third visit to the cabin to persuade her to join him had annoyed her.

"I'm not standing up there getting my hair all tossed in the wind. Go back up yourself if you think you can help them speed it up. We won't arrive any sooner, you know."

Johanna did her final check in the mirror, adjusting the red hat to a jaunty angle and pulling a comical face as she stuck her tongue out to remove the sensible 'kind' reflection that looked back at her.

She did one last check in her bag. Yes, everything present and correct – all the important documents there. The corner of an envelope caught her eye, a small edge of it poking up over the material of the separate pouch. Declan's letter. Unopened. She'd had no intention of allowing it to take up any of her precious time in Ireland or spoil her visit. No, it could wait until she was back at home and good and ready to read it in her own time. Closing over the top of the bag, she picked it up and took one last look around the cabin before shutting the door for the final time.

The stairs were narrow. She was sorry she hadn't given

the bag to Hugh to bring up on deck. It was difficult to negotiate the steps with the bag in one hand and her other employed holding up the hem of her coat to avoid stepping on it as she ascended.

It was windy on deck and she was glad of the hatpin Ellen had given her as she headed across to join him at the rail. She laid her bag down on the deck. It was a wonder he wasn't first in the queue.

"Would you stay easy?" She pulled him back as he made to move forward too close to the family in front.

"What's keeping them at all?"

Impatient as ever, shifting as he did from one foot to the other, moving forward whenever he got a chance even though the gangplank hadn't yet been put in place. No change there so.

"It'll take as long as it takes. Have you learned nothing from the visit home?" She grinned at him. "Just relax, will you?" She watched the wind go out of him. "That's the stuff. You're going nowhere."

She scanned the crowds waiting on the dock.

"Oh look, Hugh, there they are! And some of yours too. I don't think they've spotted us yet." She waved, glad she now had a hand freed up to hold onto the wide brim of her flamboyant red hat. Yes, she did look forward to surprising her children.

THE END

CPSIA information can be obtained
at www.ICGtesting.com
Printed in the USA
FSHW020751300521
81945FS